Once Upon a Summer

GW00372819

This one is for me.
For as long as I can remember,
I've wanted to write a 'big story'.

Once Upon a Summer

Patricia O'Reilly

WOLFHOUND PRESS
Celebrating 25 Years

Published in 2000 by
Wolfhound Press Ltd
68 Mountjoy Square
Dublin 1, Ireland
Tel: (353-1) 874 0354
Fax: (353-1) 872 0207

This book is fiction. All characters, incidents and names have no
connection with any persons living or dead. Any apparent
resemblance is purely coincidental.

The Arts Council
An Chomhairle Ealaíon
Wolfhound Press receives financial assistance from
the Arts Council/An Chomhairle Ealaíon, Dublin.

British Library Cataloguing in Publication Data
A catalogue record for this book is available from the British
Library.

ISBN 0-86327-795-0

10 9 8 7 6 5 4 3 2 1

Cover Illustration: Chris Brown
Cover Design: Mark O'Neill
Typesetting: Wolfhound Press
Printed in the UK by Cox & Wyman Ltd, Reading, Berks.

ACKNOWLEDGEMENTS

While writing *Once Upon a Summer*, I listened for my voice and, when I heard it, followed it through a maze of twists and turns to muddy the line between fact and fiction. Characters and incidents which started with recognisable traits escaped into a deliberate fictional anonymity. Several of the set pieces were first outed in RTÉ Radio 1's *Sunday Miscellany*.

The locations are real. The suburbs of Dublin. The town of Tralee. And Fenit village where I spent many happy summers. Regrettably, I never met a Mikey, though I did pick carragheen. In the interests of fiction, I have taken some geographic liberties, such as relocating the 1959 Rugby Senior School Final; Tansey's gate and woods and the sandy beach of Fenit do not exist outside my imagination. However, the remains of the graveyard are still there, as is Samphire Terrace, now mainly converted into trendy holiday homes.

Thanks for help and assistance to the staff of The National Library of Ireland, Tralee County Library, the Garda Síochána, The National Maternity Hospital Dublin and The Sacred Heart Hospital Cork, The Catholic Press Office, Maynooth College (Department of Theology), Irish Rugby Union (Leinster Branch).

And thanks for the 'Nativity Play' story to the Most Reverend R.H.A. Eames, Archbishop of Armagh and Primate of all Ireland. It was part of his speech during Irish PEN's 1998 annual dinner.

PROLOGUE

Dublin, Present Time

The monthly Sunday lunch would not be the same without Zoë. As usual, railing against discipline. 'Gran, don't you think I should be allowed to the disco?' Dressed in black from head to toe, cropped hair the colour of cranberries, Zoë demanded attention. 'Fearless' was the word Rose used to describe her favourite grandchild. The only one of them with a bit of spunk.

All the family here today. Rose at the head of the oval mahogany table. In the man-of-the-house place. Hers now for the past five years, since the death of her husband. The table was laid with damask linen, gleaming silver, sparkling crystal; and a centrepiece of late roses, 'Schoolgirl', planted with great ceremony the day Viola, their eldest, had started school, the blooms picking up the pinky-peach cross-stitching of the luncheon mats. Well Rose remembered her mother embroidering them.

So many happy memories tingeing the grief for her man. The legacy he had left helped, she supposed. Loneliness in luxury and all that. Still, she often said she would trade this house and her portfolio of shares for another day with him. Another hour. Probably even ten minutes. Though of recent times in the velvet quiet of the night she was beginning to accept that he was gone from her. For ever. Gradually, she was starting to recognise that it was time to take up the reins of her own life.

Her children were some comfort. Not that she saw much of them — they were adults now with their own lives. Busy, busy. Rushing from one appointment to another. All of them successful in their chosen careers. It was intriguing, Rose thought, how different they were, given that they had the same parents, upbringing and environment. But, most importantly, hadn't they lived with the example of their father?

Zoë reminded Rose of the way she would like to have been at her age. Full of courage, recklessly outspoken. Zoë had a good head on her shoulders. Too sensible to be harmed by a disco. Still, she would not interfere. 'That's a matter for your parents,' she heard herself say, rather prissily.

'Everyone's going. All my friends.' Pouting dramatically as only Zoë could, the silver ring in her nostril catching the glint of September sunlight, she addressed her mother, 'Do you want me to be a social nerd?'

'No,' said Viola, fashionably thin; with blonde hair, immaculately dressed in scarlet designer casuals and fighting not to show her irritation. 'I wouldn't want to be responsible for that.' Viola was riding on a high at the success of Imagine, the PR company she had started on a whim, which had taken off beyond her wildest imaginings. 'But I certainly wasn't going to discos, or anywhere else, at your age,' she assured her daughter, refusing to meet her own mother's eye, fiddling with her cigarette pack, resisting the urge to light up before dessert.

'I'm not a child. I'm nearly sixteen. You have to let me grow up,' Zoë insisted, stabbing at the air with her knife. Dark purple varnish on the childishly bitten nails.

'You're still fifteen. Neither your dad nor I are stopping you...' Viola began, a definite touch of asperity creeping into her voice.

'We'll talk about this later. When we get home.' The patient voice of reason from Richard. Zoë's antics amused her father and he found it difficult to take her seriously. Twenty years Viola's senior, he was a prosperous barrister who had settled contentedly into early old age. His passions were his wife, his daughter and Beethoven. He appreciated good wine too and, taking another sip of St Emilion, thought how he was never disappointed with his mother-in-law's choice of wine.

Zoë sighed. 'There weren't discos in your day, sure there weren't, Uncle Trev?' Zoë adored Trevor, Rose's youngest, and deferred to him constantly, taking as gospel his every pronouncement on the social scene.

Trevor was a maker of television documentaries, unmarried, flitting successfully from job to job and from relationship to relationship. Variety in all aspects of life, a necessary part of the creative process, he assured his mother. He had been late arriving. Something about running someone to the airport. Probably his latest girl.

'No. No discos. Nothing modern.' Devilment glinted in Trevor's eyes, which were the same deep blue as the denim of his shirt. 'All kinds of demonstrations, though. Greenham Common, bra-burning and, of course, streaking.'

FR, the eldest, looked up from his plate, check waistcoat straining across his torso. Rose often said he was born sensible. He had been plump from babyhood, with that placid curiosity so often the precursor to success. An accountant with a golden touch for investment, he tucked into his food as though there was no tomorrow. The slender, out-going girl he had married had gradually taken on his body shape and disposition over the years. Their three daughters, fourteen, thirteen and ten, and their eight-year-old son, were miniatures of their parents.

'Really, Trevor,' he remonstrated, placing his knife and fork tidily across his plate.

'What's streaking?' It was Julie, FR's eldest.

'Taking off your clothes. And running stark naked. Usually across a football pitch.'

Julie blushed the delicate pink of her cardigan, and FR started again, 'Trevor. Do you have to…?'

From the end of the table Cissie met Rose's eye and chortled. Cissie still looked much the same as Rose remembered her from more than forty years back. Not that Cissie would allow any of them to know her age. Despite the stiletto heels kicked off under the table, and the false teeth in for the formality of the occasion, she was still the same no-nonsense Cissie. As pragmatically capable and as caring as ever.

Back from one of her frequent visits to Donegal and on her way home to Kerry tomorrow, the letter from Australia, which had come as a bolt out of the blue, burning a hole in her pocket. No more chickening out on that. No further stalling. She would show it to Rose. It was high time Rose started living again.

Zoë was intrigued. 'Do you think sex has replaced streaking?' she asked Trevor.

'Quite likely,' he answered, deadpan.

'Which is best? Sex, hash or booze?' Zoë asked.

'Good sex,' her uncle replied without hesitation.

'I knew you'd say that!'

'Why?' Julie asked Zoë.

'Because sex is cool,' Zoë, with a toss of her head, answered her cousin.

Rose looked from one to another. How incredibly open conversation had become. Was that a good or a bad thing? Having lived through three generations, she still was not sure. Though today's honesty was appealing, she had to admit, it was so different from her time — and how varied the reactions of her family were, she thought with a smile. Humour, embarrassment, outrage, interest, curiosity.

Zoë was not one to be diverted. 'Times have changed. Everyone goes to discos. Can I, Mum? Please, please,' she pleaded.

'Discussion. Later.' The more annoyed Viola became, the more clipped her words.

'Dad. Make Mum say yes.'

'When have I ever been able to get your mother to do anything she didn't want?' countered Richard cheerfully.

Yielding to temptation, Viola lit up. 'You're too young. That place has a reputation for drugs and drinking. And God knows what else. Probably sex too.'

'Mum,' Zoë pleaded, 'I told you. Our crowd don't do drugs. Everyone drinks. And, of course, we shift. But we know all about safe sex and unsafe sex, AIDS and getting pregnant.' A mischievous smile lit up her face, and, licking her thumb, she made a sign around her heart. 'Cross my heart and hope to die, I promise not to be an unmarried mother.'

Richard, used to his daughter's dramatic behaviour, ignored it. And topped up his glass. This Bordeaux — a *grand cru*, no less — was particularly good.

'Everyone of your age doesn't drink,' said FR tartly. Zoë should not be allowed to get away with this behaviour. Heckling, hogging the conversation, ruining a good lunch. He ignored the issues of sex and drugs, on which he suspected she would best him. 'Julie won't drink until she's of age, sure you won't?' he asked his daughter.

Zoë snorted with derision, Rose smothered a smile, even Cissie looked amused. Difficult to imagine squeaky-clean Julie anything other than parentally compliant.

'No, Daddy,' Julie said, her concentration total as she constructed her next mouthful. A piece of roast potato, a corner of pink beef, a wedge of Yorkshire pudding, topped with purée of carrot and parsnip — mission accomplished. Before transferring the forkful to her mouth, she smiled good-humouredly around the table.

'No wonder the world's the way it is. The majority of today's youth running wild. No parental discipline,' proclaimed FR, red-faced with annoyance. 'Faces pierced, rainbow-coloured hair. A law unto themselves.' He thanked God for his own children. And looked forward to a dessert of warm Kerry apple cake smothered in cream.

'Sex mad. Drugged out of their minds. And totally irreligious,' Trevor finished for his brother with a wicked grin at Zoë.

'FR, you've no right…' began Viola, casting a despairing look at Trevor.

'It's my body. And I'm a millennium person,' interrupted Zoë, well able to defend herself. Then, to her grandmother: 'Growing up must have been awful in your day.'

'It wasn't. We'd great times.' Zoë looked dubious. 'I did my real growing up over one summer in Kerry. Do you remember, Cissie?'

Cissie nodded.

Zoë yelped, 'In one summer?'

Rose laughed at her granddaughter's reaction. 'The foundations had been well laid over the previous months.'

The semantics of the situation did not interest Zoë. 'So was your real growing up done with Great-aunt Babs?' she asked.

'No. They were the early days of teenagers. Babs had the hotel to run. And we were considered so wild she organised a sort of second mother, a surrogate mother, I suppose you'd call her, to mind us. My cousin Kate and myself.'

Zoë's eyes widened. 'Is that true? You were that wild?'

'Yes. Indeed. Ask Cissie,' said Rose with a fond look down the table to a beaming Cissie. 'She was our surrogate.'

The three sisters looked mildly animated, Zoë amazed. 'What kind of wild?' she asked Rose.

'The same as all young people, wanting to live life to the full, I suppose.'

'Boys?'

'Of course, what else?'

'Boys, like sex, you mean?' Rose smiled at Zoë's amazement. 'Cool. Did you know Granda then?'

'I did indeed.'

Turning to Viola triumphantly, Zoë commented, 'See, Mum.' Then to Rose, 'Can you really remember how it was? The feelings and all that stuff?'

'I do believe I can....'

CHAPTER ONE

Dublin, February 1959

Rose Horn was a thinker. A thinker of slumbering thoughts which she hugged to herself until she decided they were ripe for release into conversation. This particular thought, the one she had been consumed by for weeks, was not quite ready for its freedom, but she was so bursting to tell, she knew she could not resist for much longer.

Still she hesitated, reluctant to mention this boy she had noticed since the start of the second school term. It was now the beginning of February. From his tentative smile and the way she straightened up on his bike and looked at her across the divide of the road when he passed, she thought he must be interested. The first boy to pay her any attention, and just as she was beginning to panic that she would never have a boyfriend.

Rose was dying to be infected with this love bug which had bitten the class of 4A, desperately wanting to report on these deliciously new and strange sensations invading her body. Since the beginning of the year, boys had been the main topic of conversation, everything else — even the Intermediate Certificate examinations — was relegated to second place. She had felt excluded while the other girls drooled over various boys, rhapsodised about their latest conquests, or went into decline if the object of their affection did not reciprocate.

'There's this boy…' Rose began hesitantly, a soft smile lighting up her heart-shaped face. Her best friends, Barbara and Monica, skidded to a halt on the highly polished linoleum of the corridor. They were on their way to cookery — cherry buns this week.

'What boy?' they asked in unison.

'I don't know his name,' Rose admitted. She was the shyest and quietest of the threesome. 'But he wears a blue and white scarf. I'm certain it's the 'Rock one.'

'Blackrock. Not bad. Wonder if he's on the rugby team,' speculated Barbara. She had a dimply smile and gingery airborne curls. 'Lucky old you.' Blackrock College had a reputation for rugby, and was the undisputed master at both junior- and senior-school levels. A boyfriend on the team would be a real status symbol.

'What else about him?' asked Monica sharply, her flat face alive with interest, her protruding teeth resting on her lower lip. She liked to know everything that was going on.

'I don't know.'

'Does he walk? Ride?' asked Monica impatiently.

'Ride. A red and silver racer with dropped handlebars, and sometimes he has a tennis racquet strapped to his carrier,' rattled off Rose.

'Not a rugby player so,' Monica deduced gleefully. She was interested in the Terenure College stand-by goalie and didn't want the limelight deflecting to Rose.

'Girls, girls. No talking in the corridors. Shouldn't you be in the kitchen?' It was Mother Mary Magdalene, mistress of studies — a force not to be argued with.

While creaming butter and sugar, Rose received a whispered message, passed surreptitiously from one aproned girl to the other. To her dismay, Monica and Barbara would cycle part of the way home with her to have a look at him. Rose was not sure she was ready for what she knew would be a rigorous probing, particularly from Monica.

It began to rain at 3.30 as the class ended — a drizzly but determined downpour that did nothing to dampen her friends' enthusiasm. In between mouthfuls of hot buns, Monica announced to the cookery class that Rose had a boyfriend — an exaggeration Rose let rest.

Rose liked being the centre of attention, enjoying the camaraderie and the initiation into this special sisterhood as her classmates danced ecstatically around her, welcoming her to the inner circle of 'being in love'. Their enthusiasm unnerved her though, and for a moment she had a horrific vision of all fifteen girls running or cycling home behind her. But Monica took control, insisting that as she and Barbara were Rose's best friends, only they should accompany her.

Rose had often wondered about being in love, speculated on how it would feel and wished it would happen to her. She was sure the body quivers and tingles she had already experienced were the beginning of it; and she was certain that when she really fell in love they would be intensified into one enormous vibration of delight. She couldn't wait for it.

Cookery was not Rose's forte and, rather than subject her rock-hard buns to her mother's scrutiny, as they left the classroom, she dropped them into the waste bucket. The three friends, books loaded into satchels, raced to the bicycle shed, turning up the collars of their school gabardines against the rain. Oblivious to the rat-tailed hair trailing below their mushroom-shaped school berets, sodden lisle stockings and saturated uniforms, Barbara and Monica were in high spirits cycling through Donnybrook village.

Rose wished she had stayed quiet, wished she was still hugging her dream to herself. She would die if he thought she fancied him. As they had not even spoken, she could not be sure of her feelings, though it would be nice to be in love, to have a special somebody to daydream and to sigh about.

'Pretend you don't notice him,' she begged as he loomed into view at the bottom of Eglinton Road, hating the blush that spread upwards from her very toes.

However, after all the anticipation, the vetting process turned out to be a damp squib.

'Hi, Frank,' said Monica gaily, full of herself that she was one up on the other two by knowing him. He looked startled, half smiled, then put his head down and cycled on quickly. 'He plays tennis with Tom,' explained Monica who, having an older brother, was the envy of the class.

'Do you really think he fancies you?' Monica asked

Rose after she had once again given a blow-by-blow account of what her would-be goalie had said to her and what she had said back to him. The girls had pulled in to the side of the road, sheltering under dripping foliage to swap further notes on the boys of the month, their cheeks bulging with bull's-eyes, the sweets of the minute. Monica asked the question with an air of doubting cynicism, as though the idea was as preposterous as the moon raining gold. Rose shrugged.

'Maybe you think so because you fancy him,' Monica pursued her point. She was very outspoken.

Rose did not know how to answer, so she said nothing. She liked the name Frank. It suited him.

Barbara said, 'I think he looks nice.'

Rose shot her a grateful look. Barbara, the peace-maker, could always be guaranteed to say the right thing.

Monica agreed. 'Yeah, he's nice, but wet.' 'Wet' was her description of most of her brother's friends. 'Too stuck up even to stop to talk to us. But he's always in and out of our house.' She shrugged and took the last sweet from the rumpled brown paper bag.

Monica gave the impression that while hordes of boys fancied her like mad, they were beneath her notice. Rose had seen the current object of Monica's fancy in action during a friendly rugby match she had sneaked into one Saturday afternoon while she was supposed to be returning her mother's library books. Big, red-faced and mud-covered. Hard to judge his looks, but she had known enough to sound enthusiastic.

During the summer holidays, Barbara had acquired a boyfriend. A real boyfriend. Though boarding in Castleknock College, he got out at weekends, and she brought him home for tea. That, in Rose's opinion, was really going with a fellow. Barbara did not talk much about him, though she smiled whenever his name came up and kept his latest letter in her uniform pocket.

Next day after school, Frank wheelied across the Stillorgan Road and stopped with a squeal of brakes in front of Rose. Close up he was taller, blonder and more handsome than she had realised. With front wheels nudging, they smiled, making shy eye contact, and ended up grinning delightedly at each other.

Talking came easily to them, each revelling in discovering the other. From then on, they waved and shouted laughing comments as they cycled back and forth, stopping after school to chat at the edge of the road wherever they happened to intersect. Over the following days and weeks Rose decided she really liked Frank, probably loved him. But what she liked even more was the way her status had grown among her classmates.

By any standards Nance Horn was a handsome woman, if a little austere. Her looks were classic and understated — she was well built, with a regal bearing, her immaculately French-pleated hair beginning to be sprinkled with silver.

Her opinions were forceful and positive. She was a woman of definite ideas on many subjects, her current favourites being the importance of Rosemary holding on for as long as possible to her childhood, followed closely by her belief that women's best interests were served by domesticity.

One evening during the early days of Rose and Frank's 'going', Nance was stirring scrambled eggs in her green and white kitchen, a frilled apron protecting her pale blue twin set and toning kick-pleat skirt. It was their live-in help's afternoon off. Not that Nance would trust Agnes, or indeed anyone, with the finer points of domesticity. Certainly not the cooking. That, as mistress of the household, she reserved, like a badge of authority, for herself. Rose was peering into the saucepan when she asked, 'Is it possible Auntie Dolores could have seen you talking to a boy on the side of the road?'

'I don't know,' Rose replied, not really telling a lie. She could not be sure who Dolores Luke had seen. Nosy old busybody. And her not even a proper aunt.

'Are you hanging around corners with boys?'

'No,' Rose answered truthfully, regretting having even bothered to come into the kitchen, much less pretend to be interested in cookery.

Against the chill dark of the February evening, Nance had drawn the kitchen curtains. Cheerful check with insets of apples and oranges. This was her favourite time of day. Her children, Rosemary and George, safely home from school, and husband, Trevor, on his way back from Trinity College. The house gleaming, comfortable and warm. A meal on the ready. Caring for her family. That was what life was about. Though she wished they had more than their two children. Four, or even six, would have been nice, but Trevor had been adamant about only replacing themselves. Still, two could be given quality time. It was nice to see Rosemary taking an interest in cooking. It just went to show, perseverance paid off.

As for George, with his face-splitting smile and little-man mannerisms, he was the apple of Nance's eye, though she hotly disputed it. And she was even more vehement in her denial of spoiling him. Justifying herself by saying that the rearing of a boy had to be different. Boys had to be encouraged to stand on their own two feet, learn from experience and make decisions from an early age. After all, they were the ones who had to have careers and the ability to head up a family.

Though, that said, at every opportunity she trotted out her favourite 'George' story.

The year he was six, George's heart had been set on playing St Joseph in the school Nativity play. When he was cast as the innkeeper, he cried, great gulping tears of anger, begging his mother, then his father, to intercede on his behalf. He received a parental lecture about team spirit and pulling his weight. Rose, siding with them, explained the importance of the show going on. Not to forget he was a vital character.

With a sigh of relief, the household settled back as George, appearing to accept his role, asked lots of questions about the story and the various characters.

Nance heard his few lines over and over again until he was word-perfect.

One evening he called Rose in on her way to bed. Rumpled and earnest, he sat up in his blue winceyette pyjamas, which were strewn with gambolling yellow teddy bears. He was full of chat, wondering what would have happened had there been room at the inn.

'Baby Jesus would have been born in a cosy room, not a draughty stable,' Rose told him. 'Now, go to sleep.'

'Could the wise men and the shepherds still have come?'

'Yes. Sleep.'

'I think the innkeeper should've made room, like I do in my bed for Teddy and Golly,' he said drowsily.

For the next few days, George was quietly confident. On the afternoon of the performance he was first into his costume and raced into make-up. When he was told that, as he was not really on stage, cosmetics were not necessary, he became so upset that the make-up artist gave in and gave him the works. A grey beard, orange face, black eyebrows and red lips.

An hour later, when Joseph knocked on the innkeeper's door and asked for accommodation for his wife, heavy with child, and himself, to the astonishment of the cast, teachers and audience, George shot centre-stage through the makeshift door, looked to right and left, then, pitching his voice out over the lights to the auditorium, said, 'Do come in. It's Christmas. We're full up, but we'll make room for you and your wife.' With a final triumphant glance into the wings and at the wildly gesticulating director, he led a mystified Joseph and Mary into the inn.

Thanks to the quick-thinking director, within a short space of time a bewildered Joseph and Mary, cushion slipping to around his knees, were back on stage. Joseph read laboriously and with painful precision the block-capital words on a page of a copybook. 'It is too crowded in there. We will look elsewhere.' And so they did, to the delight of the audience.

The nuns were furious over George's 'deliberate sabotage', as they put it. 'Nonsense,' said Trevor at the party afterwards, as he sipped at a glass of Mi-Wadi orange, puffed on his pipe and rumpled George's hair. 'He was merely putting into practice the kind and charitable generosity he learns from you. Weren't you, son?'

Nance, unsure whether to laugh or cry, ended up laughing. But not until they reached home.

Now, as she stirred the eggs around the edges of the saucepan with the wooden spoon, circling the bottom to prevent sticking, Nance began one of her 'little talks' with Rosemary:

'Don't be in too much of a hurry to grow up, or to be thinking of boys,' she advised. 'All this raucous music, wild dancing and running to the pictures won't do you any good. You'll regret it when you're my age.'

Rose, watching the eggs solidify, wished she resembled the modern Jezebel of her mother's imagination. What a wonderful life she would have! She didn't even get to play her one and only record on the radiogram. Whenever she put on Elvis Presley's 'Love Me Tender', no matter how low she kept the sound, as though fitted with special antennae, her mother materialised tut-tutting out of nowhere.

She had seen only a few decent films. And those by accident. *Rock Around the Clock*, because her mother didn't know about rock 'n' roll then and thought it sounded 'nice and cheerful'; James Dean's *East of Eden*, presumed to have religious overtones; and *Seven Brides for Seven Brothers* which, luckily for her, had been promoted as 'wholesome family entertainment'. Rose certainly would not count in this category *The Song of Bernadette*, shown in the school hall as a special treat.

Rose was sure that when she was as old as her mother, her major regret would be having been thwarted and imprisoned during her teens. Usually she spoke out on perceived injustices, but today she did not. Having a secret boyfriend, she had crossed the threshold from child to woman. That made her one up on her mother.

By the time Nance had finished, the eggs were so well cooked that they were inedible. Still, Rose ate with gusto.

Rose and Frank's relationship was easy and natural, their conversation full of the latest rock music, the newest films, school talk, gossip about friends. And grumbles about parents — Frank afraid of not living up to his father's expectations, despite getting five honours in last year's Inter Cert; Rose raging that her mother treated her like a child.

While enjoying the status of having a boyfriend, Rose was dying to be loved, kissed and petted, to have first-hand experience of this boy/girl business, to hold her own with her classmates; to match Monica's blow-by-blow accounts of her activities with her stand-by goalie which, if she were to believed, grew more passionate by the day. But for now Rose was unsure of how to handle this new blast of feeling that weakened her knees and made her crave Frank's touch.

The highlight of the second school term became the party. That it was her brother Tom's party in no way deterred Monica from taking a proprietorial interest in the guest list. Among the class, she wielded invitations as tools of blackmail, as leverage for having homework projects done, or for acquiring lunchtime chocolate biscuits and sweets which she ate behind the raised flap of her desk. Rose was not worried. As Frank's girlfriend she was a definite. Her concern was getting her mother's permission to go. She would have to choose her time of asking carefully.

One March evening when Rose was stuck into a geography project at the table in the corner of the living-room — functional, mushroom-coloured, with leather armchairs and brown velvet curtains — Nance raised her head from her most recent project of cross-stitching luncheon mats. 'Don't you agree girls of fifteen are too young to have notions about being grown up?' she asked Trevor, sitting across the fire from her, engrossed in *The Irish Times*.

Trevor Horn, not the most practical of men, was the personification of an absent-minded professor of literature, which, in fact, he was. Kind and cuddly, his air was one of abstraction and he had a great fondness for tweed suits. Despite being an internationally respected expert on James Joyce, he could be unsettled by the most minor of domestic practicalities.

That said, he considered Rose perfect. As well as rejoicing in her academic ability and the twinkling gravity of her manner, he was delighted by her squeaky clean looks. To himself, he thought of her as an apple person. Crisp, rosy flesh, dancing eyes, snowy teeth. Glowing. Sometimes, looking at her, he felt as though he would burst with pride.

Rose's heart plummeted. With the party looming, the last thing she needed was her mother band-wagoning yet again on the benefits of childhood. Dammit. She was nearly sixteen. Cocking her ears, she kept her head down and ran nervous fingers through her short, brown hair.

Listening to grown-up conversation was beneficial for acquiring insights into attitudes and information to which she normally would not be privy. Knowing that adults were far from partial to eavesdropping children, she had learned that if she kept her head in a book, they presumed she was not paying them attention.

'Wouldn't a summer in Kerry with Babs put a stop to Rosemary's nonsense about being a teenager?' Nance continued, in a low voice, having re-threaded her needle with pinky-peach silk.

When Trevor was reading, the house could go up

in flames around him and he would hardly notice. On this Thursday evening, he was even more absorbed than usual, as he analysed the implications of the funding for education requested in the Dáil by the Minister for Finance. Certainly £260,500 would make a considerable impression on university and college accommodation, though given the current political climate, it was unlikely they would receive the whole allocation.

It was only after being called by Nance three times in ascending tones of shrillness that he came out from behind the paper, looking confused, and nodded — a gesture she triumphantly took as affirmation of her plan. Rose turned a page of Butler's geography.

Having Trevor's attention, Nance went into full flight. She had recently read in one of the English Sunday papers that, when the 1950s began, teenagers did not exist; now, at the end of the decade, there were five million of them in Britain. Ireland's ratio would be about the same, wouldn't it? Not only had teenagers a name, but they had found an identity and invented their own distinct culture, on which they spent £800 million a year. This included trips to the cinema, clothes, records and cosmetics. 'If that's the way the world is going, it's worrying, isn't it?' she finished.

Trevor nodded in an unworried way.

Rose tried to visualise £800 million. She could not even manage £800, or, now that she thought of it, even £80. But she could imagine the bliss of frequent visits to the cinema, and the rapture of buying stacks of records, and vast amounts of clothes and cosmetics.

Glancing at her daughter, pleased to see her still absorbed in homework, Nance dropped her voice a few octaves: 'I'm worried about Rosemary. She's not as biddable as she used to be. I'm afraid there's a streak of wildness there. I wouldn't like to see that developing.'

Conventional by nature, Nance was uncomfortable with her family background. Kerry wildness, she called their behaviour. Generations of drinking, gambling and carousing. Imagine, her mother had been married at sixteen to a man old enough to be her grandfather. You would not get that kind of behaviour in Dublin. Certainly not in the circles in which she and Trevor moved.

Trevor was inbred traditional. The Horns were English Protestant, the ultimate in conservatism, settled for three generations in Dartry, one of the more prosperous suburbs of south Dublin. 'She'll be all right, dear,' Trevor said fondly, wishing he could return to his paper and, not for the first time, pondering Joyce's statement about how you could always see a fellow's weak point in his wife. How Nance had changed since their marriage.

Rose realised that getting permission to attend the party required more than watching her every word and action; she would need to rustle up skills in diplomacy and ingenuity as well.

Over the weekend a brainwave hit. She would complete and give to her mother the tapestry she had received from Grandma Laetitia on her last birthday. Nance had been so rapturous that she had almost, but not quite, hugged her mother-in-law.

The decision made, Rose took the stairs two at a time and retrieved from the bottom of her wardrobe her sewing box — Nance's gift to her three Christmases ago. Shaking out the tapestry from its crumpled repose, she loathed it anew. The subject was three improbably shaped tulips, rigidly placed in a shallow container. The design was harsh, the colours garish, Rose's workmanship inferior.

That weekend she sat in the rocking chair in her bedroom, her feet on the windowsill, the sewing box and its ugly wool by her side. She threaded the needle, knotted the wool, stabbed the needle into the canvas and out again. One stitch. Then another and another. Double stitch to prevent ravelling. Snip. Finished with that colour. Time to swap insipid pink for bilious green.

Despite the fact that with each passing stitch her initial indifference to the project grew to active loathing, she persisted. Hour after hour. Emerging only for meals. Dampening her mother's curiosity by saying it was a surprise for her. At last it was finished. Battle fought and won, she presented it with a triumphant flourish, a blatant bribe that Nance accepted enthusiastically as a gesture of filial love.

Her mother's pride and delight took Rose by surprise. Holding it at arm's length, squinting at it with a professional eye, Nance announced, 'I'll have it framed. And hung. But where?'

Forsaking her fireside chair, the bag of pink and white iced caramels, and her Sunday-night radio listening, she held it against this wall and that. 'Up here? Over there? What do you think?' She then crossed the hall, heels click-clacking on the parquet floor, and into the drawing-room. Rose and Trevor trailing after her. 'Would it look well over the mantelpiece? Better than that mirror? Don't you think? Or wouldn't it be perfect above the china cabinet?'

Rose did not doubt the tapestry would become a conversation piece for visitors and a constant source of embarrassment to her. The ultimate outcome was immaterial; Rose's strategy had paid dividends. She was certain — well, almost certain — she was going to the party.

CHAPTER TWO

After chatting for a few weeks at the side of the road, putting up with lots of ribbing from their pals, and with Rose increasingly nervous of being spotted by more of her mother's eagle-eyed friends, Frank found a quiet archwayed entrance leading into the drive of a large house on the Stillorgan Road. Once inside the gate and with their bicycles propped against the wall, it became their own private bower.

There they were shielded from prying eyes on the roadway, and a lavishly evergreen laurel bush protected them from discovery from the house. They continued their discussions, agreeing that Tom's party was a real bonus, and graduated to holding hands. Exploring each other's palms and fingers. Running index fingers up and down wrists, sliding under shirt cuffs, Rose discovered to be amazingly titillating.

She veered from being sick with excitement at the thought of the party to despair at the thought of her clothes. Not that she had many to despair of. So few, in fact, that she had reduced her only decent outfit to an over-worn disaster. A passionately loved pair of black drainpipes, a roomy black V-neck pullover and suede flatties to complete the Audrey Hepburn look she so admired. With her short dark hair, secretly she felt she looked quite like the film star.

She tried on the clothes, adjusting them this way and that, substituting a white shirt for the pullover. Adding and subtracting the silvery medallion, Aunt Babs's Christmas present. No matter what the combinations, the results, she decided, were the same. Disgusting.

Of course, there was her Sunday outfit. The dress. Black Watch tartan with a white collar. She would die if she were reduced to that. Or the suit. The one she got for Aunt Josie and Uncle Bart's wedding. Her mother's choice, yucky green tweed. So awful that she had hardly stood up for the whole day. If she were seen in either outfit, she would be laughed out of it.

With the party looming on the horizon, clothes chat superseded boy chat. Everyone was getting a new dress. A real party dress.

Nance, while far from enamoured at the idea of Rosemary gallivanting to parties, recognised the importance of socialising. Correct socialising. Dublin was a small place. It was never too early to think about a suitable match.

Quietly she congratulated herself on Rosemary's friendship with Monica Doyle, whose parents were leading social lights. Peter, an up-and-coming gynaecologist, and Mysie, whose work as a fundraiser for medical charities took her as far afield as America.

'We'll have to get you a suitable frock,' Nance told a delighted Rose. Only then did Rose really believe she was going to the party. Grown-up shopping. Rose could not believe her luck. Just like Barbara and her mother. 'We'll go into town on Saturday, have a look around and get the material.'

Nance's own clothes were made, or designed — her preferred description — by a Miss Meek, who she praised as 'a gem of a find', though whenever anyone asked, Nance adroitly sidestepped divulging her whereabouts.

'Wouldn't it be easier to just buy a dress?' Rose asked, nervous of ending up in something in her mother's style.

'We'll see,' promised Nance, who was becoming increasingly excited at the thought of fixing Rosemary up with her first formal dress — well, semi-formal. Wait until her debs; or even better, the wedding. 'But the one thing you can be sure of when you're having an outfit made is the quality.'

Rose had seen the dress of her dreams ages ago in a movie magazine at a sale of work. She had eased out the page, secreted it in her atlas and occasionally drooled over it. She had never shown it to Nance. There wouldn't have been much point. Dare she now?

Trevor drove them into town. He would spend a few hours in Trinity library; it would be quiet on a Saturday, and he would pick them up at the top of St Stephen's Green, outside Geary's toy shop, at one o'clock. Nance looked smart and vibrant in her bottle-green coat and matching hat; Rose dowdy in her school gabardine. Handing Nance a signed blank cheque, Trevor joked, 'Get a nice frock now. Without breaking the bank.'

Rose and Nance started off with coffee and custard slices in Bewley's in Grafton Street. Nance loved custard slices, the romantic connotations of them. Her elbows on the marble of the table, she told Rose, 'The first time we met, your father bought me a custard slice.'

It was her third year of nursing at the Mater Hospital and Nance Clifford was happy in her choice of career, considering that she had found her true vocation. She had a great affinity with her patients and enjoyed even the goriest aspects of hands-on nursing. But she was always hungry and, as she was poorly paid, constantly broke.

As she came out from saying a prayer in Clarendon Street Church one damp November evening, the waft of warmth and the aroma of food drifting from Bewley's side entrance were tantalising. But financially, a cup of coffee — much less one of the custard slices to which she was inordinately partial — was out of the question. She piled her books back into the basket of her bicycle and made for Grafton Street.

The bicycle's front wheel stubbed on the uneven granite slabs, Nance's basket slewed sideways and the books spilled out, landing on a pair of scuffed brown shoes. They belonged to Trevor Horn, recently appointed Lecturer in English at Trinity College. Between them they retrieved and re-packed the books.

On a sudden impulse, he asked, 'Have a coffee with me?' His breath puffed silvery clouds, his hair was a mop of dark curls and his tweed jacket had leather elbow-patches. To the amazement of both of them, in a warm Kerry accent and with a shy look from under her lashes, Nance agreed.

Their rapport was instantaneous. Before they had eaten the last flake of pastry and finished their first cups of coffee, Trevor was smitten and Nance knew that this was LOVE in capital letters.

After just a few weeks, the idea of life without each other had no meaning for either. Trevor wooed her, in a gentle, insistent manner. He also paved the way for their wedding, facilitating the necessary permission for a mixed marriage, signing documents promising to raise their 'issue' in the Catholic Church, making it as easy as possible for her and her mother. He need not have worried, Annie Clifford took to him on first sight. In Trevor she recognised the same unwavering love that she had enjoyed with her late husband.

The difficulty lay with Trevor's parents, whose unbroken line of Protestantism dating back to the eighteenth century they waved like a banner. Even with Trevor's best intentions, Nance's integration into the Horn family had been, and still could be, fraught with difficulty.

Despite her feelings for Trevor, Nance knew that, by marrying him, in the eyes of the Catholic Church, she had flown in the face of God. In all her confessions, she had never come across a priest who confirmed that her marriage had been a good thing. Thus she wanted Rosemary to grow up slowly, to take her time about boys. Not to end up, as she had, hoist on the petard of passion.

When Rose first realised the implications of mixed

marriage, she considered her parents' defiance of Church authority positively heroic. She was even more impressed on discovering that the ceremony had taken place without music, choir, or flowers. And in the porch of the church. They did not even receive a papal blessing. Such a sacrifice. And all for love.

For herself Rose dreamed of a wedding full of pomp and ceremony: a flower-decked altar, organist and choir in full voice, white crinoline dress and puffed tulle veil, with yards and yards of train trailing along the red carpet. A bouquet of roses, red surrounded by maidenhair fern, like she had seen in a magazine. And, of course, despite having reservations about religion, she would have a papal blessing all the way from Rome.

Her parents were the most unlikely candidates to flout protocol. She wondered had they been driven by a consuming passion which could not be denied. Or could it have been plain and simple rebellion? From what she knew of them, neither explanation made sense.

'Now you know why I'm so fond of custard slices,' Nance finished, having given Rose an edited version, and thinking how lucky she was to have a daughter to confide in. Over the years what fun they would have, shopping and doing things together.

Basking in the warmth of her mother's confidence, Rose, judging the climate to be as right as ever it would be, removed the picture of the dress from the side pocket of her gabardine and daringly spread it on the table. 'Look, Mammy. What do you think? Isn't this gorgeous?'

Worn by red-haired Rita Hayworth, the dress was black, diaphanous. From shoestring straps the neckline plunged to a deep V which revealed a generous amount of cleavage. The bodice was tight and the skirt fluidly figure-hugging.

'Very nice,' Nance said, to Rose's amazement, not batting an eyelid. 'But she must be as old as me.'

'She's a film star,' explained Rose. 'Lives in Hollywood.'

'Well, yes, but a redhead. They are limited in what they can wear. You're lucky, Rosemary. Being a brunette you'd get away with something softer.' Peering closely at the picture, she pronounced, 'And that looks like chiffon — a dowdy fabric. Come on, let's look at materials.' And Nance whisked her daughter down the street to Switzer's.

Today Rose was contented in Nance's company and it gave her a good feeling. Usually she had the impression that she didn't come up to her mother's exacting standards. On this outing it was like having the big sister she had always wanted. 'What do you think of the straps?' she asked, trailing through Cosmetics to Fabrics, wishing she had a load of money to spend on make-up.

'Very fashionable.'

Rose wanted to discuss and analyse each aspect of this dress. 'And the skirt?'

'Looks really well,' said Nance over her shoulder, resting her bag on the counter. 'We're shopping for a party dress for my daughter, here,' she confided to the sales assistant who had a badge pinned over her heart proclaiming her to be Miss Love. 'And we've run into a bit of a problem. My daughter is keen on a black dress, but I feel with her colouring she could take something softer.' Leaning across the counter, she flattered, 'We thought we'd call on your expertise.'

The first Rose had heard of it. There was a short, shiny silence. The two older women looking at each other. Miss Love shot Rose an appraising look which Rose interpreted as admiration for her dress sense. She came out from behind the counter. Stood Rose in front of a long mirror, prodding at her to straighten up. Hands clasped behind her back, she paced around Rose, sizing her up from the tip of her un-polished shoes to the top of her slightly greasy hair. 'You're lucky,' she pronounced. 'I have just the material.'

Rose opened her mouth to reinforce the importance of its being black and chiffon, but Miss Love was gone, bounding over to a shelf, removing a bolt of turquoise brocade. Quick as a flash, Rose, still in her school coat, was swaddled from neck to ankle.

'Lovely,' the two women breathed in unison.

'It drapes beautifully,' enthused Miss Love, jerking, plucking and smoothing the fabric this way and that. Rose knew that, despite her name, nobody could love her.

'It brings up your skin tone,' said her mother.

'I don't like it,' Rose ventured, hankering for the fluidity of chiffon while struggling out from stiff brocade.

'Nonsense,' they assured her.

By now it was too late. Miss Love was wielding her shears and Nance waving the cheque.

Nance's gem of a dressmaker was mousy, but she was so complimentary and Nance so enthusiastic that Rose ended up delighted by her choice of material. Turquoise. The word 'free' roamed around her head in delicious expectation. A dress the colour of the sky.

No trouble visualising herself at the party. Frank, seeing her for the first time out of school uniform, totally entranced. Hair up, with a few strategically pulled tendrils brushing her cheeks and the nape of her slender neck, bronzed shoulders, pert bust, hourglass waist, skirt falling seductively to strappy four-inch heels.

Nance said she would deal with Miss Meek. As she had for years. Miss Meek would be insulted with a picture. She had served her apprenticeship in London with Norman Hartnell, the Queen's dress-maker, no less, and was trained to follow instructions down to the last detail. During measuring, Rose wished she had a brassière, satin, pink and pointy. Like Monica's. But she stuck out her bosom anyway, and sucked in her stomach.

She couldn't really judge from her first and only fitting — all pins, tailors' chalk and red tacking threads, though her mother assured her the dress was shaping up nicely. But Rose did ask Miss Meek to make sure the straps were really narrow and to nip in the waist, tight.

The completed garment arrived some days later. Beautifully presented in a royal-blue box, nestling between layers of tissue paper. Nervously Rose extracted her dress and held it against her. The front of the bodice came up to her collar-bone without even the suggestion of a dip, much less a plunging V; and the back to her shoulder-blades. The straps were two inches wide and sturdy; the bodice bag-of-flour shaped, the waist roomy and the skirt substantial.

When she stood contemplating herself in the full-length mirror attached to the door of her wardrobe, Rose looked just like herself. Herself in a turquoise dress. A frisson of loss or, perhaps, sadness flicked over her; the dress bore no relationship to the one in the picture that she had stashed away in her atlas all those months ago. Then she realised that, despite the dress, the lisle stockings and school shoes, she felt good, even quite gorgeous. She ran down the stairs.

Agnes, eyes shining, confirmed her self-assessment; George said she looked like a real grown-up. For once Trevor did not have to be prodded out from behind *The Irish Times*. He called her his princess and assured her she would be the belle of the ball.

A touch wistfully, Nance said, 'You look beautiful,' adding, 'Don't let this give you ideas about growing up too quickly.' Then she nearly gave Rose a heart attack by asking, 'Trevor, do you think we're doing the right thing, letting her go?'

Trevor put his arms around his daughter, gave his wife a hug and said into her hair, 'As James Joyce would say, "It's the reality of experience that's important."'

CHAPTER THREE

Rose would never forget the reality of her first party. And not just the party. The excitement of the whole occasion.

She began the evening with a bubble bath, the bubbles so dense that they made a boa. Flirty white feathers flickering on her shoulders, glimmering as she moved.

She imagined she was a film star getting ready to attend a gala opening in her figure-hugging, spaghetti-strapped dress: diamonds at her ears and around her neck, sparkling on her wrists. Luscious red lips, matching ovals of nails. Arriving in a limousine, escorted by Frank, of course, on a waft of Chanel No. 5 — what else?

Writhing with delight, she pushed the bubbles down until the tops of her breasts were visible. Touching her nipples, she sighed with pleasure. She liked her breasts, liked feeling them, liked the way her nipples stood rosily to attention, making her feel all womanly and tingly.

She imagined Frank seeing them. Would he touch them? Kiss them? She thought she would like that, but wondered was that something boys did. And then blushed beetroot at the very idea. She climbed out of the bath and away from the temptation of impure thoughts, or, even worse, impure touching, though she was none too sure of the semantics of either. Wishing she had a bra and hating her school roll-on. Monica said she had the loan of her mother's black garter belt which had little pink roses surrounded by dotey green leaves.

Still, even though she had to wear the scuffed flatties, which were better than her brown laced-up school shoes, and she did not have any make-up, Rose felt truly beautiful.

At the last minute, Nance came up trumps with a string of pearls, a pair of nylons and a dab of 4711 cologne behind each ear.

The Doyles lived in Rathgar, in a sumptuously elegant Victorian house in its own grounds. The informal living-room at the back of the house had been given over to the 'children's party', as Mysie had labelled the occasion, much to Tom and Monica's disgust. The room had been cleared of most of its furniture, carpet lifted, floorboards 'Luxed' to slithery perfection, and bunting and balloons decorated the walls and ceiling. An impressive stack of seven-inch EPs of skiffle, rock 'n' roll and slow numbers awaited the turntable.

On a crisply starched damask cloth, bottles of Pepsi-Cola and jugs of orange were flanked by dishes of crisps and peanuts, baskets of tiny sausages, trays of skewered triangular-shaped sandwiches. There were even whole grapefruits spiked with cocktail sticks on which were impaled cubes of cheese, glacé cherries, chunks of pineapple and pickled onions. The food and its layout had come from the teenage section of one of Mysie's American magazines.

A stickler for etiquette and chicly hospitable, Mysie had a fire blazing in the formal drawing-room, and drinks and nibbles (another American innovation enthusiastically adopted by her) were laid out as refreshment for parents dropping off and collecting their offspring.

The Doyles encouraged their eldest children to entertain at home. They liked to know their friends and where they fitted in socially. Mysie approved of both Barbara and Rose as friends for Monica, though she totally disapproved of this stand-by goalie. She particularly encouraged Tom's friendship with Frank Fennelly, explaining, 'His father's the only Harvard-experienced banker in Ireland. And there's nothing like the old-boys' network. Nowadays, it's who you know rather than what you know.'

As Trevor drew up at the bottom of the steps, he gave Rose a hug. 'Enjoy yourself. I'll be back later to collect you.'

'Not too early, Daddy,' she begged.

'You know me. I often forget the time,' he chuckled, leaning across to let her out of the car.

Now that she was here, actually pressing the door-bell, Rose's excitement bordered on terror. She wanted to flee down the granite steps, across the gravel, into the car and home.

It was too late.

An efficient maid took her coat, and further along the hall, Monica and Tom, backed by Mysie and

Peter, welcomed her warmly. Rose had no experience of parties, but from the first blast of warmth when the hall door had opened, she knew this was the best.

With the exception of Monica who looked dead sexy bursting out of black lace, there was a conservative sameness to the girls. They stood around giggling in self-conscious little bunches, body language too exaggerated, talk too forced, too aware of the boys. Their tidy hair and borrowed strands of pearls, the royal blues, rich wines, bottle greens, quiet pinks and muted reds of their party dresses were a perfect foil for the boys in their social uniform of grey trousers, white shirts, striped ties and navy blazers.

Monica was in her element playing hostess, laughing and chatting, flirting like mad. Even her protuberant teeth added an air of rakish gaiety to her behaviour.

After meeting the would-be goalie, she had removed her brace and dropped it down a drain in Donnybrook, maintaining that he refused to kiss train tracks. The brace had been Mysie's idea — every teenager she met in the States had a mouthful of metal; all the adults had gleaming, even teeth, and every one of them seemed to have attended an orthodontist. The class was not only envious of Monica's sex life, but full of admiration for her defiance of her parents.

The boys hung around in hard, tight circles, smoking cigarettes held inwards towards the palms, aping nonchalance, ostensibly and determinedly unaware of the girls. In both groups flickering glances appraised and astute eyes assessed. Though inexperienced and untried, they were sexually aware and tuned in to the mating game.

Rose and Frank saw only each other. He caught her hand immediately as she came through the double doors. The look he gave her was one of admiration. Unselfconsciously, as though it were the most natural thing in the world, they danced to the strains of Acker Bilk, Guy Mitchell, Buddy Holly and Bill Haley.

Gradually the floor filled up. Barbara, dimpling but unavailable, in wine velvet. Secure in her boyfriend, who was incarcerated in school, she was a non-threatening dancing partner. Jiving and rock 'n' roll quickly gave over to smooching, and fellows and girls were wrapped around each other. Only Frank and Rose held themselves apart; they were still too shy for public affection, though he did get her a mineral and she saved as a memento the red, white and blue Pepsi bottle-top.

Then Mysie and Peter came and stood in the doorway laughing. His arm was around her waist, her head resting on his shoulder. Rose thought they looked like film stars, he in his broad-shouldered, taper-leg, navy suit in the latest Italian mohair, she with her polished blonde hair and multi-petticoated silver-blue dress. She was gorgeous, like a Dresden figurine.

He whisked her into the centre of the room and they smooched, like teenagers, to 'Strangers on the Shore', her pointy-toed high heels quicksilvering between his Italian winkle-pickers. The young people stood back and gave them the floor.

Tom and Monica were mortified. Red-faced with shame. Parents should know their place. Should not go in for close dancing.

'Some dancers,' said Frank.

'A hard act to follow,' remarked someone else.

'Would you want to?' wondered another.

One half of Rose wished she had parents like the Doyles; the other half knew she would hate such exhibitionism. Still, she was in awe of Mrs Doyle whom she considered the ultimate in sophistication. Imagine the romance of having a husband who brought you to London to see the stage show, *My Fair Lady,* for a wedding anniversary. Imagine seeing the stars, Julie Andrews and Rex Harrison, in person.

The way Mysie had told the story the last time Rose was up for tea, you would think she knew all about shows transferring from New York's Broadway to London's West End, and the cultural pluses and minuses of Alan Lerner's adaptation of George Bernard Shaw's *Pygmalion*.

'Not at all,' she had said, tossing her head and giving a tinkling laugh. 'It was just such a fascinating experience. A total surprise. And I love surprises. And the clothes and décor by Cecil Beaton were exquisite, particularly the Ascot scene. It's my dream to go to Ascot. I'll have to start dropping hints. But I hope I won't have to wait until my twentieth wedding anniversary. I don't want to be too old to enjoy the experience.'

Suddenly flushed and laughing, Mysie broke loose from Peter, whipped the red crêpe paper off the lamp-shades, lifted the needle off the record and rooted among the sleeves. She made her choice and out blared 'The Yellow Rose of Texas'. Not content with musically shattering the romantic mood, she disturbed sofa-bound couples by plumping cushions, standing them on their tippy-toes, briskly suggesting playing games, before finally linking her husband out of the room.

The ice was broken. With much whooping and hollering from the boys, it was spin-the-bottle time. Players sitting in a circle on the floor, a bottle twirling, the person the neck pointed to choosing his or her kissing partner. Rose was mesmerised. Wondering would she get a real kiss. Hoping it would be Frank. Terrified in case it was not. Thinking she did not want her first real kiss to happen here, like this.

Eventually the bottle did stop at Frank.

Hauling her to her feet, he said to nobody in particular and to the party in general, 'We'd like some privacy', and they went into the hall where they looked at each other.

From inside came the slow count, 'Six … Seven … Eight …'

Mysie appeared up from the kitchen, a cocktail glass with a cherry on a stick in her hand. She directed them towards the toilets — pointing Rose upstairs, Frank off the hall. All the time the count continued, 'Fifteen … Sixteen …' Interspersed with whoops.

'A good game?' she asked as Rose climbed the stairs. 'Lots of fun from the sound of it.' Rose nodded and Mysie wondered had mousy Rose Horn really got off with Frank Fennelly.

'Ninety-one … ninety-two,' came the chant as Rose descended the stairs to Frank. He took her by the hand and gave her a quick kiss that landed somewhere between her mouth and nose. It was the smell of him — soapy and cigarette-y — she remembered most. Also that she wanted more, much more. They returned to the party to a crescendo of caterwauling applause.

It was some weeks before Rose got her first proper kiss. During which time she was consumed with the thought of it. She had not admitted even to Barbara, and most certainly not to Monica, that she and Frank had not really kissed. She dreamed how it would be, the romance of it.

A few weeks before, Monica had perched on the edge of her desk, legs swinging, and had given the class a crash course in kissing techniques. Using her index and third fingers as lips, she had shown them how to manipulate their own lips, tongue and teeth for maximum sensation. Eyes wide at the wonder of her knowledge and experience, they had listened intently and watched in fascination. With a toss of her head, she had asked Rose, 'Isn't this right? This the way Frank kisses?'

Rose, too mortified to do other than nod, determined to put her lack of experience to rights.

In the end, the kiss occurred unexpectedly. In 'their place', as they had labelled the bower. Propped against the wall, they were holding hands, fingers loosely laced, discussing the latest instalment of

Rose's difficult mother, and Frank insisting he had an even more difficult father.

Frank's thumb strayed under Rose's sleeve, as it had done on many occasions, circling her inner wrist, moving up her arm, making little soft round motions. She shivered at the thrill of it. He looked at her. Suddenly their arms were wrapped around each other.

Of one accord, their lips met. Softly and gently, tentatively exploring. 'Is this all right?' Frank asked.

'Oh, yes,' she assured him, drinking in his masculinity, feeling that this was the best day of her life. The greatest thing ever. Like her whole body was falling through something warm and moist and lovely. Wanting more and more.

Rose was disappointed when Frank pulled back. Even more disappointed when he cracked a joke, 'What's a three-legged donkey called?'

Rose looked at him in amazement.

'A wonkey, of course.' He laughed, told a few more daft jokes and the intensity between them dissipated. Though Frank was full of a protective tenderness, and Rose was quiet, her body seething in a new delicious turmoil.

Next day their kiss was instigated by Rose. It was longer, more lingering. Frank told no jokes. She emerged from it with collapsing knees and the certainty she had committed the sin of sex.

Sex and religion. In Rose's mind they were irrevocably entwined. Boundary subjects, not for discussion.

Such as the gentle flow of conversation she would sometimes hear from her parents' bedroom. Her father's voice growly gruff; her mother's girlishly giggly. Invariably this would be followed by strange sounds and bed-creaks. And she knew an intensely private and personal act was taking place. From which she was excluded. Occasionally, though, she was certain, she could make out her father's pleading voice and her mother sobbing.

She used to think their arguments had to do with God, because when she was little she had gone to sleep every night with her mother's prayers ringing in her ears. As she grew older though, she suspected their arguments might be about sex.

Whatever about Monica and her goalie, the idea of adults, particularly mothers and fathers, especially her own mother and father, kissing and going on was disgusting. These nocturnal activities made her so uncomfortable that she found it hard to look her parents in the face the following morning.

With Frank in her life, sex and God became even more intertwined. Unburdening herself in confession, Rose saw as the only solution.

Twelve o'clock confession in the Church of the Sacred Heart, Donnybrook, after Saturday-morning school was quite a social occasion. The girls removed ties, unbuttoned shirts, hitched up gymslips, and the lucky ones swapped lisle for nylon stockings.

Of recent times not the least attraction was the dishy new curate with the crisp dark curls and shy brown eyes. Monica spent as long as she could in his confession box and betted he had a past. Rose did not think so — he came for afternoon tea with her mother.

On this particular March Saturday with spring in the air and cotton-wool clouds gambolling across a virginal sky, Rose determined to make a general confession, to wipe clean from sin the slate of her soul. The combination of skimping on previous confessions and her recent sexual activities niggled like a very large uncomfortable burr. The curate had the reputation of being sympathetic.

Impure thoughts were hard enough to live with. Impure actions even harder. And as for continuous occasions of sin, the worst of all. The bower where she and Frank met, she knew, had to be an occasion of sin. A 'mortaler'.

The fact that only Father Crosby was on duty that Saturday was disturbing. As well as being old, he was cranky and deaf. His voice a penetrating, piercing kind of whisper-shout. From a penitent's point of view, it was off-putting to have their confessor's views heard throughout the church. Even worse, he was a priest who not only asked a lot of questions on even the most simple of sins, but also commented in a most authoritative manner. In between ejaculations of 'You what?', 'Repeat yourself' and 'Number of times?'

As well as being a thinker, once Rose set her mind on a course of action, she was a doer. She had listed her sins and their frequency, and had practised the order in which she would present them. While she waited in the wood-panelled sweaty gloom of the confessional box, her own hands were wet with nerves and her heart palpitating.

The silence within the box was thick and dark and dusty. A good omen, she thought, knowing that if

Father Crosby were in full voice she would hear his comments to the penitent in the other side of the confessional.

The tiny curtain jerked open. Through the mesh grille, the priest was a slumped profile and a musty smell. 'Yes,' he snapped, turning his face, bestowing on her the full blast of bad breath.

She went through the formulaic, 'Bless me, Father, for I have sinned and it's a week since my last confession.' Rattling through disobediences, the omission of morning and night prayers, minor lies — important to stress the minor, otherwise he might start asking questions. And, of course, not doing homework, a handy filler-in. Then cursing. She shouldn't say 'dammit'.

Rose breathed a sigh of relief; she was getting away with it. Screwing up her courage, dropping her voice, easing nearer the grille, she murmured about 'kissing'.

Shooting upright, chair creaking, the priest's voice pierced like an arrow. 'What? What? I can't hear you.'

Dammit.

From the shuffles and sniggers of her classmates, Rose knew he was audible. With her lips against the grille, she repeated herself several octaves lower. 'Speak up, boy. You what…?'

'Please, everyone can hear,' she entreated, reduced to tears, devastated that he thought she was a boy. Unrelentingly, he lectured her and those within the vicinity, on the degradation of carnal sin. At some point Rose shut off, unable to absorb his spewed platitudes on God's mercy, honouring Our Lady, and the body being the temple of the Holy Spirit, not a vessel of wilful depravity. His voice reached a crescendo on the last two words.

Rose escaped the box feeling abused, unable to remember if she had been given penance and not knowing if she had received absolution. Mortified, she fled the church and cycled home, head down, a gnawing pain in the base of her belly.

When she tiptoed into her father's study and looked up 'carnal' in the dictionary, it proved even worse than she had imagined. Words like 'fleshly', 'sensual', 'unspiritual', 'bodily', 'sexual', even 'murderous' leapt off the page. She closed the dictionary with a bang, secure in the knowledge that if she were to die now, she would burn in the fires of hell for all eternity.

She waited for something awful to happen.

Chapter Four

The something awful never happened. What did happen a few days later was that Frank finally French kissed her. And that very same day, invited her on their first formal date.

When he tentatively put his tongue into her mouth, Rose was so startled, despite Monica's coaching, that she did not know what to do. But she knew that finally this was it. French kissing. The ultimate in sexiness.

Monica, flat face earnest, had insisted, 'You aren't really going with a fellow until you've French kissed.'

Barbara, curls bobbing, confirmed this, adding, 'It is special.'

Well Rose remembered the conversation which had taken place only a few days previously in the locker room as they had changed into their boots, prior to hockey practice; feeling unsure and childish, wishing she had an experience, or even a comment, to add.

Now here she was. Experiencing life. With a capital L. Frank's tongue tasted odd, rough and smooth at the same time, rather like suede. The sensation was quite disappointing and she remembered wondering why anyone would want to do this. Tongues still locked, she decided to keep her disappointment to herself.

Their date was to the Schools Cup Senior Final at the Bective Rugby grounds in Donnybrook. Castleknock versus Newbridge. Appearing with your boyfriend at a rugby match, particularly the finals or semi-finals, was a mutual and public sign of commitment, and Rose's status among her classmates had escalated. The custom was to meet outside the grounds, and the boy would pay as they went through the turnstile. The problem for Rose was that kick-off was half an hour before school ended.

Hating herself for not having the courage to ask Nance for a note excusing her from last class, she consoled herself that she would be unlikely to get it anyway. Telling lies did not come easy to Rose. She also knew, though, that no way would she miss being paraded in public by Frank.

Not one to leave happenings to chance, Rose planned the operation carefully, on Wednesday morning, offering to catalogue books after school.

To Sister Concepta's horror, this year, as well as her duties as librarian, she had been assigned the class of 4A for Christian Doctrine. A slight, nervous woman, best known among her students for urging them to 'make their hearts a garden for Jesus', her bad eyesight was not much helped by thick whirlpool glasses.

More at ease with books than people, she regarded as a nightmare trying to impart even the basics of religion to those girls. Daily she dreaded the way they could turn any aspect of religion around to sex. Modern sex. Men had never appealed to her and even the thought of sex she considered disgusting. As a group, the class was appalling. Boy-mad, they were. Sex-mad. And egged on by that Monica Doyle.

Never would Concepta forget the newspaper incident. The nerve of Monica.

'Please, Sister, if we have to sit on a boy's knee, should we use a newspaper?' she had asked out of the blue in the middle of the Gospel of Mark. And looking as though butter would not melt in her mouth.

Concepta, who had no idea what she was going on about, but found herself becoming flustered at the giggles, had answered, 'I suppose so.'

'Why?' asked Monica to gales of laughter.

To her everlasting mortification, that evening Concepta had had to make enquiries in the nuns' common room and the sisters' amusement only added to her misery.

'That is,' Rose continued, jigging from one foot to the other, 'unless Mammy's cold gets worse.' Concepta quite understood, thanked Rose for her offer, and complimented her on her consideration for her mother. Individually, she grudged, the girls were not all bad.

Wednesday lunchtime when Nance realised that Rosemary was not eating with her usual appetite, she felt her forehead, checked the glands behind her ears, got her to stick out her tongue.

Certain she was running a temperature, she dispatched Agnes for the thermometer from the bathroom cabinet. Nance was a great believer in catching chills in their infancy and dosing them with rest and hot lemon with cloves and honey. She loved the opportunity of putting into practice her nursing skills and enjoyed mollycoddling her family, but Rosemary disappointed her by registering a temperature slightly below 98.6°.

Nance, who had recently learned to drive, had use of the family Ford Prefect on Wednesdays. Driving had not been an easily acquired skill. She still handled the car with the total concentration of insecurity. Today was car day. She would drive Rosemary back to school.

No, Rose insisted, panicking. She would cycle; the air would do her good. She might be late coming home; she had promised to help out in the library and could not really let Sister Concepta down. Nance, being a convent girl herself, appreciated Rose's dilemma and admired her for her integrity of purpose.

By the time Rose left the house, after all the hassle, she did feel feverish. Dammit. She was angry with herself for having lied, but angrier still at having a mother who forced her to.

It was perfect rugby weather, sharp and cold with a clear blue spring sky with a few cotton-wool clouds and the promise of a crackle of frost later. People said it was the largest turnout anyone could remember. Wearing Frank's blue and white school scarf, Rose was soon caught up in the buzz and dramatics of the occasion. She envied Barbara who legitimately had the afternoon off, courtesy of a note from her parents, to attend the match with her boyfriend. It was a big thing having a boyfriend from one of the competing schools.

The élite of the spectators, muffled in coats and hats, wrapped in rugs and sipping from hip flasks, occupied the stand: clergy, the parents and families of the players, old boys, rugby aficionados, a journalist from *The Irish Times*, and a smattering of talent-spotters from rugby clubs like Palmerston, Old Belvedere, Lansdowne and Wanderers.

'Look at the alickadoos.' Frank pointed to a group of sober-looking men. 'No rugby gathering complete without them.'

'The what…?' asked Rose.

'Alickadoos,' said Frank. 'Didn't you ever hear of them?'

When Rose shook her head, he explained how the name 'alickadoo' had been coined during a rugby tour in the 1930s. While on a train journey (point of departure and destination unknown) one of the players (unnamed) chose to read a novel by an Alec Kadoo rather than play cards with Lansdowne club member Ernie Crawford. From then on, for no good reason, rugby club officials or committee members were known, particularly by the younger generation, as alickadoos.

The masses wandered the sidelines. Children sucking on lollipops and playing tag; rugby enthusiasts; socialites busy seeing and being seen. Past pupils in trilby hats, crombie coats and Paisley scarves were standing as close as they could get to the action on the pitch, reliving their own glory days, commenting on the teams' strengths and weaknesses, criticising the state of play and analysing individual performances. They scrutinised moves, passes, kicks, thumping and hugging old friends, shaking hands with new acquaintances.

The atmosphere of sporting rivalry and camaraderie was beyond anything that Rose had ever experienced, or even imagined. Swaying crowds, waving banners. Roars. Chants. Razzmatazz. School songs. Wooden clappers. Teddies in team colours.

Leaning close to her, his breath hot in her ear, Frank told her that old Irish football maxim about rugby being a bowsies' game played by gentlemen; soccer a gentleman's game played by bowsies; and as for Gaelic, that was a bowsies' game played by bowsies. Rose liked Frank's droll way of imparting information. Much better than his joke-cracking mode.

After a particularly spectacular tackle, one of the Newbridge forwards staggered across the pitch, his face a red smear, blood darkening his jersey. The referee, a slight man moving like greased lightning on bandy legs, had him pinch the bridge of his nose and hold back his head. With the heel of his boot he dug out a sod of turf, weighed it, shaped it in his hands until it was like a small cushion and positioned it at the base of the player's skull. Within a few seconds the bleeding had stopped.

Shortly after play resumed, one of Newbridge's backs dived in across the ball and knocked it into touch, resulting in a scrum to Castleknock. After a successful eight-man push and the scoring of another try, Castleknock's star kicker and universal heartthrob lined up to convert the try. Collectively the spectators held their breath. The only sound to be heard was the blur of the traffic beyond the grounds. With the successful conversion, the heart seemed to go out of both the Newbridge players and their supporters. Castleknock carried the cup.

Nance, still fretting, rang the convent and spoke to Sister Concepta who said not to worry, she would check that Rosemary was all right. After the usual social exchange of pleasantries, Concepta said that she hoped Mrs Horn was feeling better. 'Very well,' Nance assured her. 'Thank God, not as much as a touch of a cold this winter.'

Sticking her head around the door of the class-room where an analysis of the character of Juliet was in progress, Concepta asked for a quick word with Rosemary. From the class reaction it was clear she had put the proverbial cat among the pigeons. For the past twenty minutes they had unsuccessfully been jostling to discuss the obsessive love aspect of the play, so the interruption was enthusiastically received. In one voice they shouted, 'Rose wasn't back after lunch.'

When asked if anyone knew Rosemary's where-abouts, Monica, in her capacity as one of Rose's best friends, stood up from her desk and asked the class in general, 'Didn't Rose say something about her mother not being well?'

'There's nothing wrong with Mrs Horn. It's she who made the enquiry,' said Concepta firmly.

Nuns are renowned for their expertise at reading facial expressions and body language, smelling out guilt and scenting cover-ups. Eyes batting frantically behind the whirlpools, but in a clipped voice quite unlike her usual insecure self, Concepta went for a quick follow-up, 'Are you absolutely sure none of you know Rosemary's whereabouts?'

'No,' the class answered in unison, experts too at plastering puzzled looks on their faces, their justification for the falsehood being that they did not know at that precise moment exactly where she was.

To the disappointment of the remainder of the students, who recognised the unfolding of a drama far greater than in any Intermediate Certificate text, even the romance of *Romeo and Juliet*, Concepta asked for Monica to be excused. After a short conference, the nun was even more convinced she was being played for a fool. But Monica stuck to her story and Concepta had no option but to phone Nance. On hearing that her daughter had not been seen for the afternoon, she became hysterical and summoned Trevor home from the middle of delivering a lecture.

By the time Monica was dismissed by Concepta, it was too late for her to make even an appearance at Bective.

The only word Rose could think of to describe the reception she received on returning home was 'awesome'.

Nance, a pessimist by nature, was red-eyed from crying. Trevor, the eternal optimist who regarded his lecturing as sacrosanct, was tight-lipped and angry at having been disturbed. George had been banished to his room with a jigsaw. Agnes's eyes were downcast when she opened the door to Rose.

A kind girl, Agnes was the eldest in a family of ten and loved little ones. Loved helping her mother rear the babies who appeared annually, and wanted nothing more from life other than her own babies. Eleven years ago she had been devastated when her father, in conjunction with the parish priest, had arranged this position. Mrs Horn was not easy to work for, but Rose and George made life bearable.

Before Agnes had a chance to warn Rose, Nance rushed into the hall and managed simultaneously to hug, shake and subject Rose to a barrage of questions. Rose, trying to gather her wits, was evasive. Trevor joined them, determined not to have the situation escalate out of control.

'The truth, all we want is the truth,' he said.

Rose, feeling guilty enough anyway, tried to gather the shattered remnants of her thoughts. She had no idea what information her parents had, nor from which source it had come.

Suddenly, without warning, Nance, acting totally out of character, smacked her across the face with her open palm. It made a whacking sound, made Rose's nose water, and she began to cry with anger.

Rolling her eyes to heaven, muttering, 'Jesus, Mary and Holy Saint Joseph,' Nance moved away so she would not be tempted to hit her again.

'Where were you?' Her father's voice was velvet quiet. His princess. This behaviour was unlike her.

'Nowhere, really.'

'Where were you?' His voice was even velvetier.

'At a rugby match.'

'A rugby match?' Nance shrilled. 'What happened?'

Rose, who in times of stress often became flippant, due to nervousness rather than boldness, answered, 'Castleknock eleven, Newbridge nine.'

'Why did you go to a rugby match without permission and lie into the bargain?' Her father was now more interested in her reasons than he was angry.

'Because I wanted to go. And you wouldn't have let me,' answered Rose.

'In that you're right.' Nance, tight-mouthed, thumped her hand down onto the marble of the console table. 'We wouldn't. I won't tolerate this wildness in you. And who were you with?'

'My boyfriend.'

'Your boyfriend?' screeched Nance, unable to continue, sinking into the hall chair.

'Your boyfriend,' echoed Trevor, amazed at his lack of knowledge of what was going on in his own home.

'You, girl — go to your room.' Nance pulled the remnants of herself together. 'I'm going to phone Mrs Doyle. Right now. And get to the bottom of this.'

'Oh no,' wailed Rose, visualising becoming the butt of Monica's comments. 'Don't phone her, please don't.'

Mysie Doyle, returning home from a reception where her latest fund-raising campaign had not been its anticipated success, was met by Monica, red-eyed with rage, railing at having missed the match.

Inputting 'quality' time, a phrase Mysie had picked up in the States, she listened 'sympathetically', made appropriate clucking sounds and looked suitably distressed at Monica's rantings. Mysie had no intention of encouraging this infatuation with the stand-by goalie. Ridiculous nonsense, and Terenure College not even in the Finals. This boy was not at all suitable. Though she knew better than to intimate any of this to her strong-willed daughter.

Monica, thought her mother, was still looking peaky, acting erratically and picking at her food. Weeks ago Mysie had mentioned this to Peter. Medically relaxed where his family was concerned, he calmed her by quoting the latest from a paper about teenagers. All kinds of statistics about rampaging hormones and unpredictable mood swings.

From her sojourns in America, Mysie had seen at first hand teen power. This new emphasis on their bodies, on clothes, make-up, dating. Parental tolerance was promoted at all costs. Communication lines were kept open, twenty-four hours a day. At times like this she abhorred the progressiveness which prevented her from giving Monica a well-deserved smack.

Highly relieved by the interruption of the phone, Mysie was saccharine social to Nance. Totally sincere in her insincerity.

You'd think in this day and age Nance would be more liberal being married to an academic; though, Mysie supposed, academics were not known for their progressive attitudes. Extricating herself gracefully, she hoped everything would work out all right, urged

Nance not to worry, assured her Rosemary was a good girl and a credit to her upbringing. In her opinion, you couldn't put a lid on your children's growing up. Sooner or later they'd become involved with the opposite sex.

She only wished it was her Monica who was going with Frank Fennelly.

CHAPTER FIVE

The day after the rugby match Rose designated the worst day of her life. She and her parents were summoned by an 8.30 phone call to the office of the Mistress of Studies. To be there at ten o'clock. Rose's presence was not required in class.

Mother Mary Magdalene was a disciplinarian with an uncanny ability to cut right to the heart of the matter. Her office, small, brown and austere, oozed a rigidly controlled atmosphere, as though the combined authority and knowledge of generations of previous occupants lingered on in distilled form.

Like a judge, her black veil unwrinkled, her white wimple starched to uncomfortable perfection, the Mistress of Studies sat erect behind a large oak desk covered with neat bundles of papers, a glass ashtray of paper clips, and tiered wooden baskets, clearly labelled In, Out and Pending.

The three Horns lined up in front of her on uncomfortable stickback chairs. Concepta, wimple awry, puffing in at the last minute, blinked nervously.

Raising her right hand, in a magisterial gesture, and inclining her head towards Rose, Magdalene said, 'We would like to hear an account of your movements, who you were with and where you were yesterday. Take your time.' Her voice was flat and emotionless. More deadly than Nance's explosion of temper and Trevor's hurt. 'And stand up. Give Sister Concepta your chair.'

Facing Mother Mary Magdalene, feeling isolated, responding psychologically as though to a flogging, Rose did not even consider burnishing the details. There was peace in telling the whole truth and nothing but the truth. Once started, there was no stopping her.

Yes, she had a boyfriend. Frank Fennelly was his name. She filled in what she knew of him. Yes, they had 'been keeping company', as Magdalene put it. Yes, they did meet alone. Yes, they did kiss.

'Impure touching?' staccatoed the nun, leaning forward avidly.

Concepta wiped her glasses on the corner of a blue-bordered handkerchief.

Rose hesitated; she had never been sure exactly what 'impure touching' was. Could it be as simple as the tingle of Frank's finger up her arm; or was it French kissing? Probably. Tongues would be more impure than arms and fingers. Wouldn't they? As she dithered, her hesitancy was taken as affirmation.

Nance looked both disgusted and embarrassed.

The nuns stared smugly.

Trevor drew in a deep breath. His princess. Puffing at his pipe, he felt sick. Well he remembered buying her a doll. The innocence of those days. They seemed like only yesterday.

The day before Nance was due home from the nursing home with their son, Trevor had left the confines of his office. Hands jammed in the pockets of his tweed overcoat, he strolled .across the cobblestone quadrangle, out the gates of Trinity College between the statues of Oliver Goldsmith, Irish poet, and Edmund Burke, British politician, onto College Green, down Westmoreland Street and, as he always did, smiled in reminiscence at the waft of coffee from Bewley's.

He stopped outside Clery's in O'Connell Street, looking at the brightly displayed windows of the department store. On a sudden impulse, he stepped through the revolving door and found himself in Cosmetics, where he looked around bemusedly.

'Can I help you, sir?' asked the doorman.

Trevor scratched his head, murmured something about dolls.

Down in the basement was a mind-boggling display. Dolls of all shapes and sizes. In all sorts of costumes. Then he saw it. The most beautiful doll ever. He knew it was the one for Rose. Never before had he bought a toy. Not even for himself, as a child.

That evening he called Rose into his study. It was her favourite room. She loved its bottle-green atmosphere and its tobaccoey aroma. He did his work at a giant Victorian pedestal desk beneath wood-panelled walls covered with framed old maps, and shelves laden with dictionaries, encyclopaedias, the works of James Joyce, Samuel Beckett, William Shakespeare, Charles Dickens and many more famous writers, as well as books of Irish and international history.

It was Rose's dream someday to be let loose in here to climb the library steps, pick and choose to her heart's content and lose herself reading in her father's fat armchair.

From under his desk Trevor conjured the most beautiful doll Rose had ever seen. Curly blond hair. Blue eyes that opened and closed. A smiling rosebud mouth.

His daughter's reaction was everything Trevor had hoped for. Like a miniature prima donna, she clasped her hands in front of her and, eyes shining, reached out for the doll. She picked her up and it was love at first sight.

'What's her name?' she asked, stroking the doll, hunkered down in front of the fire, the flames softening her strong features to prettiness.

'Whatever you like,' he answered, wishing the naming of his son was as easy. A right battle that was proving. Sometimes Nance could be so intransigent.

'Susan, I think. She looks like a Susan, doesn't she?'

'Yes. A real Susan,' he told her, watching with wonder, as he often did when viewing the world through the freshness of his daughter's eyes. How he wished he could stop time ticking away, encapsulate this moment for ever.

She laid the doll across her knees, all the better to explore her. Tiny pink fingers with pearly nails poked under the pink coat. Rose stroked the fur-trimmed bonnet, oohed at the white frilled dress and lace-edged pantaloons, smiled at the tiny socks and rosy little shoes with their minuscule buckles. When she turned the doll upside down and it said 'Mama', Rose's happiness was complete.

'What's the baby's name going to be?' she asked.

Trevor noticed she never referred to him as her brother. 'It's not been finally decided. But probably Bardolph George — after your grandfather.'

Rose looked at him, her brown eyes serious, giving her doll a little hug. 'She looks like a Susan. Does the baby look like a Bardolph George?'

'Not really,' her father had to admit.

Nance returned home untidy and tired and fat. She didn't pleat her hair and spent most of the next few days in her pink Foxford dressing-gown, milk-stained and baby-dribbled. To add to her misery, at every opportunity Rosemary pointed out the baby's wrinkles, redness, baldness and the loudness and frequency of his crying. Her assessment of the newest member of their family was so accurate that Nance wanted to strangle her.

In the throes of post-natal depression, Nance cried a lot and, if the subject of their son's name came up, veered between logical passion and blubbering inconsistency. 'After all, it's I who has given birth. For God's sake, it's nearly the 1960s, not the Dark Ages. Don't I deserve a say? Bardolph George. An awful mouthful to impose on an eight-pound baby. How about Peter or David? Even John?' she suggested, tears rolling down her cheeks.

Amazingly, Trevor, puffing on his pipe, tweed jacket more rumpled than usual, stuck to his choice while trying to mollify Nance. 'As you well know, naming sons after their paternal grandfather is a Horn family custom going back generations. It's also a tradition that girls be called after flowers. I'd have

71

liked Viola for Rose. Still, I gave in to you and we've ended up with a daughter called after a herb.'

'I'm heartily sick of constant compromise,' shrieked Nance. 'Don't you realise that's what Rosemary was? Naturally I'd have liked Mary. For the Virgin Mary. If you had any consideration you'd have known that. Compromise does nothing but leave everyone dissatisfied.'

Trevor tried to hug Nance, but she brushed him aside. He rumpled Rose's hair and gave a short sad laugh and Rose wished she had been called Viola.

'We could call him BG II, American fashion,' suggested Trevor next day.

'Over my dead body,' answered Nance, bursting out of a Donegal tweed skirt. Still, even making the effort to dress had her feeling more like herself.

'Do you know the actual meanings of Bardolph and George?'

'No, I don't. And couldn't care less.'

Trevor refused to be daunted by Nance's attitude. 'According to the *Oxford Dictionary*, Bardolph means "Bright wolf", and George, "Treasure-bringer". Good strong names for a son. Well, aren't they?'

'Yourself and that *Oxford Dictionary*,' was all Nance said. But with a half smile.

The following Thursday, a spring day of lemony sunshine, frost silvering the lawn, skeletal trees reaching skywards and a fat robin in full voice, hair tidily French-pleated, face powdered and mouth lipsticked, she tapped on Trevor's study door.

Rose, curled up in the wing-chair, Susan tucked in beside her, was engrossed in a Beatrix Potter book.

Trevor, upright behind his desk, was deep in the Molly Bloom soliloquy, a text which, for unfathomed reasons, he found enormously soothing in times of domestic strife. Unsure of Nance's humour, he welcomed her with polite reservation. But he need not have worried. Never one for prevarication, she came immediately to the point.

'I'm so worn out with all this nonsense about names. To put an end to it, I'll agree to George. On its own,' she warned.

Trevor was highly relieved. 'Good choice. St George and the dragon.'

Nance burst out laughing. He came out from behind his desk and they hugged and laughed together. Rose held Susan tightly, feeling lonely and excluded from their private joke.

For Trevor, this current situation had deteriorated into a voyeuristic confessional-like purge — this bullying of his daughter and the stripping of her dignity was alien to his idea of Christianity.

The more he learned of the mechanisms of Catholicism, the more incredulous he became. The power of the Catholic Church in post-colonial Ireland, and its involvement in politics and particularly censorship, he considered both perversive and an infringement of human rights. He feared that if the power of John Charles McQuaid, Archbishop of Dublin, were not controlled, a wealth of Irish literature — from the likes of James Joyce, Sean O'Casey, George Bernard Shaw, Liam O'Flaherty, Kate

O'Brien and Oliver St John Gogarty — would be lost to the people of Ireland. Strange, he had often thought, how Catholicism was seen as nationalistic Irish, whereas Protestantism was perceived as loyalist English.

It both amused and saddened him that the vision of a Catholic spiritual utopia was based on the premise that by eliminating sin, society would be perfect. The worst sin of all, as far as he could see — indeed the only sin for Catholics — was sex.

When he was a student in Trinity, he had often heard and, indeed, laughed at the expression, 'You can take the girl out of the convent, but you'll never take the convent out of the girl'. Today, if never before, he knew the harsh reality of the saying.

This so-called sin of sex was ruining their marriage. Nance and her ideas that they were flying in the face of God if they did not welcome the idea of one baby after another. A barbaric situation. Even worse, her solution. Abstention. Or that new daft method of calculating fertile days, or was it the infertile ones? He could never remember. Not that it made a bit of difference. It was no way for a married couple to live.

He wanted to stand up, throttle Magdalene, give Concepta a boot up the backside, shake sense into Nance, gather Rose to him and run with her to a better place. But he did not. A man of honour, his word, once given, would not be broken. On his marriage to Nance, *Ne Temere* and all that, he had sworn to uphold her religion and to bring up their children accordingly. Sometimes he knew he must have taken leave of his senses. Other times, when he and Nance looked at each other and she gave him that special little smile — her invitation to love-making — the old magic was still there.

Reaching out, he put a restraining hand on Rose's arm. She shook him loose, hell-bent on riding this roller-coaster of guilt to the terminus of absolution. Spewing on, citing harmless incidents, times and places. With each word, Trevor feared, entrenching herself deeper in the mire of a psychological quicksand.

This was a situation in which the two nuns rejoiced. The breaking of a spirit, the forerunner to humility and absolute obedience. Purity of mind and body. Character building.

Well Magdalene remembered her own baptism of fire. Scrubbing endless tiles with freezing water. Her chapped hands raw and bleeding. And just as she finished, the Mistress of Postulants kicking over the bucket. Watching the dirty water spew across her pristine floor. Starting from scratch again. And again. She knew all about humility and obedience.

What, Concepta racked her brains, was the precise wording of that Nietzsche quotation she had come across recently? Something about, 'That which does not kill us makes us stronger.' A sentiment she believed, though she chose to ignore the philosopher's passionate rejection of what he called the 'slave morality' of Christianity.

'With your permission, I want to put Rosemary on her honour that she will have no further contact with this Frank,' requested Magdalene after lecturing Rose sternly on the importance of adherence to the Ten

Commandments, and the dangers to her immortal soul of company-keeping.

Nance and Trevor nodded agreement — she enthusiastically, he with a sense of inevitability.

A squeezing band around Rose's chest was so tight that she had difficulty breathing, but her head was up and her expression mulish.

'Speak up, Rosemary,' said the nun, impatiently drumming her fingers on the desk. This interview had taken longer than anticipated. Eating into the time she had allocated for administration. 'Let us hear you promise.'

'I won't.' Rose amazed herself at her own courage. She stood squarer, tilted her chin even higher.

'Let me talk to her,' said Trevor.

They stepped out into the bleak brown corridor with its well-worn linoleum. When the door had closed behind them, Rose burst into uncontrollable crying. But even with Trevor's arms around her and her face pressed into the comfort of his tweed, she would not shake in her resolve.

Stroking her hair, he told her that if she wanted to survive in the world she would have to learn the skill of negotiation. 'Things are seldom black and white, positive or negative, attitudes change. Remember, princess, because you were less than honest and as it's up to us as parents and the nuns to ensure your welfare, this is a necessary short-term arrangement.'

'No,' Rose shouted. 'I won't.'

'Didn't you hear what I said? Short-term. Give in. You'll be watched like a hawk and won't have the opportunity anyway.'

The fight was gone out of Rose and in a perverse way, she was glad to do her father's bidding. To get the whole horrible experience over and done with.

Driving through Donnybrook, out the Stillorgan Road and turning down into Booterstown Avenue, Nance's silence was stony and Trevor's knuckles blue-white on the steering-wheel. When they reached home, unusually, he took charge, ushering Nance into the drawing-room, pointing Rose towards the kitchen.

Half an hour later, he asked Agnes to prepare a tray of tea for Mrs Horn and himself. Never did Rose remember her father having anything to do with tea, much less carrying it anywhere.

CHAPTER SIX

Nance had never seen Trevor in such a rage: narrow-eyed, his expression angry. Pacing up and down their bedroom, he repeatedly slapped his right fist into his left palm.

'Calm down,' she urged from the safety of the bed.

'Dried-up old bags, frigid biddies. What would they know about feelings?' he demanded, yanking off his tie. 'How dare they?' he stormed, heeling off his shoes. 'Who gave nuns the right to ruin my daughter's life?'

Stripping off his shirt and trousers, he stood indignantly in underwear, socks and suspenders, presenting a comical figure, though there was no amusement in the air that night. Despite her woolly bed-jacket, Nance shivered under their sky-blue quilt.

When, as usual, she demurred, without rancour and all the more frightening for his acceptance, he said, 'Look at what the Catholic Church has done to us. I don't want Rose to become frigid. How could priests or nuns know what it's like for a man to lie with the woman he loves and not touch her?'

His hurt tore into Nance's very essence. 'It's hard for me too,' she whispered, nestling close to him, putting her arms around him. After a while, she felt him relax.

This was an awful way to live. Married people should not be denied lovemaking. Yet in the eyes of her Church she was damned to hell for all eternity unless she made love with the purpose of creation. Put like that, it sounded like a philosophy of the Middle Ages.

Then his hand was slipping under her nightie, wandering the familiar path of her body. To her horror, despite only intending comfort, she found herself responding. It had been such a long time. Perhaps some good would come out of this bad, she thought. Maybe there would be another baby. It was the right time of the month. She could feel the familiar sexual glow invading her body. Languor overtaking her limbs. Fire in her belly. Still stroking her with one hand, Trevor ruined it all by reaching into his bedside drawer.

God, how she hated those condoms. The rubbery feel of them. Hadn't she told him time and time again? In the beginning, he had laughed, riposting that if she were a good Protestant, she would have been weaned on them.

When she said no, and rolled over to her own side of the bed, he slammed out of their bedroom, shouting down the stairs. Never before in their seventeen years of marriage had that happened.

This was the worst night of Rose's life. Worse even than her day. It was the night her father's anger, followed by her mother's sobs, reverberated through the house.

Rose had not wanted to know what was being said in her parents' bedroom. Had not wanted to so badly that she stuck her face into her pillow and brought up the edges around her ears to block out the sound. Still, she heard enough. And knew that it was all her fault.

Then George came into her room. George, with freckles like farthings, was known for his determination, a trait over which the Horn grandparents claimed proprietorship. He was tough, full of self-confidence, the kind of child who, even when very young, resorted to tears only when thwarted or frightened.

Tonight Rose was glad to comfort him. Drawing him into bed beside her.

When Rose came down next morning, teeth brushed, ready for school, relieved to have the past twenty-four hours over with, Nance was waiting in the hallway. Camel-hair car coat and rattling keys. She announced, 'I'll be driving you to and from school until you can be trusted.'

That Trevor was relegated to the bus did not disturb her in the least. In the light of day, she considered her husband's behaviour of the previous night to be unforgivable. Her duty lay in Rosemary's salvation, valid justification for his minor inconvenience.

Knowing better than to argue, Rose was pleasantly amenable. Refusing to be put off by her mother's coolness and monosyllabic responses during their first few journeys, she chattered away as though nothing was amiss.

Gradually it worked, with Nance's natural loquacity winning out as she detoured to pick up shopping, drop in something, call on somebody. Rose was certain her mother's tactics were to avoid her even catching a sight of Frank. And dammit, they worked. She had no idea of when this ban on her 'freedom' would be lifted.

After a few days, making contact with Frank assumed a new urgency. They were not in the habit of ringing each other at home. Anyway, Nance controlled the phone and, while Rose hoped he had rung, she had not received any message. Agnes, when sounded out, looked at her with such frightened eyes that Rose dropped the subject.

One evening when the coast was clear, she dialled Frank's number, but killed the call on hearing the cheery voice of a woman who she was sure was his mother. Frank often said she was great fun. Fun and all as she might be, Rose had neither the nerve nor the opportunity to try again.

Rose could not imagine adults being fun. Not fun, fun the way she and her friends could be. The only adult Rose knew who could be described as even remotely approaching fun was Babs, her favourite aunt. Rose loved her perfumey smell, bright-red nails and enthusiasm for whatever happened to be going on around her.

Glamorous, big-bosomed, slender-hipped and very fashionable, she came to Dublin twice a year to shop for clothes in Brown Thomas and antiques from Vine's in Grafton Street. Usually without her husband, Foxy. Rose liked him too. He was so different from her father or other uncles. Not like an adult at all. She never called him Uncle; none of his nieces and nephews did. Well, you couldn't seriously call anyone Uncle Foxy, could you?

Invariably when Babs visited, she and Nance would spend hours closeted together, gossiping, catching up on family news, checking the younger generation's academic prowess, sporting ability and musical progress, as well as height, and, of course, who they took after.

Family likeness was a big thing with her mother's relatives, but of no consideration with her father's people whose focus was on character. Rose had horrible visions of Babs pronouncing her the image of some hag of a great-aunt living in the wilderness of Kerry. But no. Each time, Babs insisted that Rose was growing more and more like her grandmother. 'The same wonderful bone structure,' she never ceased to compliment.

When Nance's enquiries came to Tommo, her attitude changed. She pursed her lips, lowered her voice, smiled too widely and adopted a too-caring attitude. Nineteen, Tommo was. Everything about him was a boundary subject. Rose had never even seen him.

'A terrible cross to bear,' Rose once heard her mother whisper to her father. Nance always whispered about Tommo.

In spite of her determination not to be censured for eavesdropping on adult conversation, Rose had not been able to resist raising her head from the 1798 Rebellion. 'What's wrong with Tommo?'

Nance, in the throes of finishing off the luncheon mats, muttered something about, 'There but for the grace of God....' She shook her head, and said accusingly, 'I thought you were doing your homework? Tommo's better not discussed. Time enough for you to have to know the hardships of the world.' Rose knew that Tommo was a subject that made her mother very uncomfortable.

Last year Rose had come upon a conversation never intended for her ears and, to her horror, had discovered that Babs was into sex too. Peeping through the open drawing-room door, she saw her mother and aunt ensconced on the sofa, the tea trolley in front of them.

Initially lingering on the off-chance she would be offered a butterfly bun, she heard conversation worth ten buns.

Dabbing at her eyes with a small lace-edged handkerchief, Babs was saying, 'Tommo being the first and a boy was a particularly difficult burden to bear. What with Foxy's problem and no guarantee we wouldn't have another like Tommo, I'd have preferred not to risk another baby. It was an awful birth too.' She stopped for a sip of tea. 'I didn't let Foxy near me for months after, you know. Not as much as a finger did I let him lay on me.'

Nance gave a gasp of incredulity and Rose settled herself more comfortably on the stairs.

'Foxy went around to the priest. Complained about me withholding his conjugal rights — I didn't even know he knew the words, much less their meaning. I was so embarrassed. Going like that behind my back. But you know what men are like. Can't do without IT when they get used to it on a regular basis. In the end, despite myself, I had to give in.'

With a proud little laugh, she explained, 'Foxy's hard to refuse. He knows how to get around me. And he was so upset at the idea of not having the boy — well, you know, one that was all there...' Babs tapped with her index finger on the side of her head — 'to take over the business. There was no good to be got out of him.'

Yes, thank you, she would have a top-up. Nothing to beat a nice cup of tea. And another bun too, she might as well.

'Doreen arrived. Then Timmy, thanks be to God. But Foxy didn't feel it right to stop there. Wouldn't an extra son be a blessing and if it turned out to be only a girl, sure weren't we giving thanks to God by bringing another child into the world? All difficult births that had me wanting to die. But, sure, in the end, God was good.'

The 'another child', Rose realised, was Kate, her favourite cousin.

Then she heard her mother: 'God is good, but there's no such thing as an easy birth. That's a rumour started by gynaecologists and all of them men. I can put up with a lot of pain. But I thought I'd be torn in half with my two.'

Rose had heard more than enough for one day. Enough to decide that no matter how much she might want a baby, no baby would be worth such agony. Her memory of her one and only toothache and the subsequent attempt at extraction was bad enough. She couldn't help wondering if God was really all that good.

Rose's dissatisfaction with religion was gradual, rather than sudden. Probably the seed was sown by the picture of the Sacred Heart in the heavy black frame, which hung on the opposite wall to her bed. Even as a small child, she was scared and appalled that anyone could worship such a disturbing image. Every night, with great fervour, Nance, eyes closed and hands clasped in prayer, asked the Sacred Heart to watch over Rosemary and to keep her safe until morning.

Rose, in her pink checked pyjamas, tucked up in her own little bed, never considered she would not be safe. But obviously Mammy did. This was worrying. Rose's mind conjured up all sorts of horrible fates, spawned by the Christmas pantomime, and by her mother's bedtime reading of the fairy tales of Grimm and Hans Christian Andersen.

After Mammy kissed her, snuggled the blankets around her neck, turned off the light, tiptoed out and closed the door, Rose was left all alone with a God who terrified her and certainly, in her opinion, not only offered no protection but increased her vulnerability to all sorts of horrors. Suppose a wolf got her? Or she was cooked in the witch's oven? What if she ended up lost in the forest? Or below stairs in rags? She knew God was more powerful than any witch or bad fairy. If she was bold, He could do anything he wished to her. And she could not be good for ever.

Rose wished Mammy would leave God alone, not be asking favours on her behalf. With thorns sticking into His forehead, blood dribbling down His face and the anguished eyes, you had only to look at Him to know He had enough troubles of His own.

The day she was eight, Rose plucked up the courage to ask for the picture to be moved. Nance was delighted, concluding that Rosemary, even at her young age, had taken literally to the concept of being watched over. It would not be sensitive to discuss the matter with Trevor, though she did ask him to hammer in a nail over Rosemary's bed. Rose did not like the idea of God looking down on her while she slept, but it was better than meeting his eye last thing at night and first thing in the morning.

For as long as Rose could remember, Nance's attitude to Trevor's religion had been ambivalent. Most of the time she ignored it, but when it had to be acknowledged, she did so uneasily, saying something like, 'It's a matter between your father and his maker — when they meet.' This 'meeting' sounded like the ultimate spiritual test.

It did not worry Trevor, who seemed so secure in his faith that Rose often wished she was a Protestant. He attended services, sang in the choir, supported badminton tournaments and would never miss the annual church garden party. It all seemed such fun. It was so unfair. By even entering his church, Rose was committing a mortaler, whereas it was not even a venial sin for Trevor to come to mass with them.

Sister Concepta not only insisted that the immortal souls of non-Catholics were destined to burn forever in the flames of hell, she also made Rose feel that the sins of the father were truly visited on her, his daughter. Rose hated the implication that, because of his religion, her father was an inferior being.

Religious discussions were sure-fire methods of diversion from the boredom of the proscribed texts. However, Monica had the ability to disrupt a whole class with her red herrings and seldom missed the opportunity. Such as the time when, from her place in the third row, she had raised her hand, interrupting Concepta's enthusiasm for making their hearts gardens for Jesus.

'Yes, Monica?' The nun's voice had a resigned, martyred tinge to it.

'Please, Sister, would it be better to marry a white Protestant or a black Catholic?'

For a moment the nun froze. As often, when unsure of how to progress, she threw back the question. 'What do you think, girls? A white Protestant or a black Catholic? Remember your immortal souls.'

With the exception of Rose, the class sat twitching, grunting in contemplation of the enormity of such a decision.

Out of the blue, Rose heard herself say, 'My father's a Protestant.' The ensuing silence was shiny with the wonder of difference. Rose's classmates looked for guidance to their teacher, still standing motionless on the dais. Under her wimple, her glasses seemed more whirlpool-like than usual and she remained silent.

'Is that true?' asked somebody from the back row.

'That's for her to know and you to find out,' said Barbara, shooting Rose a dimpled glance of allegiance.

There and then, Rose decided how simple life would be without religion. Instantly she felt more grown-up. Closer to her father. More of a woman for Frank.

Not that Frank had seemed in any hurry to have a 'session', as Monica labelled heavy petting. Despite what Rose perceived as the lack of real passion in their relationship, she was pleased enough: it was romantic and she loved having a boyfriend. When she and Frank kissed, she heard music, saw whirring particles in the air; the sound of their breaths, even the dappling sunshine combined in one joyous chord. Afterwards there was the closeness of whispering sweet nothings in the musical silence.

Regularly, Monica, perched on the edge of her desk, the class grouped around her like acolytes, regaled them with tales of male lust, men's uncontrollable sexual urges and what happened when passions were unleashed. Dramatically rolling her eyes and flashing her teeth, she justified her stand-by goalie's urges: 'He's experienced. He's had a lot of girlfriends.'

Such antics did not sound very romantic to Rose and she was glad that she was Frank's first real girlfriend. Much and all as she might crave passion, she could not cope with all this raging tornado stuff which Monica seemed to take in her stride; no way would she publicly discuss intimate moments either — they were slumbering thoughts for private savouring. To Monica's annoyance, Barbara, too, refused to go into detail, despite the fact that occasionally after the weekend she sported a love bite or two on her neck.

'Keep him above the waist, never let him below,' advised Monica blithely. 'Unless you want to become pregnant. Though if you're really in love, you'll let him go all the way. You know, do IT.' Raising her eyebrows, smiling mysteriously, 'And you don't even think of what might happen. Not when you're on a roller-coaster of passion.'

No matter what, Rose could not imagine herself and Frank doing IT. Anyway, she did not know how.

While the girls of 4A were full of sexual longings and avid for information, despite their best efforts, the majority were more into talk than action. Digesting but abandoning the enormity of doing IT, they moved on to less torrid territory.

Somebody's cousin had a boyfriend who could open her bra with one hand. 'Handy,' said Monica, to gales of laughter.

'What about touching under your clothes?'

'Fine, as long as you're careful.'

'Are breasts safe?'

'Yes,' Monica assured. 'E.R.O.G.E.N.O.U.S.' The word slid unfamiliarly, but safely, off her tongue. She had discovered it in one of her mother's books, knew it was something to do with sex, but was unsure of its precise meaning.

'Isn't touching a sin?'

'Everything to do with boys is a sin. You just have to keep going to confession.'

'How do you actually get pregnant? Is it anything to do with the belly button?'

Monica's hesitation gave Rose her chance. She jumped in, dying to prove that Monica was not the only expert. She might not be informed on the nitty-gritty of getting pregnant, but courtesy of Nance and Babs, she did know the gruesomeness of birth. 'Having the baby is the worst ever. If you don't die during it — and my aunt nearly did with all hers — you feel as though you're being torn asunder. That's why there are only the two of us. Mammy couldn't face it again,' she improvised madly.

Monica hated the limelight being taken off her. 'How do you know? Bet they didn't tell you.'

Rose shrugged. She was not going to admit that her information had been gleaned by eavesdropping. 'If you're that smart,' Monica taunted, 'go on, tell us, how are babies born?'

Rose was saved from answering by the bell ringing for next class.

CHAPTER SEVEN

The following Thursday, while sharing a washbasin after Art class, Monica asked Rose, 'How's Frank these days?'

'Don't know. Haven't seen him.' Rose did not want to get into a discussion with Monica, who knew she was grounded yet never stopped asking about Frank. Teasing out yellow ochre from under her nails, Rose rubbed scarlet from the pad of her index finger.

'Still being driven to school by Mammy?'

Shaking droplets of water off her fingers, Rose shrugged, but did not answer. Monica could be so mean sometimes.

'I'll give Tom a letter for Frank, if you like,' offered Monica in conciliatory mode.

It was the best offer Rose had had in ages. She did not hesitate. 'Would you really?'

Registering Rose's interest, Monica drove home her bargain. 'For a bar of chocolate. A large Cadbury's — fruit and nut. And the next English composition.'

That night Rose went early to her room, leaving Nance and Trevor engrossed in Radio Éireann's mid-week play. Sitting at her dressing table, gnawing at the skelp of skin between thumb and forefinger, she started the letter in the middle of her Latin copy. Less likely to be noticed when she pulled out the pages. This letter was much harder to write than any composition, she decided, after much sighing and crossing out.

Distracted by her face in the mirror, she examined but was not duly impressed by her bone structure, though when she smiled at her reflection, she liked her strong white teeth, the way her face lit up and her eyes danced, invoking all kinds of merriment.

Then she thought, what kind of an eejit was she, grinning into the mirror! Get on with it. The play wouldn't last for ever. What she needed for inspiration was proper notepaper. Opening her door carefully to minimise squeaking — theirs was a house of creaking doors and groaning floorboards — Rose tiptoed across the landing, eased down the handle of her parents' bedroom door, unlocked the Davenport, and removed her mother's writing case. Nance used luscious cream vellum notepaper, with fluted edges and matching envelopes.

Safely back in her room, Rose inserted the lined sheet into the pad — couldn't have crooked lines. Picking up her fountain pen, she wrote with easy fluency. A real love letter. Full of passion. It was good. Very good. Maybe she would be a writer of romantic love stories. But she couldn't send it.

Rose decided she couldn't bring herself to destroy it either, so she enveloped it, addressed it and, in a moment of pure whimsy, added a stamp from the sheet tucked into the writing case. Then, as though the letter were red hot, she stuck it under the large oval mat of her dressing-table set. A safe place. Agnes, in spite of Nance's admonishments, still dusted around rather than under impediments.

Rose covered another sheet of paper with several lines of 'Mrs Frank Fennelly'; a few lines of 'Mrs F.S. Fennelly' (Frank's second name was Sylvester, after his paternal grandfather); a further half dozen with 'Mrs Francis Sylvester Fennelly'. She tried a few with 'Mrs Rose Fennelly', even 'Mrs Rosemary Fennelly'. But decided that, despite being a modern girl, she would be an old-fashioned wife and adopt her husband's Christian name for correspondence.

She had better destroy this, she decided. It was evidence she would not want falling into her mother's hands. Allowing herself a moment of horrific imagination, she shivered at the conse-quences and, after tearing up the page, placed the fragments for eventual disposal in her school bag. It was then the thought struck. Dammit. Would her mother notice that notepaper was missing? Knowing her, very likely. Better not risk using more, Rose decided, returning the writing case.

Then it was back to the Latin copybook. To her chagrin, the finished 'official' letter was stilted and childish. Couldn't be improved on, she reckoned, without an injection of passion. Giggling at the very idea of passion, she enveloped the letter and tucked it for safekeeping into *Harte's Doctrine*, their Christian Doctrine textbook.

Instead of going through Tom, as she had originally proposed, Monica delivered the letter to Frank in person, lying in wait for him as he cycled home from school. A turn of events which disturbed

Rose. Monica, her bottom toasting against the radiator, devouring her chocolate payment, was uncharacteristically noncommittal about her mission.

'What did he say?' Rose hated having to ask.

'Nothing.'

'Come off it, Monica.' It was Barbara. 'Don't tell us neither of you talked. Bet he asked about Rose.'

'Our conversation was private,' smirked Monica. 'No, Rose, he didn't ask about you.'

'What did he do with the letter?'

'Put it in his pocket. His right-hand blazer pocket, if you really want the details,' Monica answered with a touch of asperity.

'But how is he?'

'Still wet.' Monica's eyes shifted away from Rose's direct look.

'What about a reply?'

'What about it?' Monica asked with a toss of her head, finishing off the last square of chocolate.

Barbara, dimpling earnestly, consoled Rose with a bull's-eye and advice: 'Don't read anything into Monica's going-on. She's dreadful. Did you hear her parents caught her and her goalie hot and heavy at it Saturday night, in their bed? There was a terrible scene.'

It was as simple a matter as Trevor needing the car which resulted in the lifting of Rose's purdah. This particular Thursday, with its packed itinerary, would be one of the most significant days of his career, and no way was he going to let Rose's punishment upset his arrangements.

He was taking a visiting professor from Oxford on a tour of James Joyce's Dublin and environs. Bringing him to the Christian Brothers in North Richmond Street and to Belvedere College where the young James enjoyed school; then to University College in St Stephen's Green where Joyce considered his lecturers obtuse and cliché-ridden.

Trevor also planned to take in the many residences in which the Joyce family had lived, including Martello Terrace in Bray, County Wicklow, where most of the children were born; Carysfort Avenue in Blackrock, reputed to be the place where James wrote poems and the draft of a novel, long lost.

While living in Fitzgibbon Street in the heart of old Georgian Dublin, Joyce had wandered the nearby streets, making 'a skeleton map of the city in his mind', and the seeds of *Dubliners* were sown. A downturn in family fortunes necessitated moving to Millbourne Lane, Drumcondra, near the Tolka River on Dublin's northside. The year 1894 found them in North Richmond Street, which became the 'blind' street of the story 'Araby'. Later, as family fortunes declined further, they had three addresses in Fairview.

It was Trevor's dearest dream to set up a Joyce Trail, where Joycean enthusiasts could follow in the footsteps of *Ulysses*'s Leopold Bloom. With the amount of international academic interest being shown in Joyce's work, and the number of erudite and, indeed, ordinary publications blossoming into print, he dared hope.

'I don't like the idea of letting Rosemary so easily off the hook,' said Nance, tying the clasp of her single strand of pearls, while Trevor battled to insert his silver cufflinks into too-stiffly starched cuffs.

'Sorry, dear,' he said cheerfully. 'Can't be helped. This isn't the kind of opportunity that comes along every day.' Giving up on the right cufflink, he held out his arm to her. 'Anyway, you've enough to do without driving Rose here, there and everywhere. I'm sure we can trust her now. She'll have learned her lesson.'

Rose, cycling along the Stillorgan road, sniffed the air of freedom. She felt as though a yoke had been hoisted from her shoulders. It was one of those warm early-summer mornings with a skittering, flirty breeze and clouds chasing each other across an azure sky. A nectar-like morning with a promise of the lusciousness of summer to come. Spotting Frank in the distance, her happiness was complete.

With a broad grin and a whoop, he wheelied across the road, his tennis racquet wobbling precariously on the back carrier. 'I'm late. Have to see The Bull before class. Meet you after school.' And he was gone.

At four o'clock Frank, palpitatingly attractive in his rolled-up shirt sleeves, pullover knotted around his shoulders, cycled across the road, with scant regard for personal safety. If missing someone was being in love, Rose reckoned, Frank was the passion of her life. Certainly, absence had made her heart grow fonder.

'About time the ban was lifted,' he told her enthusiastically, drinking her in with his eyes. 'I mitched tennis just for you.' Rose protested but secretly was delighted. It proved he really cared.

They stood close, glad to be back in each other's company. 'I tried to ring you — twice. But your mother said you were doing your homework. Thanks for the letter. Boo for the messenger. Monica's a pain in the neck….'

'Why didn't you answer?'

'She warned me not to. Said you didn't want a reply, that your mother was on the warpath. Was keeping you prisoner.'

Rose digested that piece of misinformation. 'Mammy was cross.' And not wanting to be totally disloyal, amplified, 'She hates lies. But she's okay now. Though I'm not supposed to see you again.'

Frank burst out laughing. 'You're joking.'

'I promised.'

'Who?'

'The nuns and my parents.'

'Never mind that. Who's going to stop us?'

'I gave my word.'

'They can't treat you like this. We're not in the Dark Ages.'

'We'll have to be careful.'

'We will,' he promised. 'Anyway, now that it's lighter in the evenings, I've loads of extra tennis practice to get in before the start of the championships, so I mightn't always be able to make it.'

Frank reached over their combined handlebars, hugging her goodbye.

Rose forgot her earlier caution and enthusiastically returned his embrace.

It was just her luck that at that precise moment her mother's friend, Dolores Luke, happened to be passing on the 46A bus! This time she craned her neck to be sure her eyes were not playing tricks on her. Her first impression had been correct. It was Rosemary Horn. Kissing. On the public road. In broad daylight.

Next day, Rose and Frank reverted to meeting in their bower. 'I'm torn between obedience and passion,' Rose whispered dramatically to Barbara a few afternoons later as they changed for tennis. From the far toilet cubicle came a sound like vomiting. Monica emerged, her flat face looking drawn and pale.

'Are you okay?' asked Barbara.

'Of course,' she snapped. 'Why wouldn't I be?'

'It sounded as though you were getting sick.'

'It's nothing. What were you whispering about?' demanded Monica.

Rose told her, finishing with, 'And we weren't whispering.'

Monica laughed. 'Frank, passionate? You must be joking.'

Rose flushed.

'Everyone has hidden depths. Bet he is in private,' said Barbara kindly.

Monica splashed water on her face. 'There's no way I'd allow myself to be dictated to the way you are,' she said dismissively. 'Times have changed, you know. It's the 1950s we're living in.' These days Monica never seemed to miss an opportunity to try to undermine Rose.

Barbara, ever the peacemaker, said, 'Give it time. It'll die down. But maybe you'd have been better telling your parents you were seeing Frank.'

'Not *her* parents,' jeered Monica, with such spite that Rose instantly wanted to fly to their defence.

'Come on,' said Barbara, grabbing her racquet and pushing Rose in front of her. 'We don't want to add to our troubles by being late on the courts.'

Rose's no-contact stipulation made her trysts with Frank a nightmare of guilt. She hated skulking behind walls, as though they were doing something so wrong it had to be hidden. Frank wanted to go public with their relationship, take in a film or a walk over the weekend. Drink espressos in the Coffee Inn or in the New Amsterdam, the latest places for hanging out, setting the world to rights and listening to jukebox music. Rose did not even try to ask for permission at home.

Talk about being plagued by guilt on all fronts. When she was apart from Frank, she was consumed by thoughts of him. When they were together she craved the physical contact of kissing and touching. Alone, she soul-searched. So indoctrinated was Rose on the destructiveness of sex that she began to doubt her relationship with Frank. Began to wonder if she were wrong. Was everyone else right? Surely her mother, teachers, priests could not all have got it wrong?

'This is nice, isn't it?' she asked Frank as they stood one afternoon, coats opened, bodies straining together. She wished he would tear the clothes off her, kiss her bare flesh, like in the *Angélique* books. Fat chance.

The school uniform was a real passion-killer. Not like the tight sweaters and plunging evening dresses worn by Hollywood film stars. Stiff material. Baggy shape. Awkward buttons. And underneath, what would he find? Dammit, a liberty bodice. Some turn-on.

'Are you okay?' Frank asked, his breath warm against her ear.

'Yes,' she assured, snuggling further into him, remembering the day she had asked her mother for a bra. A real bra. A pink, pointy satin bra, she had hoped. Pulling her school blouse taut over her budding breasts to illustrate the necessity. To her way of thinking, a bra was a natural progression into womanhood. Just another item of clothing. But Nance pursed her lips in that lemony embarrassed way of hers and gave Rose the standard lecture about there being plenty of time for that, not to be in such a hurry to grow up, et cetera.

A few days later, Rose found a bag from Madame Nora's on her bed. Madame Nora's, one of the nicest lingerie shops in Dublin. She dared hope. Breaking one of Nance's house rules, she sat down on the side of the bed, crushing not only the rayon olive-green eiderdown, but also the matching frilled spread. With eyes closed, Rose hoped again. When she opened the bag, it contained not one, but two, liberty bodices.

Still, she and Frank managed to consolidate the friendship they had laid down over the previous months, swapping details of their day, complaining about their parents, grumbling about homework.

This secrecy was alien to Frank too, particularly as his parents — well, his mother anyway, he assured

Rose — was quite modern about him having a girlfriend and would love to meet her. Rose believed him. Mrs Fennelly had sounded nice on the phone.

At home, Frank's name was not mentioned. Trevor considered Rose's romance to be water under the bridge. Nance, presuming her daughter was honouring her promise, subscribed to the theory of 'least said, soonest mended'.

CHAPTER EIGHT

Frank got as far as the finals of the Leinster Schools Senior Tennis Championship, where he was beaten by the previous champion. He said his father was more disappointed than him. Rose and he celebrated with a shared bottle of Pepsi, their drink.

Reaching for her hand, hair tousled, eyes serious, he said, 'I've something to ask you. It's important. Think before you answer.' No jokes today. This was a more solemn Frank than Rose was familiar with. She sensed she was not going to like what was coming next.

'There's a tennis do on Saturday in Fitzwilliam. My parents are going, the Doyles and Tom and whoever he brings. I've a ticket for you. Say you'll come.'

Rose took a deep breath. 'I can't. You know I can't.'

'What I'm hearing is you won't.'

'You know the situation. I'm not supposed to have anything to do with you. No meetings, no contact.'

'You're not a baby. You've to choose.' Exasperatedly: 'We can't go on like this. Look, let me talk to your father.'

Rose wished it were her father who held the power over her social life. She shook her head, her brown eyes troubled. 'It wouldn't matter. Mammy's the one you'd have to persuade.'

'All right so. I'll do it.'

'Frank, you can't. She'd be furious.'

'Well then, let me get my mother to ring her.'

'No. You'll have to go without me.'

'What am I supposed to do for a partner?'

'Do you have to have one?'

'Yes. I bloody well do.'

When Frank turned his bike around and rode out the gate without even saying goodbye, Rose felt awful. Cowardly and childish, abandoned and alone. She did not know what to do. Who to turn to. While she blamed her mother, she was honest enough to realise that she should have had the courage to stand up to her parents and the nuns and, as Barbara had suggested, come clean about her relationship with Frank.

Two days later, something even more awful happened. Barbara grabbed her as the class split, half to take Physiology, the remainder Latin. One of their last classes before the Intermediate exam. 'There's something you should know.' Barbara took a deep breath. 'I'm really sorry. And hate being the one to tell you. Monica's going to Fitzwilliam with Frank.'

Rose stood stock-still. 'But she doesn't even like him,' she wailed.

'Aren't you lucky?' soothed Barbara. 'Wouldn't you really have something to worry about if she fancied him?'

Rose was not comforted. Thousands of butterflies fluttered in her stomach. The only way she could deal with the situation was by ignoring it.

With the exams coming up, she had a lot of

revision to do. It was impossible to get through the whole syllabus, but she found peace in losing herself in study. Her preoccupation with sex abated, leaving her mind freer to concentrate on the exams.

But nothing worked the night of the Fitzwilliam party. She had earmarked the romantic poets in her textbook. How stupid can you get, she thought, undecided whether to laugh or cry at the absurdity of her choice. She just ached. And hoped Monica was not wearing the black lace. It made her look really grown-up. Like a film star. And she had got gorgeous and thin. And her protruding teeth were looking particularly stylish.

On Monday, Monica came into school wearing a smug expression that had Rose imagining the worst. And to crown it all, she was getting her period.

She had been frightened when it had first happened. Cramps tearing at her stomach, pains down her legs and across her back, hunched into her rocking chair, wondering whether she was going to bleed to death.

When Agnes had burst into her room waving her feather duster, Rose explained through tears as best she could. Agnes touched her shoulder awkwardly, the first time in years they had had any sort of physical contact, and said kindly, 'Go on down and tell the missus.'

Nance, humming softly to herself, was chopping vegetables for a brown stew. Onions, celery, carrots. Rose's news broke her good humour. Now the trouble really starts, she thought. Her reaction to Rose, conveyed with few spoken phrases but with eloquent body language, reeked of embarrassment. As her hand flashed up and down, chopping faster and faster, Rose had backed off in confusion.

That night, when she opened the centre drawer of her dressing table where she kept her hairbrush, she found the accoutrements of womanhood — a packet of sanitary towels with loops, a belt with clips and pants with a rubber gusset. She managed as best and as secretly as she could. Three months later, she was regarded as the class expert when Barbara and Monica both got their curses within two days of each other.

Usually her cramps were not all that bad; today was an exception. Complaining about the curse and the bother of having to take Anadin was nearly as important a status as having a boyfriend. Fainting, the way Monica did, was the ultimate. Nobody in the class could better her performance. Even today, bad and all as she felt, Rose knew she would not be fainting.

Rose had escaped to the toilets for a breather. The last person she expected to follow her was Monica. These days when they had to communicate, they did so in feathery undertones of avoidance. Shunning the one subject neither would mention. To avoid contact, Rose dived into the nearest toilet, clicked over the bolt and sat on the seat, feeling pathetic.

Monica entered the adjoining cubicle, flushed, and over the sounds of the gushing water Rose was certain she could hear gaggy, vomiting noises. Then more flushing. Rose stayed still, hardly daring to breathe. From over the partition floated Monica's voice: 'Frank's a great kisser, isn't he?'

Rose could think of nothing to say. The tiny cubicle went around and around. Maybe this was fainting?

She shuttered her mind against Frank and silently hated Monica.

When it came to sitting the first papers, which were English, Rose enjoyed pitting her knowledge against the questions and reckoned she had done well. The pattern repeated itself for the remainder of the exams.

If she and Barbara wondered about Monica's absence from the final Art paper, they were not unduly worried. By this stage, Rose had decided she would eschew sex for ever and devote her life to academia. And in between, maybe, dash off the occasional romantic novel.

As the exams concluded and summer term wrapped up, Nance was preoccupied and addled. She had heard on the social grapevine that Monica Doyle was ill. Very ill. All very hush-hush. Monica had collapsed after getting out of bed on the last day of the exams and had just crumpled to the floor. Rumours flew. Mysie and Peter were desolate. Some said Monica was pregnant, others that she had TB, and more that she was in the throes of a nervous breakdown.

The Monica situation only confirmed Nance's reservations about this whole teenage nonsense. Unhealthy, it was. When she heard Monica was suffering from a recently diagnosed illness which affected teenage girls and was associated with dieting — Anorexia Nervosa and Bulimia, starving, stuffing and vomiting — her fears were compounded.

The visit from Dolores Luke was the last straw. She and Nance had been best friends from the age of twelve, when they were both new girls from the country sent to boarding school in Dublin.

Dolores, determinedly cheerful, talked in gushes, throwing back her head, laughing uproariously. Her long, thin body was coiled into Trevor's armchair, her short black skirt riding up to the tops of her stockings and black suspenders. She asked Nance for whiskey rather than tea, drank two in quick succession, and lit up one cigarette after another, which she smoked through a black and gold holder.

'How's Rose? Growing up, I suppose?' she said, blowing smoke out her nostrils.

'Indeed, yes,' said Nance, still full of the news of Monica.

'Got a boyfriend yet?' Dolores's question was studiously nonchalant.

'Certainly not,' Nance jumped in sharply. 'She's much too young.'

Dolores studied her bitten nails. 'I feel I should tell you. I saw her. With a boy.'

A shudder of alarm drifted down Nance's spine. 'When?' Trying to sound casual.

'A few weeks ago. When I was coming home from work.'

'Are you sure it was Rose?'

'Certain. They were on the Stillorgan road.'

Nance breathed a sigh of relief. Rose could not be up to much on the Stillorgan road. 'Probably a friend. Though I don't like Rose hanging around the roads with boys.'

'Remember us … every chance we got … anything in trousers.'

Dolores brought Nance back in time. Made her remember the way they were. The chances they took. The heat of her own passion seemed like another era. Where had it all gone?

'Girls have to be careful. It doesn't do to get a reputation,' Nance said, without thinking.

Dolores looked sharply at her friend. And wondered if the news of her behaviour had reached Nance. Dolores knew that she and her capacity for whiskey were well known around Dublin, particularly in the Wicklow Hotel, and in the Shelbourne's Horse Shoe Bar. Oh, she had a reputation all right. The only person who did not seem to know about her affair with her boss was his wife.

Dolores wanted to hurt, to lash out at her smug friend. 'By the look of them, they were more than friends, I'd say….'

'What do you mean?' demanded Nance.

'They were kissing. Good old-fashioned snogging.'

'On the side of the road?'

Dolores's nod confirmed Nance's worst fears. If they would kiss in public, what would they get up to in private?

Nance did not pursue the matter with Rosemary. In fact, she was afraid to. Action rather than discussion was required, she decided. That evening she rang Babs — she should have listened to her instincts and done it before — and asked whether Rosemary could spend the summer with her. Nance might not approve of her elder sister's lifestyle and many of her attitudes, but where her children were concerned, she was strict. Right now, in her opinion, the simple Kerry life and a dose of external disciplining was just what Rosemary needed.

Babs's air of distraction came down the phone line, but Nance ignored it. Her sister was often distracted: her hands were full running the hotel, keeping an eye on Foxy and bringing up the children. In any case, her reply was typically warm and effusive. 'Of course. Delighted. Kate and she'll get on famously. I'm sending the girls to a house in Fenit for the summer. Better to have the children out of town, what with all the going-on leading up to this Festival of Tralee.'

Nance agreed. There had been a lot of publicity about this new competition which, according to the newspapers, was targeted at bringing back emigrants. Funny way to go about it, Nance thought — a beauty competition, of all things. As if the young people were not bad enough. Filling their heads with such nonsense.

And, despite her upbringing, Rosemary was not immune either. It must have been around April when she had bounced in from school. Full of the joys of spring. 'Guess what? I'm the only one in the class qualified to enter the Festival of Tralee. Because you were born in Kerry. I could go forward as the Dublin Rose....'

'You what? Enter a beauty competition? The Rose of Tralee? You most certainly won't.'

Rose's exuberance deflated, her voice trailed off. 'Well, not now. When I'm old enough. Maybe…?'

The house in Fenit was a blessing. Now that Nance thought of it, of course Tralee would be packed coming up to the Festival. All sorts of undesirables too, she was sure.

'Will you be going out yourself?' Without even asking, she knew Foxy would not.

'No. I couldn't leave the hotel. It'll be a great opportunity for business, thanks be to God,' said Babs. 'A woman called Cissie Something will be minding them. Comes highly recommended. Father Michael has made all the arrangements. She was in service in Cork. Came back to nurse her parents, stayed and never married.' As the final selling line to her sister: 'I believe you could eat your dinner off her floor.'

'Are you sure Rosemary won't be too much?' Nance fussed, delighted at this turn of events. Fenit. A God-forsaken seaside village, full of simple people who fished for their livelihood. No harm could come to Rosemary there.

'Take no nonsense from her,' Nance urged. 'I want her out of Dublin, away from this teenage nonsense they're all going on with. Plenty of fresh air is what they need at that age.'

At the other end of the phone, Babs clucked sympathetically. 'Is she into the boys?'

'Certainly not,' lied Nance. 'She's much too young.'

Knowing the rigidity of her sister, Babs had a

110

fleeting moment of sympathy for Rose. But only fleeting. Hadn't she romance blossoming under her own roof? And one that couldn't be more unsuitable. You would think marrying Trevor would have loosened up Nance's attitudes. Not a bit of it. If anything, she was becoming more inflexible.

Still, she would be glad to have Rose keep Kate company. For a moment she had an urge to confide. But only for a moment. She could just imagine Nance's reaction if she were to tell her about finding Doreen and her bar boy Jack kissing in the yard. Passionately too. Almost eating each other. And as if that wasn't bad enough, the two of them surrounded by the bottles Jack should have been washing.

For now, Doreen was confined to her bedroom until Babs decided how best to handle the situation. Now the solution came to her. So obvious. Why hadn't she thought of it before? 'I'd love to send Doreen up to you for a few weeks.'

Silence. Then Nance asked, 'Are you sure you'd want her in Dublin?'

'In your hands, yes. Let her get a bit of culture. She won't know anyone, so she can't get into trouble,' finished Babs with considerably more optimism than she felt. These days there was no knowing what Doreen could and would get up to. And no getting through to her either.

'By all means,' replied Nance unenthusiastically. 'When were you thinking of?'

'As soon as possible, like right now?' joked Babs.

'How about the middle of July? Trevor and I are heading off for a little break, while Agnes is on

111

holidays, and George is going to go and stay with his grandparents.'

Babs, who had hoped for an instant solution, settled for what was offered.

Nance had a qualm of conscience about her lack of generosity, but rationalised. Doreen, nearly a year older than Rose, was likely to be that much more troublesome. She had hoped for a quiet summer. It had been a difficult year.

CHAPTER NINE

Before she had time even to get used to the idea of spending the summer in Kerry, Rose found herself on the morning train to Tralee. Her first journey on her own. Grown-up but scary too. Her heavy leather suitcase had been sealed for extra protection with two wide tan leather belts, formerly used for holding up Trevor's holiday trousers.

Inside were presents: for Babs, from The China Showrooms in Lower Abbey Street, a green pottery dog with a rakish air and a crooked ear to add to her collection of 'purties', as she called the hundred-plus ornaments she had built up over the years; and a round tin of Mackintosh Carnival Assortment for her cousins. For Granny a pound of Bewley's coffee — Café Blend, medium ground. Ringing in Rose's ears was Nance's insistence that she pay a visit to her in Castlemaine. She would anyway, she loved Granny Annie who was a real granny, much better than Grandma Laetitia who tried to be modern, wore make-up and even talked about rock 'n' roll.

Also, tucked far into a corner of her case was a doll's head, Rose's beloved Susan.

Trevor had got her a copy of *Schoolfriend* and had insisted on accompanying her onto the train to settle her in. Dammit. Even her own father still considered her a child. He had always bought her the occasional comic for what he called a 'naughty treat' and to avoid, as he said, 'academic overload'. But Rose had never been a comic person. Even when she was younger, the *Beano* and the *Dandy* had left her cold. She wouldn't have minded a *True Romance*, though. Fat chance, she thought with a grin, only half listening to her father's fussing.

'Don't put your head out of the carriage window. You could be blinded by flying sparks from the engine,' he told her, wrinkling his forehead worriedly, totally out of his depth with such practicalities. 'Though if there's an emergency, you'll have to open the window.' Pipe clenched firmly in the corner of his mouth, he battled unsuccessfully to close the recalcitrant window.

A tall fellow, the most teddy-boyish teddy boy Rose had ever seen — gorgeous, he was — shouldered his way through the corridor, and closed the window with one effortless shove. Trevor was profuse in his thanks, but Rose, still hugging to herself a life devoid of men, feigned indifference.

When her father left, after embracing her as though she were emigrating for ever, she sat in the middle of the plush, wine-coloured moquette seat, just in case she was targeted by a shooting stray spark, knowing that no matter what calamities occurred, she would never manage to open the heavy window with its heavy leather strap and fiddly brass knob.

At Nance's insistence, Rose had dressed rather formally for train travel — bursting out of her two-year-old wedding outfit.

Her burgeoning shape had now stretched the yucky green tweed pleated skirt beyond credibility, together with the matching jacket with its too-nipped-in waist, three straining buttons and brown velvet collar. Underneath she wore a white blouse with a strangling Peter Pan collar. Her toes curled to accommodate Clark's well-polished, brown-buckled sandals. For unknown reasons, her ankle socks, with their lime-green turn-downs, were so large that their heels still climbed several inches up her legs.

She congratulated herself that, while posting her letter to Barbara outside the Ladies' toilet, on a sudden impulse, she had stuffed into the maw of the post box the white fabric gloves which completed her outfit.

The journey was over too soon.

She spent it, nose jammed against the window, looking out at the countryside, trying not to think about Frank, eating squelchy egg and parsley sandwiches and swigging from a bottle of red lemonade.

The hurt of Frank would always be with her. It was bad enough his asking Monica to Fitzwilliam, but kissing her was the pits. Rose felt let down, ashamed. As though it was she who had done something wrong.

Still, standing on the platform in Tralee, her natural optimism asserted itself. She was on an adventure.

Then she heard it. 'There she is. There she is,' and what seemed like an army approached — an untidy army — her cousins and their friends, boys and girls, brown shining faces, flashing white teeth, shorts and shirts awry, grubby plimsolls, waving tennis racquets, bouncing balls.

The only exception to this joyous spontaneity and ragbag clothing was an unsmiling girl in a red princess-line dress, with blond bobbed hair. It was Doreen. She sauntered over to Rose, with a sad look, and parroted, 'You're welcome to Kerry. Mammy's sorry she couldn't meet you. She said to bring you straight back.'

Skidding to a halt beside them, a boy, with tousled brown dishmop hair and freckles like George's, grabbed Rose's case in one hand and, with his other, shook her hand so vigorously that she felt her bones would be forever crushed.

'How'ya? I'm Timmy.'

Followed by the others, he rushed her out of the station, down Edward Street, yanking her case along the ground, around to the right into Castle Street, the lot of them in an untidy straggle across the footpath, saying 'Hello' or 'How'ya?' and introducing her to all and sundry as their cousin from Dublin. Only Doreen dawdled behind.

All the time they talked, gesticulated, bombarded her with questions, not caring whether or not she answered, not even expecting a reply. 'Did you've a nice journey?'; 'Do ya like travelling by train?'; 'It must be awful living in Dublin?'; 'Don't you just hate school?'

It was the first time Rose had come across the soft Kerry accent in quantity and it sat easily on her ear. But their rumbustiousness terrified her.

They turned the corner into Denny Street and when they reached the hotel, they climbed up the stone steps and spilled through the open doors into the hallway.

The lobby was quiet and cool after the heat of the street. Wood-panelled walls and a square of luscious red carpet set off a circular, centre-pod, claw-legged mahogany table, topped with a large colourful floral arrangement: a profusion of pink-belled lupins, cathedral-spired delphiniums, pincushion corn-flowers, and sunshine-centred daisies in a chamber pot, handle and all. Rose could not believe her eyes — a chamber pot as a vase!

Babs came out from a doorway at the end of the hall, wearing a yellow dress, patting immaculate copper-coloured hair. Holding her arms wide, bracelets jangling, she came forward to hug Rose, assuring her in a rather abstracted way that she was more than welcome to Kerry.

Checking her watch, a man-sized affair with a thick gold expanding bracelet, she informed Timmy that he should be at his tennis lesson. Rose thought Timmy was quite like Frank, though younger.

'So I should,' he said cheerfully, swinging out of the doors, racquet first, followed by his entourage, bouncing balls on their racquets.

A beanpole-thin boy, enveloped in a green apron, materialised from the back of the hall, a lick of dark hair skimming impudent eyes.

'Jack, I told you. Stay in the yard. I don't want to see or hear you until those bottles are finished.' Babs's voice was decisive. With a shrug of good-humoured resignation and a jaunty grin lighting up his narrow face, he backed out of view. Babs looked warningly at Doreen, just catching the tail-end of her daughter's eye contact with Jack.

'Doreen, take Rose upstairs and get her sorted out. And don't let me find you near the yard. Kate, your hair's a mess. God made it your crowning glory. It's up to you to look after it. And the rest of you, outside. Have you no homes to go to?'

Her bidding was obeyed by two girls and a boy who said, 'See you around,' to Kate. Kate, a few months younger than Rose, was of a lean greyhound build, green-eyed and sooty-lashed with rippling blond hair, the colour of ripened wheat.

'Come on,' said Doreen — impatiently, Rose thought.

Rose and Kate followed Doreen through the door at the end of the hall, along a narrow corridor, up a few flights of stairs and into a bedroom. 'That's your bed,' Doreen said, dumping Rose's case on a chair. 'And tea's at six in the kitchen.'

A red and white checked gingham cloth covered the table; the dishes were all blue willow pattern and there was heaps of food: slabs of ham, slices of beef, whole tomatoes, lettuce, hot scallions, tiny radishes, strips of cheese, a whole platter of hard-boiled eggs swimming in Chef salad dressing, and a bowl of parsley-topped cold potatoes. And four kinds of bread — brown and white soda, spotted dog (the traditional Kerry currant bread) and even shop turnover.

They were a noisy group, but despite Babs, from her vantage point at the top of the table, controlling Timmy's tennis prattle, Kate's know-all comments and Doreen's monosyllabic contributions, their table talk bore no relationship to the political, theatrical and literary conversation Rose was used to at home with her own family.

Then there was Tommo. Terrifying, the way he snuffled and grunted and yelped. Too tall and too thin, constantly in motion, windmilling scarecrow arms and legs as though trying to expand the universe of himself. But it was his face which marked him as different. His eyes were a slithery, vacant blue, his ears very small and very red, his lips thick and rubbery. His mouth would often drop open and a dribble run down his chin.

He sat on his own at the end of the table, his eyes on his plate, cramming food into his mouth with both hands. Spasmodically and seemingly involuntarily, he jerked and he yelped. Strangulated sounds, scattering food in all directions. The others took no notice of Tommo, and while Babs too appeared to be oblivious to him and his behaviour, as always when she tried to see him through the eyes of a stranger, her heart broke.

Six months after his birth Dr Leslie Coward had called Babs into his surgery. Sitting very straight behind his desk, eyes avoiding hers, he said, 'I'm so sorry, Babs. There's no easy way to put this. But it's unlikely your son will grow up normal.' He un-steepled his hands and ran them through his hair until it stood on end.

The fact that Foxy was on another celebratory skite, honouring yet again the birth of his son, did not help. Babs was pragmatic enough to realise that life must go on, and if she did not take control, the family and the business would fall apart. 'How abnormal?' she asked after a while of trying to conjure up a suitable word.

'We don't know.' The doctor was reluctant to commit. It was difficult to project how such cases turned out. And he had an aversion to hysterical women. Not that he classed Babs as such, but you never knew. 'We'll need to run further tests.'

'From your experience, what's the likely outcome? I need to know to plan things…' said Babs calmly.

Now Leslie Coward really admired Babs's strength of character. 'Sometimes children like Tommo can do quite well. Basic educational skills. Simple tasks — in your case, like washing bottles and brushing out the place — should not be beyond his capability.' He steepled his hands again. 'The problem is, they can become obstreperous when they reach adolescence.'

'What exactly do you mean by obstreperous?'

Trust Babs. He had specifically chosen the word 'obstreperous'. It sounded harmless in a way others describing mental and physical handicap were not.

'Sexually aware, I suppose. And a bit aggressive. They haven't control over themselves and can be physically quite strong. Often it's nothing more than playfulness,' he assured.

'And if this playfulness can't be contained?'

'That's when problems can arise. But it's not a bridge we need to cross now.'

120

'So what happens when we do have to cross the bridge?' Babs wanted to know the worst. Confronting life head-on was her way.

'Killarney. The asylum.'

'The lunatic asylum?'

'Yes, they're well looked after. In the circumstances. I'm sorry.'

Babs kept her knowledge to herself, watched over Tommo like a hawk, and breathed a sigh of relief when his behaviour did not become obstreperous with adolescence. Her pluses in life — and she often thanked the Lord — were multitudinous: health, drive and ability, a good business that could be worked up to better, and three fine children.

The minuses in her life were a dipsomaniac husband — as her mother pragmatically classified Foxy — and her poor idiot, Tommo. She had loved Foxy since they were children together and still did, but for many a day it had been with realistic reservations.

Except when he was on one of his benders, Foxy Mac was a good businessman with a practical as well as a visionary attitude to life. It was he who had converted the dilapidated Georgian town house, left him by his father, into an exclusive hotel. He was the first in Ireland, so he claimed, often in the process executing a joyous little skip and a jig, to come up with the idea of tapping the North American tourist market. Long before the idea was even a twinkle in the eye of Fógra Fáilte, the Irish tourist board's incipient promotional arm.

The response to his first tentative, one-inch, single-column advertisement in both the *Washington Post*

e New York Times was so overwhelming, and
peat business so good, that the hotel and him-
ad ridden on the crest of his little ads for three
ons. He never bothered to mention that, although
y were his idea, it was Babs who had implemented
s vision.

Rose wondered about Foxy. Where was he? He
was fun and she wished he was sitting around the
table with them. She felt shy and out of place in this
noisy, self-confident group. Babs, after a few abortive
attempts to draw her into the conversation, leaned
across the table, bright-red nails rumpling her hair,
and said, 'We'll leave you alone. Give you a chance to
adjust. You'll shine in your own time.' Rose believed
her, and looked forward to this shining.

Next day, while not actually shining, Rose felt
more in control and relieved to be away from
Tommo. The bus to Fenit was old, swaying, dusty-
windowed, bumping determinedly along the narrow
potholed roads, sideswiping hedges and overhanging
branches. A green single-decker that badly needed
cleaning, it had cracked maroon-coloured upholstery
and a conductor with watering eyes and a constant
snuffle. 'It's old Snots Healy,' Kate informed Rose.
'He thinks he owns the bus.'

Rose and Kate were in high spirits. They could
not have been more different in looks and manner,
yet were perfect foils for each other. Rose, the quieter
of the two, had a serenity which held a great promise
of beauty. In gesture and sentence, Kate was vital,
dramatic and given to flashes of mood change.

'This is punishment,' she assured Rose blithely.

'We're being punished for Doreen and Jack. And you're a kind of trade-off.'

'What do you mean?' Rose had no idea of the finer intricacies of her sojourn to Kerry.

'If Mammy hadn't caught Doreen and Jack snogging, we'd be in town for the whole summer. Instead, we're missing the fun leading up to the Festival. You're here and Doreen's going to Dublin so Aunty Nance can keep an eye on her.'

'What's Fenit like?' Rose asked, hurt she had not been privy to family plans for the summer holidays.

'Wait till you see it. You don't want to know.'

'And this Cissie who's minding us?'

'Don't know. Haven't seen her. But she comes highly recommended by Mammy's passion,' said Kate blithely.

'Aunt Babs's passion?'

'Yeah. Old Lehane. A real crawlie priest. Always buttering up to Mammy. He knew Cissie in Cork. Said she's so reliable that he'd trust his life to her. Imagine? She sounds like a witch to me. She heals people. Herbs and things, I think.'

'How do you know all this?'

'By listening.'

Rose was impressed. She and Kate had something in common.

'Have you a boyfriend?' Kate asked, jumping from one subject to another.

'I don't want to talk about it.'

'You do, so you do,' she chanted. 'Don't be so mean. Tell me about him. When I've a boyfriend, I'll tell the whole world.'

'Bet you won't. Your mother's as bad as mine about boys. Worse. Look at the way she went on about Doreen. And you're even younger than me.'

'Only a few months.'

'Eight.'

Kate ignored Rose's precision. 'Well, I wouldn't tell her. Do you think I'm daft altogether?'

'Mothers don't like daughters growing up and having boyfriends,' stated Rose, in the definite way of one with personal experience.

Tossing back her hair, Kate said that when she had a boyfriend she would not be as stupid as Doreen. 'Anyway, imagine going with Jack,' she said disapprovingly. Then, brightening up, 'I suppose he must be a great kisser.' Rose had only caught the one glimpse of Jack. From her experience he did not look much of a kisser and certainly not boyfriend material for the glamorous Doreen.

Kate nudged Rose and whispered gleefully, 'Wait until Doreen finds out I've taken her best bra. Have you one?'

'No.'

'Don't worry. I'll give you a lend.'

The other passengers on the bus were shapeless old women, wearing dark coats, their lined faces framed by sombre headscarves; gnarled old men hunched into themselves, sucking on clay pipes; and a selection of boxed and crated poultry — cheeping day-old chicks, a cranky gosling and an agitated cockerel.

Kate, jigging around on her seat, kept up non-stop chatter on inconsequentials and a running commentary on the countryside. As the bus careered around a particularly sharp corner and trundled to a sudden stop, she said, 'This is the Spa, a very dangerous corner. Loads of accidents. Imagine, in the old days, people used to come here on holidays to drink the water.'

The idea amused her so much that she craned her neck backwards to peer out the window, the better to size up the few bleak buildings.

'Look. Look at him.' She nudged Rose, as a young man got on the bus. 'Isn't he gorgeous?'

If it was not the helpful teddy boy from the train, Rose decided it had to be his double.

'Isn't he the image of James Dean?' hissed Kate, so excitedly that her voice travelled the length and breadth of the bus.

When Rose risked another peep, she could see he had that James Dean moody look, and the Brylcreemed flop of hair. His long, drainpiped legs stretching out into the aisle finished in black suede crêpe-soled shoes, the kind that were called 'brothel-creepers'. Kate was mightily impressed when, whispering right into her ear in case she would be heard, Rose passed on this snippet of information about the name for the shoes. It had come from Monica whose brother Tom knew somebody who had come back from London with a pair — from Carnaby Street, no less.

Kate craned her neck back down the bus, staring openly, giving Rose a blow-by-blow account of his every gesture. 'He's having a cigarette. He has his eyes closed.' With a quivering groan and a dramatic sigh, she stretched her hands above her head and whispered, 'He's divine.'

125

When Rose turned around to check for herself, their eyes met. He raised his eyebrows and winked, and his smile was lazy and half mocking. Just like James Dean's in *East of Eden*.

Mikey Daw winked to play tough man-of-the-world. The girl up the front of the bus looked like the one he had noticed on the train. There was something about her that reminded him of his mother. The same expression. A sweetness. But not soppy.

He could not remember much about his mother. But he would never forget her gentleness, the way she used to stroke his head, running her fingers through his hair, tingling his scalp. 'My man,' she called him. And the way she laughed and sang little songs when she brought him walking in the woods beyond Tansey's Gate.

The days they met Father Florence, or Flurry, as she called him, were the best. They played hide 'n' seek around the trees and rolled multicoloured glass marbles on the mossy paths. Sometimes the priest would pull a slim purple-papered chocolate bar from behind Mikey's ear. But when they saw him in the village, they behaved like polite strangers. With a firm hand on his shoulder, Sadie curbed her son's enthusiasm and puppy-like adoration of the priest. Funny, he had not thought of that for a long time. It must be the nostalgia of returning from London.

The bus stopped at the gate of Cissie's cottage, where she stood waiting for Rose and Kate, stocky and sturdy in a brown-flecked cardigan and skirt, her feet incongruously bursting out of yellow suede high heels. Her smile was brilliantly synthetic. That her teeth were obviously artificial, being too small, too even and protruding from too-pink gums, in no way detracted from her sincerity.

The snivelling conductor escorted them from the bus, with great gallantry, insisting on handing down their cases. He had a great how'ya for Cissie and wondered when her sister was coming.

'Soon,' she told him, her eyes twinkling blue, her cheeks all smiles. 'I'll tell her ya were askin' in me next letter.'

Casting his head down, the man shuffled and snuffled before bashfully agreeing.

CHAPTER TEN

From the moment Rose stepped off the bus in Fenit she felt at home in a way she had never before experienced. It was as though she had always known this place.

Not that Cissie's cottage, with its air of poverty, its dingy thatch and tired whitewash, looked particularly hospitable; neither was there much of a welcome in the tiny garden where the bushes grew at frantic angles and the foliage tangled and the undergrowth was dark. No, the welcome came solely from Cissie. And it was a strange one.

Head cocked to one side, to Rose's horror, Cissie pronounced her, 'Nice and fat.' To Kate's relief, Cissie's verdict on her was, 'Ya're too thin, but the Fenit air'll soon fatten y'up.' And then, tactfully, as though to take the harm out of the fatness and the thinness, she finished with the assurance, 'In no time at all, both of ye'll have roses in yer cheeks.'

Whatever about the outside, the inside of her cottage was like a highly polished doll's house. The kitchen had a range in the alcove and a table by the window. A picture of the Sacred Heart, with the same tortured expression as the one in Rose's bedroom, fronted by a votive lamp, faced the door. Off to one side was Cissie's bedroom, to the other Rose and

Kate's, complete with a creaking brass bed, a bockety chest of drawers and wooden pegs on the door for their clothes.

Rose was going to leave Susan tucked into the corner of her case, but Kate spotted her, took her out and ran her hands over her face, the way Rose herself often did. 'What is it?' she asked.

'The head of a doll I had when I was small,' Rose answered shortly, embarrassed about bringing it.

'Where's the rest of her?'

'That's all that's left.'

'Well, little one, you deserve a holiday too,' said Kate, fluffing out the tattered curls and propping up the head in the centre of the mantelpiece. At that moment Rose loved Kate. After all this time, the thoughts of Susan could still hurt. And it was nearly ten years ago.

Once George's name had been settled on, Nance picked up and returned to her familiar efficient self. She and Rose minded their babies in harmony until the day Rose wanted to bathe Susan.

'You can't, Rosemary. You'll ruin her,' said Nance, lifting George from the bath and wrapping him in a yellow towel. But she allowed Rose to dab the doll's bottom liberally with Johnson's baby powder and, using one of Trevor's handkerchiefs, showed her how to fold and pin a nappy.

Some time later, Rose hit on the idea of feeding Susan. By now she was beginning to cop on to the do's and don't's of the household and was smart enough to do it secretly. She filled a bottle from her toy box with George's leftover formula. Holding Susan in the crook of her arm, she inserted the bottle into her mouth. When the feed was finished, Rose put her over her shoulder, and rubbed her back to get up wind, and when she had burped, laid her satisfied to sleep.

She fed Susan as often as possible, and when the doll began to smell, she washed her in the sink. Some time later Trevor summoned her to his study. He put down his book, noting its place with a bookmark, and took Rose on his lap. She felt the fire warm on her legs.

'I've something to tell you, princess. Susan is sick and will have to go away.'

'How long?' asked Rose, eyes wide, lips trembling.

'Until she's better,' Trevor prevaricated.

'For how long?' Rose persisted.

'Maybe for a long time.'

'For ever?'

Trevor nodded. Rose screamed and screamed and kicked and kicked.

Nance rushed in, carrying George, wondering was someone being murdered. 'We'll get you another doll,' she promised, abstractedly, chucking the baby under his chin until he gurgled.

Next day Jill arrived, in a bottle-green box with her name written in gold lettering — a present from Grandad BJ and Grandma Laetitia. She was a grown-up doll with a grown-up expression of disapproval, staring green eyes, toothbrush eyelashes, tumbling orange hair and a long, blue satin dress.

Rose hated her on sight. Her mother said she was an ungrateful child; her father that she was upset. Jill lived on in her box on the top of the wardrobe until Nance suggested at Christmastime that perhaps there was a little girl out there somewhere who was not spoiled and would be delighted to love her.

Rose remembered the occasion well. She was in the hallway dressed in a tartan coat, fur mittens and had on a new striped jelly-bag hat, its tail winding its way down her back. She was on her way out for her afternoon walk with Agnes.

Feeling strangely grown-up and strangely empty, she told her mother, 'Yes, give her away.' She was blinking her eyes very fast and keeping her top teeth pressed into her bottom lip to prevent the tears from spilling over.

Agnes took Rose gently by the hand and, when the hall door was closed after them, hunkered down on the driveway, gave her a cuddle and a little kiss on her forehead. Rose sobbed as though her heart would break. Agnes said nothing, just wrapped the jelly-bag hat more snugly around Rose's neck. After a while she dried Rose's eyes.

When they returned, Jill was gone and Rose, looking at the God on the wall over her bed, asked Him to please send Susan back. To make a miracle. He could, if He wanted. He could do anything, she knew. She even said a prayer on her knees. But when she looked after tea, there was no sign of Susan.

As her mother tucked her in after the Guardian Angel prayer, Rose wound her arms around her neck, nuzzled in, and whispered, 'How can I get Susan back?'

Nance kissed her daughter softly on the cheek, sighed and said something about life being 'hard'.

Trevor came upstairs, lifted Rose out of bed, wrapped her in a blanket, sat her on his knees and into her hair whispered, 'Susan is gone and won't be coming back.'

Rose whispered too, 'Is she dead?'

When he answered, 'Yes, princess', Rose did not scream or kick. She felt as though she had turned to jelly and she had a funny pain in her stomach and a lump in her throat. Trevor held her tightly and rocked her to sleep. It took a long time.

That Christmas, Santa brought Rose a yellow elephant with a blue and white spotted bow. While they were having dinner — this year it was the turn of the Dublin grandparents — Rose, forking a piece of turkey with her best manners, asked slowly and distinctly, 'Mammy, who did you give Jill to?' Nance flushed and Trevor looked down at his plate.

Reaching out across the expanse of white starched damask, king's-pattern silver and Waterford glass goblets, placing a bony hand laden with rings on Rose's arm, Laetitia Horn sat very upright, her knife and fork resting in a tidy V across the few Brussels sprouts, slice of baked ham and the half roast potato remaining on her plate.

Looking from face to face in that autocratic way of hers, she said to the table in general, 'Jill! The doll we gave Rosemary?' Turning right, staring at Nance, her voice rising, but quavery, she demanded, 'You gave her away?' Her expression was hurt-funny and her neck bright red.

Her husband and her son shushed her, making motioning movements towards Rose who, eyes cast down on her plate, was chewing her turkey slowly and carefully. Not understanding, but feeling in some small way she had vindicated Susan.

Two years ago, during a particularly hot and clammy summer, Nance had put Rose to tidying the books in the attic.

A daft idea, Rose had thought, climbing the rickety wooden stairs — the magic and attraction of attics is their very disarrangement and haphazardness. Attics are seductive when they lure with the promise of yielding up their secrets.

Rose dreamed of finding proof of exotic ancestry in yellowing birth and marriage certificates; half-finished manuscripts of juicy seductions; and easels crowded with Dorian-Grey-like canvasses.

Their attic yielded nothing in the way of exotica, though a myriad of forgotten objects brought back jostling memories. Christmas decorations: gaudy paper chains in green and red, five-pointed cardboard stars in orange and yellow, sheaves of glistening silver tinsel and lopsided angels spilling out of wooden-slatted orange boxes. The pale-green papier-mâché baby bath and stand, their sturdy wooden cot and navy upright pram. And the familiar-looking oblong green box behind the pram. When she opened it, there was Jill. Still as immaculate as ever. Rose looked at her, stunned. Then she lifted her out, laid her on the floor and kicked her face in, the crêpe heels of her summer sandals making satisfyingly scrunching noises as nose, cheeks and chin caved in. With her fingers she picked at the arrogant green eyes, removing forever that look of disapproval.

Covering her up with the lid again, she crawled towards the eaves, pushing the box in front of her into the gloom behind the old pram, laying Jill to rest for ever. Backing out, Rose knelt on something soft. Omigod. A dead mouse. I will not look. I do not want to know. Then: I will not be a coward; and she backed out, dragging the object with her.

Not a mouse. A scrap of rag? No. In the poor light it showed up as tattered blond hair attached to the grimy head of a doll with a cracked face, sad blue eyes and a smiling rosebud mouth. Her beloved Susan.

'Will I tell you a secret?' Kate asked Rose, later that evening.

'Yes. I love secrets.'

'I wouldn't mind the Deaner for a boyfriend.' Kate tossed her hair, laughed mischievously and suggested they explore outside.

Much of the back garden was laid out in rows of vegetables. Potatoes, carrots and radishes and other plants Rose did not recognise. The remainder of the field stretched desolate with tufts of grass, spindles of scutch, broken furniture, stone slabs and a clothes-line, held aloft by a forked branch. Small brown hens with yellow feet and long hooked nails clustered and clucked around the few sheds at the end of the garden, one of which housed the toilet.

When Kate lifted the latch and creaked open the door, it was not the buzzing of bluebottles they noticed, but the smell — a toilet smell overlaid with Jeyes Fluid.

'Omigod, we'll have to hold our breaths while we're going,' Rose whispered.

'Jesus Fluid,' giggled Kate. 'I can't bear the thought of it.'

The 'lavvy', as Cissie called it, became the bane of their existence, particularly at night, as she insisted they make the journey down the garden path before turning in, warning them that the chamber pot reposing under their bed was for use only if they were 'short-taken'. The garden was pitch black, spooky, just bearable because they were together and had a torch.

'You go first,' said Kate generously a few nights later. 'I'll shine the torch in the cracks so you'll be able to see.'

Rose yanked open the door, forgetting the smell, then backed out again to gulp in the full of her lungs of fresh air. The 'throne' was a plank of wood with a bottom-sized circle — for buttocks much larger than Rose's — cut out of the centre. Under this sat the 'receptacle'. Rose dropped her bottle-green elasticated school knickers as far as her knees, and, still holding her breath, determined not to think of the hole.

Instead she looked around. And was sorry. It was very scary. The wavering torch from outside high-lighted concealed crevices and threw up all sorts of shadow monsters and creepy-crawlies.

From Nature Study class, she knew that the slimy cottonwool-like blobs in the corners were the larvae of butterflies and moths just waiting to be hatched out; hard-shelled black beetles patrolled the floor area, and wood lice, disturbed by the flickering light, swarmed around the door frame.

The quicker this is over, the better, she thought, putting her hands on either side of the hole, trying to suspend herself over it. But she could not and, dammit, her knickers dribbled down to her ankles and finally to the floor. Eventually having to exhale, and being stuck with breathing normally, she called to Kate, 'This is awful. Gets worse every night.'

'Any daddy-long-legs?' Kate asked conversationally.

Rose was terrified that Kate would move away with the light and leave her alone in the unknown dark and, just as she was gingerly positioning her buttocks over the hole, her worst fears were realised. Kate let out a ghostly 'whoo' into a crack, the light disappeared and Rose could hear her laughing, running back up the garden.

Rose leapt off the 'throne' and ran her hands over the wood trying to locate the door, her head filled with visions of unfurling larvae and rampaging daddy-long-legs. She reached the house gasping. Kate, her hair screening her face, was calmly reading Rose's comic by the side of the range.

Cissie said something about Rose being brave and not afraid of the dark. Rose did not disillusion her. 'I dropped my pants and couldn't find them. Maybe Kate'll get them when she goes.'

'Cissie says I can use "the under-the-bed" tonight. I'm so tired.'

'Just for tonight, so,' warned Cissie.

Kate was an expert at getting her own way. On

many occasions she managed to avoid night-time use of the 'lavvy'. And, certainly in the beginning, no matter how late or how tired they were, she insisted that the ritual of her hairbrushing be observed.

After the final cup of tea of the day, she would land into the kitchen with her bristle brush. Presenting it to Cissie, in her smiley, wheedling way which defied refusal, she would ask for the hundred brush-strokes from scalp to end, making the execution of it sound a privilege. Sitting at the kitchen table, hair spread out like a golden cloak across her shoulders, with Cissie standing behind, drawing the brush in firm, even strokes from scalp to tip, Kate wriggled with pleasure. 'You're the best brusher ever.'

'Don't think for a moment I'm foolish enough to fall for that old *plámás*,' Cissie retorted, but you would know she was pleased. Cissie took her duty of surrogate motherhood so seriously that she discouraged Rose and Kate from going to the village. Until she had the measure of the pair of them, she was happier with them under her eye.

She found all sorts of jobs to keep them occupied, one of her favourites being 'doing *The Kerryman*', as she called it. This entailed cutting the weekly newspaper into rectangles, nine to each page, skewering a hole in one of the corners, running soft wiring through the hole, and hanging the bundle on the designated nail in the lavvy.

The cousins found great reading in the paper. Rose discovered that the girl who had been voted Dublin Rose for the Festival of Tralee lived just around the corner from her in Booterstown.

'You're much prettier than her,' Kate assured, dismissing as irrelevant the coverage on Éamon de Valera and General Seán MacEoin, the candidates in the upcoming presidential election. Turning the page to ooh and aah at the idea of Killarney holding a 'Queen of Fashion' competition during the races. Wondering was there any way they could inveigle permission for a visit to Puck Fair.

Cissie also introduced them to the intricacies of trimming the wick on the paraffin lamp, laying the table and drying the dishes. Anything to keep them around. But the more she opposed the stretching of their wings, the more determined Kate became.

On a particularly clammy afternoon, she and Rose sat on the outside step, perspiration pearling their foreheads. 'She's afraid we'll get up to mischief. I bet Aunt Babs told her all about Doreen and warned her not to let us out of her sight,' said Rose knowledgeably, considering herself an expert on the workings of adult minds.

'Bet you're right,' answered Kate, twiddling a curl of hair around her index finger. 'Thinks we'll end up having passionate romances with the locals. That we'd be so lucky.' She gave a dramatic sigh. 'Not that I'd mind the Deaner. Now he'd be some boyfriend!' Squaring her shoulders, she said, 'If we're not going to end up locked up for the summer, it's up to us to let her know we're sensible and can be trusted.'

In she marched to the hot and airless back kitchen where Cissie was feeding a bunch of nettles into a blackened pot. 'What are they for?' she asked nervously.

Kate was particularly faddy about her food, though she loved sweet things.

'For me cousin Broody's boil,' said Cissie. 'He lives up Ardfert way.'

'Does he have to eat that?' Kate asked in horror.

'They'll be cooked up first. They're good for ya. And I'll make a poultice too,' explained Cissie.

Kate shuddered at the thought. 'Well, while you're doing that, we'll get the messages from the village. It'll save you the journey. It's too hot for cycling,' she offered virtuously. When Kate was being charming, she was hard to refuse.

'All right, so. A turnover and two cans of milk. Ye'll get them in the post office. And come straight back. The two of ya.' Cissie only wore her teeth on special occasions and she smiled her thanks now in an uncertain gummy way. Despite the heat and the uphill drag to the village on the bike, she reasoned that she would be happier keeping the girls here.

CHAPTER ELEVEN

The village of Fenit, smouldering in the dead heat, was bleak, dingy and silent, with a sad air of dusty somnolence.

'I told you. It's not much,' Kate said with a toss of her head, surveying the place with a jaundiced eye, hands clasped behind her back as though she were an expert on rural villages.

Kate was right. On first impression, it did not look much. Though from geography class Rose knew the importance of the harbour both as a commercial and fishing port. But this was a thin village. A mean, sandy street with a huddle of decrepit cottages, a few tired-looking houses, three shabby pubs — one having the nerve to masquerade as a hotel — and some peeling shop fronts, including the post office and shop, owned by Mags Looney.

Mags stood over the six-foot mark and was built accordingly. She had an insatiable hunger for gossip. In fine weather her favourite vantage point was her doorway from where she could keep an eye on the few comings and goings of the place.

Needles pecking as her fingers knitted fast and furiously, her buttocks spilling out over a chipped green wooden chair, she watched the meandering girls on the street outside. The news of Cissie's guests had preceded them. Cissie was being paid for minding the two girls — and well, too, Mags bet.

As postmistress, Mags considered herself a step above the others, the equivalent of First Villager. However, to her constant annoyance, Cissie was the most popular, most consulted and most revered person within the community. Mags was sure the position would have been hers, had it not been for what she now regarded as her foolish generosity of seventeen years ago.

Regularly she agonised over whether it might have been better not to have taken in her daughter and grandson when they had appeared in the village that gloomy October morning.

Sadie had returned from London a broken, pathetic figure, with nothing but the clothes she stood up in, clutching her three-month-old baby. She had no skills, no money and her only home was this corner of Kerry, and Mags had not had the heart to turn her away.

Here in Fenit, the story of her dead husband of six months had been greeted with ill-concealed scepticism, and her death five years later received with relief. Mikey had become the butt of the villagers' anger, and Mags had walked a thin line between family togetherness and wanting to play a leading role within the community. She had achieved neither, and for that she blamed Mikey.

'Ye're welcome to Fenit,' Mags greeted the cousins, taking them in from head to toe with her hooded turtle eyes. Breathing heavily, she heaved herself out of the chair. Wrapping brown wool around blue needles, the back of a cardigan she was knitting for herself, she speared the ball of wool and rolled the rectangle of knitting around the needles.

After the glaring light outside, the shop was dark and dusty, though Mags had no problem in deciphering her merchandise. Rooting behind the counter, she came up with a glass sweet jar, stuffed with small white packages. Unscrewing the lid with big square hands, she pushed the jar across the counter.

'Take your pick. It's a welcoming present.' Rose hesitated. She did not want anything from this woman whom she had disliked on sight. Mags shook out a package, pushed it across the counter. 'Don't tell me ya've never had a lucky dip.'

Rose had not. When she opened it, inside was a smaller bag of sherbet with a straw for sucking, a belt made of coloured suede pieces and a yellow lollipop. She said her thank-you politely.

Kate, an enthusiastic recipient of all gifts, got a blue elephant charm and six aniseed balls. And was effusive in her thanks.

Nor was she put off by Mags's formidable appearance, pushy manner and gasps for breath. Propped against the counter, resorting to creative liberties and artistic freedoms, she regaled the postmistress with her family's history, detailing how she and Rose came to be staying with Cissie.

Getting the inside story, from the horse's mouth as it were, had Mags in her element. She could not believe her luck. Gossip like this, and from one of Kerry's most prominent families, was powerful grist to her mill. Leaning forward across the counter to catch every juicy morsel, she nodded intently, now and again plucking a stray bit of wool from her green jumper.

When Kate began to dry up, Mags, terrified she would lose such a captive source of information, jumped in with a question. 'Will ye be going on the carragheen pick?'

It was the first the cousins had heard of it. Instantly, Kate, consumed with enthusiasm for the venture, fired all sorts of questions at Mags.

'Cissie's brother, Carragheen Mossie's the man to ask,' Mags told Kate, ignoring Rose whom she had mentally labelled as 'Dublin stuck up'. 'That's what he's known as, far and wide. He's a quiet one. Not much for talking. An expert on carragheen and its harvesting. Not only here but in the next parish.'

Rose, hating the smells of stale cabbage and paraffin oil in the shop, and feeling excluded from Kate's rapport with Mags, went outside into the clammy heat. Wandering around the back and down the laneway, sucking on her sherbet, a cacophony of bleating sounds floated on the still air. A little further on, a gate opened into a small grit-covered yard with a pump in the corner.

There he was. The James Deaner from the bus. Straddling a sheep, wielding a shears, muscles rippling, sweat shimmying down his back. With brutal grace, in swift, sure skelps he sheared, with such skill that when he had finished, the skin had not even one nick. The animal hobbled to its knees. He swiped at its rump and it scuttled out of his range. A victor. He held the fleece aloft, his hair a damp halo around his head.

Seven men looked on. One old, six young. The old man was greasy-capped and big-booted; the young ones wore thick trousers held up with wide belts. All had vacant, drop-jaw expressions on their faces. All of them in the line, hunched into the low wall and one another, tracked the shearer with their eyes. Calculating eyes.

The O'Brien men were as notorious for their roughness as for their gambling.

It was said that Jammy O'Brien and his sons would bet their last penny on two flies walking up a wall. They had lost on the shearing, but would not admit to it, determined to collect their money. Seven of them to one of him; of course they would. They also knew there was not a person in the village who would lend the shearer a hand if they roughed young Mikey Daw up.

'Ya owe us, Mikey Daw.' The old man spat into the palms of his hands, and rubbed them together.

'Don't. Not a nick on her. And me fastest time yet.' The shearer dropped the fleece, kicked the shears to one side, picked up a stained white shirt from the wall and swaggered towards them to collect his winnings.

The tallest of Jammy's sons threw a leg over the wall and dropped into the yard. Squaring his shoulders, arms hanging loosely, fists clenched, he swayed on the balls of his feet. 'Ya'll pay up.'

He was joined by two of his brothers who stood either side and a little behind him.

'Try and make me,' taunted Mikey, standing his ground.

'Pay up,' demanded the old man from outside the yard.

'And if ya know what's good for ya, stay away from Maryann,' advised the tall brother.

It was then that the old man noticed Rose. A ripple ran through him. Licking his mouth, pointy red tongue darting in and out between narrow lips, with lust in his eyes. Women were good for only the one thing.

This one standing like a frightened rabbit looked interesting. Untouched. White blouse and blue skirt. Ripe for the plucking.

The afternoon was sweltering. A silver haze writhed over the yard. The bleating sheep, staring men, buzzing flies and nauseous smells pulsated around Rose. Apprehension skittered across her shoulders. Defenceless, she stood alone against these waves of threatening sexuality. Not that she knew what they were or could label them. But these men were bad, much worse than Tommo — she knew that.

In comparison to the O'Briens, the James Deaner was like a god. A lean, clean, golden god. Young, primitive and palpable. When their eyes met, Rose's pleaded, his assessed, his stare a wondering challenge. Then he winked. But he did not smile.

He was not much older than Rose — maybe a year or two, but there was a sureness about him that marked him as different from any of the boys she had known in Dublin. The hairs on his chest were fuzzy, dark, sheening sweat. She blushed, a slow thorough flushing starting at her toes, spreading slowly upwards.

Mikey swaggered towards her, swinging his shirt. A raw energy swirled about him, like an electric current. Silky, suffocating air streamed over Rose, threatening, smothering, overwhelming her. Having no idea how to handle the situation, she stuffed the sherbet and her hands into the pocket of her skirt and, with weak knees, just stood looking at him. Then she turned and walked — no, more ran — away straight back to Cissie's, completely forgetting about Kate and the messages.

It was that girl again. She disturbed him. Mikey thought it was the way she made him remember his mother. Something he preferred to avoid. The pain of the loss was so great. Mam had encouraged him to make choices; told him there was good in everyone; urged him never to judge harshly. Funny. At the time he had not known what she was talking about. But he had not seen much sign of good around here. And, certainly, he had been well judged and harshly. His mother had done nothing more than live her own life and die tragically, and yet the villagers had never forgiven her, or him.

One sunshiny morning Mam had shown him a tin box she kept hidden at the back of a drawer in the tiny bedroom they shared at the back of the post office. Inside were papers which she spread out on the bed. 'In here is who y'are,' she said, holding him close. 'We'll find a secret place. Always remember, it belongs to you.'

That afternoon, they had climbed over Tansey's gate and buried the box in the woods, wrapped in a tarry rag, and using their favourite chestnut tree as a marker.

As they walked back, hand in hand, across the meadow towards the village, the sky was blue and the grass streaked with early buttercups and daisies. Sadie bent down and picked a mixed posy. 'Which do you prefer?' She held out one of each. He chose the daisy; he liked its yellow face, pink-tipped frill of white petals, and the way it smiled up at the sun.

They met Cissie at the gate and he ran to show her. 'Now, when's your birthday?' she asked.

He bet she already knew. Cissie knew everything. 'April, number 20,' he told her.

'Did ya know that because y'are an April baby, the daisy's yer lucky flower?'

Mikey wanted to tell Cissie he was not a baby. But he did not. A daisy, his very own lucky flower. Ever since, he had liked daisies.

Cissie was cross when Rose returned on her own, and she began to worry about Kate. Rose stuttered a half-hearted excuse about not feeling well, but Cissie's penetrating look soon had her blurting out about being frightened, and she described the incident and the men.

It had to be the O'Briens, Cissie knew. They were a scary lot. And the rumours that came down from their side of the mountain! Worse than the animals, they were. Thank God they seldom came to the village. However, after probing some more, Cissie decided no harm had been done.

Rose knew she was a bit shy, but she really didn't think she was so shy as to become immobilised by a few countrymen staring at her and a boy giving her a wink.

When Kate arrived, flushed and good humoured, a good half an hour after her cousin, with clanking milk cans and unwrapped bread, Cissie asked for an explanation.

'I was talking.'

Cissie, hands on her hips, asked, 'Who to?'

'The woman in the post office. She gave us a present of a lucky dip to welcome us to Fenit. Didn't Rose tell you?'

Cissie, looking Kate straight in the eye, asked, 'Is that all? What else were ya up to? Why didn't ya come back with Rose? Ye must stay together when ye're out.'

Hands held up in mock surrender, Kate admitted, 'I give in. I also talked to a boy.'

'Who?'

'Mikey's his name. He was on the bus on our way out here. He's divine. Like a film star.' Cissie's face tightened, but, caught up in her own enthusiasm, Kate did not notice. 'Rose saw him too. He said she ran away.'

Rose felt herself blushing again.

'Mikey is Mags Looney's grandson — the woman in the post office. He lives with her. Stay away from him. The both of ye. I'm warnin' ye now.'

To herself Cissie thought, I might have known. No matter how sympathetic her personal feelings towards Mikey, she felt that he was nothing but trouble. Now here were her two beauts raving about him. It would be just like them to become involved. What would she say to Mrs Mac? Not to mention Father Lehane?

'Why?' Rose asked.

'I'm telling ye. And keep away from Maryann O'Brien.'

'We don't know her … yet,' said Kate perkily.

'Ye will. Soon enough. Rose has met her father and brothers. There's badness in that family. Stay away from them. And that's the end of the matter.' Muttering to herself, Cissie banged the cups onto their saucers, the prelude to the production of steps of turnover, wedges of yellow butter and lashings of damson jam.

'Where's Mikey's mother and father?' asked Kate, piling jam on her bread.

'Dead.' Cissie wet the tea and poured it, and her face shuttered in a way that precluded further discussion.

Despite the scariness of the afternoon's events, Cissie was making the episode ridiculous, thought Rose. Adult reaction to fellows was pathetic. Her being forbidden Frank. Cissie fussing about a boy they hardly knew.

Later, Kate, enthusing at length about Mikey's gorgeousness, decided that Cissie had taken their silence regarding him as obedience. She was full of plans and ideas for getting to know him better, and when she ran out of steam on the subject of Mikey, she turned her attention to the carragheen pick and how to get going on that. Kate was nothing if not determined — a trait, it was said, she had inherited from her mother.

CHAPTER TWELVE

Kate, desperately wanting to be part of the carragheen harvesting, realised that getting on the right side of Carragheen Mossie was all-important. She and Rose had plenty of opportunity, as, once over his initial shyness, he was in and out of the cottage, helping his sister, Cissie, with the heavy work. Fertilising the garden with seaweed. Digging potatoes, planting cabbage, scything grass, cleaning the hen-house and doing unspoken-about things associated with the 'lavvy'.

Rose thought Mossie a lovely man, soft-spoken and courteous. Big and bulky with a stoop and features that looked as though they had been carved from mahogany, he reminded her of the Red Indian chief sitting outside his tepee, whose picture had hung in one of her junior-school classrooms.

After drinking a mug of tea, it was Mossie's habit to sit back into the low súgán chair beside the range and stretch out his feet, take a pipe from his old jacket and a pouch of tobacco from the pocket of his baggy cords. Filling the pipe, he would tamp down the tobacco, light it from a taper stuck into the range and sit, more often than not, just staring into space.

Sometimes he would spread *The Kerryman* out on the kitchen table and, with the pair of glasses he and

Cissie shared perched halfway down his nose, he would read the paper from cover to cover, his index finger picking out the words individually, his lips moving to their rhythm.

Despite Kate's being more sociable and a better communicator than Rose, her reasons for wanting to pick carragheen were transparent — she saw it as a fun venture and had no particular interest in either its benefit to the community or the protection and preservation of carragheen.

Since the 'flibbertigibbet' incident, even she had to admit she was not Mossie's favourite: one day after his dinner, when Kate had been at her chattering best or worst, depending on your viewpoint, Mossie, tamping at his pipe, announced in that quiet way of his, 'You're a real flibbertigibbet.'

To Rose, who was unfamiliar with its meaning, the word had sounded rude, but Kate was delighted. She had jumped up and given Mossie an exaggerated curtsey. 'Thank you. That's much better than being dull and boring.'

Mossie, quietly smoking his pipe, had not been impressed: 'Silence should only be broken when you've something worthwhile to say.'

Kate had perkily retaliated, 'In that case, I'd be a mute.'

Mossie had not contradicted her.

So Kate begged Rose to plead their cause. That Mossie had a soft spot for Rose they both knew. Like many a countryman, he was a natural philosopher, a bit of a poet and a mine of information on the environment and local history. When he could be got going, Rose loved listening to him; Kate's boredom was obvious.

Rose thought of history as happening in other places; certainly she would not have considered a backwater like Fenit to be a historical hot spot. Through Mossie she learned differently.

That morning, leaning on his spade, he asked, 'Did ya know Brendan the Navigator was born here in 484?' She did not. Nor did she know the meaning of Fenit in Gaelic. '*An Fianait*, the wild place,' he told her.

Rose could believe that. There was something about Fenit. An untamed spot, wild and cruel, where wind and rain, poised in the wings of sea and mountain, waited for a cue to make their dramatic entrance. It was populated by raw people, like the O'Briens and Mags Looney and more she met around the village, all seeming to be related to each other.

As with the best of Irish places, Fenit had a ruined castle, dating back to the Middle Ages, and an ancient church and graveyard, disused now for hundreds of years except for the burial of unbaptised babies. Because the unbaptised were deemed by the Catholic Church to be stained with original sin, they were denied burial in sanctified ground. The Western Cove was the last resting-place of a group of sailors, shipwrecked in the Spanish Armada. 'At the time,' Mossie told Rose, 'the English didn't take prisoners or show mercy to survivors. But they were no worse than the Irish.'

'I didn't know that.'

'How could ya? It's not something ya'd learn in school.'

He dug a few more spadefuls. 'Fishin' is a way of life here. And families have always lost their men to the sea. But it weren't until the pier joined Big Samphire Island to the mainland in 1884 it became important. Did ya know the lighthouse on Little Samphire operated until just three years ago?'

Rose decided that while Mossie was in full flight it was as good a time as ever to make her request. Cissie was around the gable of the cottage feeding the hens, and Kate was foostering in the kitchen. Mossie gave up on the digging and began hoeing the weeds between the carrot drills.

'Could I have a go?' she asked. With a grave inclination of his head — it fascinated her that he never smiled — he handed over the hoe and picked up the spade again. 'I heard you're the expert on carragheen. Could you explain it to me? I don't know anything, except it comes from the sea.'

Rose omitted to tell how one evening, as a special treat, Cissie had made a carragheen drink. After one look at its white opaque glutinousness and fast-forming skin, Kate pronounced dramatically, 'I'd sooner die than drink that.'

Dublin-polite Rose had also declined: 'No, thank you.'

Cissie, laughing good-humouredly, had gulped it down herself.

Just as Rose liked the word 'turquoise', she liked the sound of the word 'carragheen', the way it slid off her tongue and rolled out from between her lips.

In that slow way of his, standing upright, leaning on the spade, pausing between each sentence, Mossie said, 'It's hard to describe. Ya need to see it growing. Best at harvesting time.'

'Isn't that only for locals?' Rose knew that from Cissie.

'It depends.'

'Well, could I?' Kate asked, joining them. Rose shot her a look of annoyance. Trust Kate, she always had to be in on the action. 'I do live in Kerry.'

'And so you do. But d'ya need the work and the money?'

'I do,' Kate assured him, having the habit of spending her pocket money on sweets within half an hour of getting it.

'We'll see, about both of ya,' he said, moving up the garden. 'I'll have a chat with Cissie. But, ya know, she's a bit nervous about the water.'

Rose felt duty-bound to finish hoeing the remaining drills of carrots. She was enraged at Kate's refusal to help mound up the weeds.

Despite Cissie's warning, Rose and Kate began to see a lot of Mikey. He seemed to materialise out of nowhere, hands jammed in pockets, kicking stones, his backside against the pier wall, whittling away at a piece of wood; or up at Tansey's gate, throwing his knife at the bark of a tree. They had never come across anybody like him, and his difference fascinated them. In their families discipline and duty were of paramount importance. He seemed troubled by neither.

Rose likened the times Mikey spent with them to the 3-D films she had only read about, where by wearing the special green and red glasses provided in the cinema, the audience became part of the action. Mikey was a larger-than-life presence, adding spice to their day.

Often, a girl, who they discovered was *the* Maryann, would be with him. Her face round and predictable as a clock, framed by a waterfall of dark hair. Her legs stocky, her forearms strong, her hands capable-looking. Hovering at Mikey's shoulder. Big and bulky, silent and uncommunicative. Never meeting their eyes. Avoiding responding to their comments. Rose felt Maryann's hostility towards her, and it disturbed her.

'She's like his guardian angel,' suggested Kate.

More like a guardian devil, Rose felt.

Kate treated Mikey and Maryann, as she did everyone, with friendly chatter, laughter and jokes. But she did shape up to Mikey, batting the eyelashes, tossing her hair at him, wriggling her body. He paid her little attention, and Maryann too seemed immune to her overtures.

Rose was aware of Mikey watching her though, assessing, as though he could see right into her soul. He unnerved her. Made her feel so self-conscious that she tried to avoid meeting his eye.

Since what she termed her 'over-reaction' to Mikey on the day of the sheep-shearing, Rose kept a firm lid on any embryonic thoughts of him. He was a slumbering thought. Never for release into the public domain.

When she mentioned her discomfiture to Kate, with a blithe toss of her head, she replied, 'He's a divine hunk. I only wish he'd notice me.' Then, eyes narrowing, half joking, but wholly in earnest, 'Just remember, he's mine, I bagged him first.'

Mags called regularly to Cissie, often with two neighbours in tow. These women, wrapped in black shawls, heads encased in hairnets, were small and wizened and they caused Rose and Kate great hilarity. Kate admitted that when she was small she thought hairnets stopped hair from falling off.

'Inquisitive crows,' Rose labelled the women who crowded the girls in that no-holds-barred way of some country folk: quizzing them on relatives, chattering with delight when they traced ancestors back to the Famine of 1847 and shrugging shoulders in disgust on learning that Rose's father was 'all Dublin'. If they only knew he was a Protestant, Rose thought, they would probably expire on the spot. When they ran out of relatives, they interrogated Rose and Kate about school. Stabbing them in the chest and cackling with laughter, they warned them off the Fenit fellas.

Often Cissie suggested they stay for the Rosary and they never needed a second invitation.

As Rose was a first-time visitor to Kerry, Cissie bestowed on her the honour of lighting the votive lamp. Rose was still as appalled as she had been as a child at the worship of such a disturbing image as the thorn-crowned Christ, and felt more and more hypocritical. She had given up on religion, but in view of Cissie's graciousness, it seemed churlish to refuse. In the red light, Christ glowed. It was easy to believe this God to be all-seeing, all-knowing and all-powerful.

Cissie and the women would kneel on the floor in a semicircle around the range, the visiting women taking the paraphernalia of prayer from the cavernous pockets of their aprons: dark beads with heavy crucifixes, black-rimmed memorials for their dead and a long litany of petitions. Kate's beads were pearl and she wound them in and around her fingers, holding out her hands in admiration of their jewelled elegance.

Rose did not have Rosary beads. The Sunday after her last confession, she had tucked hers into a corner of the seat during 10.30 mass in Booterstown church and walked home with a quivering sense of doom. Her original plan had been to follow Monica's example with her teeth-brace, but at the last moment, as Rose's legs straddled the grating, her nerve failed. Whatever about a brace, it did not seem right to consign Rosary beads — blessed in Lourdes, no less — to the sewers.

Sometimes, however, in this wild place, there was a perverse comfort and a blanket of familiarity about the religion she had known since babyhood. 'In the name of the Father and of the Son and of the Holy Ghost,' Cissie would start, her voice ponderously and dolorously nasal. The chorused responses were lighter, sweeter. Again and again the single voice followed by the chorus. Five times for the Our Father. Fifty times for the Hail Mary. Five times for the Glory Be to the Father. Rose counted out her decades of the Rosary on her fingers.

Then came the litany, with its sonorous response of 'Pray for us', after phrases which always seemed senseless to Rose. 'Vessel of honour.' 'Pray for us.' 'Vessel of singular devotion.' 'Pray for us.' 'Mystical rose....' There was no meaning to them. Cissie had usually moved on to 'Tower of David' before Kate would react. 'Mystical Rose?' she would hiss with delight, giving Rose the thumbs-up sign. 'That's you.'

As always, Cissie clucked a warning without missing a beat of the litany. A whole sea of prayers. Tides. Waves. Ripples. As ceaseless as the pounding of the ocean. Cissie would finish off by asking God to keep Rose and Kate pure and holy. The two girls would giggle into their hands while Mags and the neighbours solemnly intoned, 'Amen.'

The bedroom Rose and Kate shared was tiny, but Rose loved it. When darkness fell, by tilting her head to look out of the window she could see a flying moon boat in a blue-clouds sea, as she snuggled luxuriously under the old patchwork quilt made by Cissie's grandmother. Frequently there was a nudge from Kate, wanting to talk. There is something about a shared bed that makes confidences easy.

'Tell us about your boyfriend.' Usually Rose fobbed her off with a minor titbit but one night, to her own amazement, she found herself confiding. The bad as well as the good. Kate nuzzled deeper into the bed, a delicious thrill of expectation running through her. Despite her sassy attitude and know-all airs, she was quite an innocent, but there was an astuteness about her. And she was more than eager to learn everything she could about boys and sex. For Rose, remembering and putting into words the pleasures and joys, hurts and sorrows, proved to be surprisingly healing. Kate's hand snaked across the bed and clasped hers in a comforting gesture.

'How d'you know Frank kissed Monica?' she asked.

'Didn't I tell you? She told me. The Monday after the tennis hop.'

'And you believed her? You're a right eejit.'

'Frank didn't ring me. Or get in touch.'

'How could he, with Aunty Nance guarding you like a jailer? Are you surprised? Did you expect him to crawl?'

Rose wondered why, all the times she and Barbara had analysed the Frank situation, they had never arrived at Kate's reasoning.

'We thought you must be down here because of a boy,' Kate consoled.

'How did you know that?'

'I heard Mammy talking to Lehane. They think I'm too young,' Kate said, sleepy now. 'But I'm not and I certainly wouldn't mind kissing Mikey. Bet he's a great kisser.' Then, 'Good night'.

One golden afternoon of puffball clouds in an azure sky, Rose and Kate lay on their backs at the end of Cissie's garden, as far as possible from the lavvy. Like poetry, the day was, thought Rose, the meadow grass alive with the hum of bees, fluttering butterflies and chirping birds, a riot of ox-daisies, pink and white clover, blue creeping veronica, and sunbursts of dandelions.

The two girls, idly picking at the petals of the ox daisies, chanted, 'He loves me, he loves me not....' The wilting skeletons of the flowers lay around them, their yellow centres studs of gold, the white petals scattered like snow.

'Hey,' said Kate, 'you must be cheating. You've loads of *he loves me*s.'

Rose, punctilious in her petal-pulling, reddened anyway.

'So who is it who loves you now?' Kate asked with a deliciously knowing grin. She was always ragging Rose. 'Who is it you want to love you? Still Frank?'

Rose had the measure of Kate's teasing even though, unlike Monica, she was without malice.

'Certainly not,' she retorted loftily, deciding she was finally over Frank. 'If I never see him again, it will be too soon. I'm off fellas....' She was going to say 'forever' when she was interrupted by a holler.

Mikey sat on top of the wall, his feet resting on the galvanised roof of the lavvy. 'So are ye coming to my hideout?' he asked.

'We are,' said Kate, jumping up, with a smile designed to please, always one for an adventure. Batting sooty eyelashes, she shook out her hair, and ran to the base of the wall to stand looking up at him.

'Come on, so,' he said, holding out his hand to Kate, but watching Rose.

'Remember I bagged him first,' Kate hissed at Rose. Then sweetly to Mikey, 'We'll meet you at Tansey's gate.'

'Don't bother going around. I'll give you a hand up here,' he offered.

'I need a cardigan.' Rose needed a breather, to digest Kate's attitude. She was disturbed by Mikey, but the fact that adults regarded him as not suitable added to his mystery and allure. She could only imagine her mother's reaction to him.

Cissie, in the back kitchen, up to her elbows in flour, was kneading soda bread in a chipped enamel basin.

'We're going to the village to get a little pink marshmallow mouse,' lied Kate.

'Haven't ya spent all your pocket money?'

'Rose's going to lend me some.' The lie tripped easily off Kate's tongue.

'Mrs Mac said neither of ye were to get extra,' Cissie told them firmly.

'Just this once,' Kate pleaded. 'And we'll save you the head,' she promised, confident in the knowledge that Cissie's weakness was for chocolate éclairs.

'Off with you so, but don't be late for tea.'

They scampered down the garden, out the gate and down the road to where Mikey was sitting on the five-bar gate of Tansey's field. Smoking. Kate was right, he *was* divine, thought Rose, though why she should feel butterflies of excitement starting in her stomach, she did not know. Mikey's eyes were astonishingly blue and his smile lazy. He tossed the butt into the hedgerow, jumped down and said, 'Come on, so. I'll show you my secret place.'

The afternoon had turned even more wondrous than the early part of the day. Clotted-cream clouds drifted across a pearl-blue sky, a frisky breeze rustled the leaves as the three of them entered the woods. Mikey stopped a little way in, cut right off the path and, after a few hundred yards, they came to a glade, dominated by a chestnut tree, against which there were propped a few leaf-covered branches.

'Interesting,' said Kate, looking around her appraisingly.

Rose said nothing, but was aware of Mikey watching her.

'It's my private place,' he said.

'A kind of a tree house?' offered Kate helpfully.

'Tree houses are for children,' he told her scornfully, but she was not in the least fazed.

'So why bother with us if you're so above yourself?' Kate asked him loftily, while at the same time keeping a flirty lilt of amusement in her voice.

'Just being sociable. Checking out the talent,' he said, winking at Rose.

Rose hated this constant blushing and wondered would she ever grow out of it.

Kate looked from one to the other, puzzled. And giggled nervously.

'Anyone for a cigarette?' Mikey asked.

'I don't mind if I do,' said Kate.

From his pocket he took a battered pack of Woodbines, opened it and offered it to Rose. Inside were three flattened, misshapen cigarettes. Rose removed one and held it between her index and middle fingers, the way she had seen her father do when he smoked his occasional cigar.

Mikey took his straight from the packet to

between his lips, then passed the packet to Kate who followed his lead.

Not wanting to be left out, Rose quickly put her cigarette to her lips. It deposited flakes of tobacco on her tongue. She took it out and fastidiously removed the offending particles with her fingers. Mikey looked amused. Realising her credibility was at stake, she stuck it firmly in place again. Sternly, Mikey told Rose and Kate to watch him. Cupping his hands professionally around his own, which was drooping from the left corner of his mouth, he lit a match and held it to the cigarette. On his second effortless puff, he chuffed smoke out of his nostrils!

Rose and Kate looked on, mesmerised. Despite Kate's in-built veneer of casualness and nonchalance, she was fascinated. Rose, as always, reacted to what happened around her.

'Pull at the flame,' urged Mikey.

After six matches, the girls' cigarettes were still unlit. Mikey took Kate's from her, shook his head in disgust at its soggy wetness, put it between his own lips and lit it with a flourish.

In a delicious sensation of fear and trepidation, Rose awaited her turn. About to call on Jude, patron saint of hopeless cases, she remembered she had given up on religion, though even if she were still a believer, she was pretty sure the heavenly bodies would frown on smoking. She was saved when Mikey counted his matches, shrugged, held out his hand for her cigarette and lit it off his own without any fuss.

Determined to save face, Rose took a few huge pulls. But she never knew that smoke could be so insidious, choking her head and throat and bringing dancing lights before her eyes. Dammit, she wished she had learned how to smoke. Red-faced, coughing, spluttering, she let the cigarette fall into the undergrowth, thankfully lost for ever.

She looked up at Mikey. He was watching her. His eyes holding the same sort of wondering challenge as they had held on the day he had sheared the sheep.

'Leave it,' he said, his voice husky thick. He took his own cigarette out of his mouth, topped it, shoved it into his pocket and moved nearer to her. Rose wanted desperately to say something, but could think of nothing.

Then Kate, puffing furiously, her tanned face a sheeny grey, said, 'I think I'm too young to smoke. You can have this back.' She pushed the cigarette at Mikey, but he did not seem to notice her because he was looking at Rose and she found herself peeping up at him out of the corner of her eye.

'Come on, Rose,' said Kate with a touch of asperity to her voice. 'We'll be late for tea. Cissie'll kill us.' With a swing of her shoulders, she took off through the trees. The spell was broken. With one last look at Mikey, Rose left him. As she crashed through the woodland after Kate, she realised they were miles too early for tea.

CHAPTER THIRTEEN

A few days later, on their return from the beach, a car was parked outside Cissie's. 'Oh, God, no. Look who's here,' Kate wailed.

'Who?' asked Rose.

'My yahoo of a father.'

'Foxy's lovely,' Rose defended her uncle. 'Great fun. Not like a grown-up at all.'

'Don't I know? I hope he hasn't been drinking.'

Foxy Mac loved his family and cursed the demon drink that took him away from them. But he did consider Babs's attitude a trifle unreasonable. Wasn't she well provided for, with plenty to occupy her? The hotel and the children. What more could a woman want?

After all, he was the one who'd to suffer the horror of withdrawal — the shakes, vomiting, diarrhoea, burning skin and, of recent times, visions of rats climbing up the walls. Real rats. Sleek and brown. With flicking tails, beady red eyes and quivering nostrils. Everywhere, they were, till he began to wonder if they had emerged from Babs's fur coat. Last time he had had to get old Coward around. He'd given him a shot which had settled him down nicely.

Foxy, off the booze for four and a half days now, was beginning to feel better. He would not drink again. Ever. Not another drop would pass his lips. He would make it up to his family. To all of them. Begod he would. He would buy Babs another ring. Diamonds she liked.

This time, while he had been gone, his children had disappeared. Scattered. Except for Tommo. Always there, Tommo. With the daft eyes. His very own clown of God. No wonder he had the few jars to forget the sadness.

Foxy was in Fenit to deliver a letter. For the occasion he had dressed his stocky, short-legged figure in navy check trousers, a matching lightweight jacket and, for a bit of colour, a red tartan cap. He didn't know why Kate and Rose were out here. Hadn't even known his niece was coming to stay.

Wading down the path, arms full of biscuits, sweets and a whole pink ham, he head-butted open the top of the door. Cissie, standing at the range, boiling sausages to prevent them from going off before the weekend, guessed who her visitor must be.

Kate dragged behind Rose into the kitchen. When Foxy saw his niece, he burst into song with 'The Rose of Tralee'. Rose looked startled.

Kate stared at her father, her eyes expressionless.

Foxy had no idea when or where he had last seen his daughter. Strange. He could vaguely recall seeing Rose, though. Something about beans. He didn't remember the circumstances.

Rose did. Only too well.

While in Dublin on one of his regular drinking skites, Foxy had mislaid his car, a rather ancient

Vauxhall Wyvern of which he was particularly fond.

One of Foxy's character traits was a reluctance to deal with being upset or rattled. The loss of his car both rattled and upset him. So, instead of standing on the side of the street worrying, he called into Wynn's Hotel in Abbey Street for another whiskey to calm him down and to think about where his car might be.

In the bar he was approached by a total stranger, Larry Dinks, a scrawny man, with an ingratiating manner, a shiny navy suit and a reputation for being hollow-legged. He had spent the previous twenty-four hours 'waking' his wife's second cousin by marriage who lived around the corner on Eden Quay. Though he had never met her in life, in death he had 'mourned' her enthusiastically until the Guinness had run out.

Foxy told him the story of the missing car.

'That's turrible,' Larry said, his Adam's apple yo-yoing up and down in sympathy, one elbow firmly placed on the mahogany counter of the bar to prevent himself from swaying. 'Have another until we think what to do.'

They both did, and then another, until one of them came up with the idea of replacing the missing Vauxhall. While waiting for a taxi which they had asked the porter to summon, they had another drink to congratulate themselves on their cleverness at finding a solution to the problem.

Ordering the taxi driver to bring them to the nearest garage, they ended up in Walden's, a few hundred yards up O'Connell Street and into Parnell Street. The charge was minor, but Foxy's tip was so generous it enabled the driver to take the remainder of the day off.

Once in the garage, Foxy's business acumen began to emerge out of the depths of the Paddy's he had drunk. He liked Vauxhall Wyverns. And wanted another. That this garage was a Ford dealership and so only dealt in Ford cars did not impress him.

The salesman, with slicked-back hair and the latest in check jackets, was, in turn, soothing, conciliatory, understanding and good at his job. Shooting his cuffs, he launched into his spiel on the benefits of Ford ownership — the factory in Cork, the cleverness of Henry Ford, the superb quality of workmanship.

Larry Dinks confirmed the salesman's patter, and the deal was struck when £10 was knocked off the asking price.

Reaching into his trousers' pocket, Foxy brought out a tightly rubber-banded roll of twenty-pound notes, from which he peeled off the exact amount. Not wanting to be worried about the necessary paperwork, he arranged to have it forwarded to his home address.

Meanwhile, the black and gleaming Consul begged to be driven. So Foxy decided to visit his sister-in-law. Naturally his bosom buddy, Larry Dinks, sat beside him on the bench seat.

They arrived at Horns' at half past five, the children's teatime. Beans on toast that day — Batchelor's, the ones with the lumps of fatty pork in them that you couldn't eat on Fridays. In Horns', whether or not you liked the food, plates had to be cleaned.

Rose and George knew all about the starving black children of Africa. Rose, and, indeed, the remainder of the class, with the exception of Monica, had been so taken by Sister Concepta's description of these children — famine-ridden lost souls, who because of their unbaptised state faced eternal damnation — that they had each willingly handed out a shilling and acquired a child of their own. Rose felt she had got a good bargain and called her child Susan in memory of her doll. Rose pictured her black Susan, in a white dress and newly twisted corkscrew curls, surrounded by her family, perhaps the whole village, sitting under a coconut tree in darkest Africa, all of them gobbling bowl after bowl of rice, courtesy of her munificence.

On more than one occasion, George left his dish of rice pudding for the black babies, but with his winsome smile and cow's lick in permanent negotiation with his eyebrows, Nance was putty in his hands.

When the doorbell rang, Rose and George were already seated, hands washed, napkins on knees, their mother in attendance, with Agnes dishing out the beans from the blue enamel saucepan onto the buttery wedges of toast.

'Who could that be?' Nance wondered, patting at her hair, glancing at the clock. 'You get it,' she told Agnes, taking over the saucepan.

Rose would have preferred their mother to have answered the door. With Agnes's connivance they could have got rid of the fatty pork bits.

Agnes shuffled along the parquet of the hall, and opened the front door. A loud male voice. Nance's face acquired a set look of annoyance.

Railroading past Agnes, Foxy, his raincoat swinging wide, landed into the breakfast room, before Nance had even crossed the rug in front of the fire. 'Beans,' he bellowed, taking the fork out of Rose's hand, scooping a forkful off her plate and popping it into his mouth. Two beans escaped and left a tomato-y dribble down his tie.

In the meantime, Larry remained in the doorway, tweed cap held like a shield across his chest, mouth opening and closing, eyes darting nervously. Agnes, peeping over his shoulder, apron awry, cap askew, was frantic. The missus would think she had fallen down on her duties yet again. Agnes could never get used to Nance's refrain of disappointment when she felt let down.

In an icy voice rich in sarcastic politeness, Nance said, 'I would like you to leave.' Foxy just laughed and stabbed Rose's fork into the loaf of bread where it seemed to quiver with indignation.

Then he stretched across the table, grabbed the spoon from the jam dish, dug it into George's plate and gobbled at beans and pork.

'I'll not tolerate anyone calling to my home in an inebriated state,' Nance said, but she seemed to lack conviction.

Foxy clapped his knee with the spoon at the good of it, leaving jammy tomato sauce on his grey flannels.

'Think of the children,' she implored.

'Do 'em good. To see a bit o' real livin'.' Still waving the spoon, he backed out into the hallway. As Nance shepherded him in front of her, whether from devilment or oblivion, Foxy pressed into her hand a ten-shilling note, with the slurred admonishment that the hospitality could have been better.

A few days later, her curiosity having got the better of her, Nance rang Babs in Tralee, ostensibly to find out if Foxy had returned safely.

'Indeed, he did,' assured Babs. 'Finally.'

The upshot of the story was that Foxy and Larry hellraised around Dublin until the paperwork for the new car reached Babs in Kerry. She promptly put into operation her network of contacts, had Foxy and his beloved Vauxhall reunited, the Ford returned, and her chastened husband back home — all within twenty-four hours.

In the boot of the Vauxhall lay an ocelot coat, unboxed and unwrapped. Foxy, who did not know how it had got there, began to get upset. Babs shushed him, told him she knew it was a gesture of attrition, kissed him forgiveness and tried it on with squeals of delight.

That afternoon, while her husband was at his most contrite, she set in motion the acquisition of long-desired wheels of her own. 'After all,' as she said to him with sweet reasonableness, 'it would be handy for me to have a car, in case you ever lost yours again.'

In the circumstances, Foxy knew better than to dispute her logic.

Foxy was not used to children, certainly not teenagers. After ten minutes of looking around, making no effort to converse, drinking a cup of tea, and drumming his fingers on the table, he left, saying he would be back to take them on a picnic. To the Macgillicuddy Reeks.

Kate just shrugged.

Foxy was halfway out the door when he remembered that the letter, addressed to Rose — his reason for coming to Fenit — was still in the inside pocket of his jacket.

Dublin seemed so removed from this life that Rose, reading Barbara's letter, sitting on the sun-warmed doorstep, felt it could be in outer space.

Last year she had written an English composition on Laika the Russian dog, orbiting the earth a thousand miles up in Sputnik. She had thought it terrible, a dog having no choice in the matter. While commending the essay and congratulating her on her individualistic thinking, their English teacher had considered pushing back the frontiers of science for the greater good of mankind more important than the likes and dislikes of an animal. Rose often wondered what the greater good of mankind was.

The big news was that Monica was in hospital because she was not eating and could starve to death. Mrs Doyle had forbidden visitors. Other than that, Dublin was boring. Boring. No action. Nothing happening. Barbara had been in Cork, staying with her boyfriend's family. They were really kind and had invited her back again. She was bursting to tell Rose all about him. But not in a letter. Oh, P.S. Frank was asking for you.

Rose's reply was full of breezy news and high socialising. Even though totally off him, she hoped Barbara would show it to Frank.

A few days later, Cissie, too, received a letter. Her sister, Elizabeth, was coming home from America for her holidays earlier than expected. It was ten years since she had been back.

Elizabeth's flight was landing in Shannon on Friday fortnight. Cissie was so excited, she went around humming and smiling, like a young girl. Amazing at her age, thought Rose. Then, like a still-life cameo, Rose had a memory of her mother standing on the half-landing.

It must have been around the time of George's nativity play. The winter light, shafting through the dimpled window, fingered the pastel of her twin set, the pearls around her neck, the silver in her hair. Caught in her shadow, little George was a dark silhouette.

For the first time, Rose had seen her mother as a person. A woman. Not just her mother. Beautiful, tender, smiling lips, joyful eyes. Rumpling her hand through George's hair. 'You'll be great,' she had assured.

'How d'you know?' George had asked.

'Because I have faith in you. And once I was your age.'

'But you can't remember that far back?' Rose had queried.

'Oh, yes I can.'

'You can't. You're too old,' George had insisted.

'Wait until the two of you are my age,' Nance had told them fondly. 'No matter how old your body gets, your feelings and emotions stay the same.'

She had continued on down the stairs, checking

with her index fingers that the banister carvings were dust-free.

At the time, Rose had thought her mother daft. How could someone as old as Mammy feel the same as when she was young? Feelings had to grow old. An old person could not understand what it was like to be young.

Now, watching Cissie's excitement, Rose conceded that maybe, just maybe, her mother had a point.

Gradually, Cissie had relaxed about Rose and Kate wandering around on their own, though she still liked to know where they were, what they were up to and who they saw and spoke to. She had no time for the locals who rented out their houses, nor for the few 'holidaymakers' who tenanted them.

The cousins were well aware of Cissie's phobia about water, particularly the sea which she regarded with a mixture of respect, superstition and fear.

Her uncle and seventeen-year-old brother had drowned from a fishing-boat, and from that day she had never let the sea wet even her feet. Still, as part of her surrogacy duties, she insisted on accompanying Rose and Kate on their daily swim. Not, the three of them agreed, that she would be much use in an emergency.

The swim was quite an expedition. Red and green togs rolled in white towels — 'A Swiss roll and a grass roll,' giggled Kate. Cissie, riding her 'Upstairs Nellie', as Kate had christened her bicycle, clucked her charges in front of her, as though they were two-year-olds, along the road, through the village and over the stile.

Fenit Strand was a typical Irish beach. Curved and ancient, with Atlantic breakers racing and plunging across it until, exhausted, they spread themselves on the fringe of moon-coloured sand.

Cissie had a favourite rock. One which afforded maximum privacy for her girls. If it happened to be taken, she scowled at the intruders before reconnoitring further along the beach, motioning Rose and Kate forward when she found what she regarded as a suitable alternative.

To their embarrassment, while they changed, she kept up a running commentary of instructions: 'Be sure now to undress under yer towels, wrap up in them on the way to the water. Wear yer caps. And make sure the strap's fastened so's ye don't lose them.'

Rose and Kate would cringe, certain they were spectacles of amusement. One of Cissie's piseogs was wetting faces before feet, believing this prevented headaches which could lead to cramps and ultimately drowning. To avoid upsetting her, they tried, though discovered it was a task easier said than done.

While they swam, Cissie would anxiously pace the edge of the water, admonishing, 'Don't go out beyond yer legs. Only swim towards the shore.'

She would look so worried that the girls would feel their selfishness at even wanting to swim. When they were dressed again, togs and towels were stowed in the basket of her bike and she would leave them to get the dinner, warning them to be back by 12.30.

Invariably Mikey appeared at this stage, like a mountain goat leaping down the black, slippery rocks that backed the pier and were one of the definite out-of-bounds to Rose and Kate. They were dangerous, but because of their inaccessibility and privacy, they were still a favourite trysting place for young people.

Mossie lived in Samphire Terrace, a row of white-washed fisherman's cottages, set at right angles to the rocks overlooking the pier. From Mossie, Rose knew that the name 'Samphire' came from the French for the Saint Peter's herb which grew in the area. Dating back to the turn of the century, the cottages had been built by the Harbour Commissioners for fishermen and crane drivers.

Rose, ignoring Kate's glare, used Mossie's location as an excuse to turn down Mikey's frequent invitations to sample the thrills of the rocks.

Rose would listen as Kate chatted Mikey up, occasionally commenting, aware he had her under constant surveillance. Kate would prattle on about her family, the ups and downs of it — though she did not mention her father — much the same way as she chatted to his grandmother, trying, though unsuccessfully, to draw out reciprocal chat from him.

The day Kate rhapsodised about her wonderful last birthday though, going to Cork with Mammy and Doreen and having a mixed grill and chips in the Metropole Hotel, Mikey left abruptly.

Hurt tore at him as he ran back over the beach to the anonymous comfort of Western Cove and the old burial ground. He was fascinated by Rose. The way she brought back all sorts of memories. Crowding memories he had not known existed.

When he was little, birthdays were even better than Christmas. That was because Flurry, their priest friend, was around. Mikey got piggybacks, swings and throws from Flurry but only in the woods. When they met in the village or after mass, Mikey always had to remember be very polite and to call him Father.

Mikey remembered the year he turned four. The best day of his life. Mam, Flurry and himself had had a secret picnic in the woods. They had sat under the marker chestnut tree on a plaid rug with a tablecloth in the middle, eating from plates of baby green chestnut leaves pink and white iced buns, decorated with red cherries, and squares of chocolate, and they had drunk red lemonade out of real cups. Mam and Flurry had smoked cigarettes and because, as Flurry said, it was such a special day, Mikey had got a pull.

His fifth birthday would be even more special.

'Are you going to be four or five now?' Flurry asked him the week before.

'Five,' shouted Mikey. He was allowed to shout in the woods. As loud as he liked. 'I'm four now.'

'I thought you were only three. Are you sure? We'd better ask Mam.'

'No. Five. Five.'

'Five's an important birthday. One that deserves to be marked in a special way. Let's put on Mam's thinking cap,' suggested Flurry. 'Now where is it? Don't tell me you've lost it again.'

The priest shook his finger at her in mock admonishment, while the little boy, his head cocked to one side, looked on with the single-minded intensity of a child enchanted by the pantomime of adults.

'Mikey, you'd better find her another one. Off you go.' The boy scampered through the pale green of the woods, scrunching over the undergrowth, rustling branches until he returned a few minutes later with a slender twig, laden with leaf buds.

The priest made a circlet of it and placed it on Sadie's head. 'Now, Queen of the Glade, it's your task to come up with a stupendous idea for Mikey's birthday.'

Watched by a wide-eyed Mikey, and Flurry who feasted his eyes on this woman he loved more than life itself, but not more than Mother Church, Sadie entered into the spirit of the game. On her hunkers, eyes closed, arms raised, she called on the Little People to help her. 'Abracadabra, abracadoo.'

That afternoon, the woods were bursting with spring life, golden sunshine, greening foliage, nesting birds in joyous call. After a few moments of clasping her hands in front of her in a gesture of prayer, Sadie raised her head, opened her eyes and said, 'Please sit here, right beside me.'

To Mikey she whispered in an aside, 'The chief happiness-maker is going to help me, so you'll have the best birthday ever. Watch and stay very quiet.' She cocked her head to one side as though listening, every now and again nodding. Then she stood up, bent down to somebody Mikey could not see, and offered her hand in a shake.

'Do ya know about my birthday?' Little Mikey

hurtled himself at his mother as soon as she straightened up.

'Yes. It's the best idea ever, but first I've to talk it over with Father Flurry.'

Stupid, wasn't it, feeling miserable like this after all those years? He who had always thought himself so tough. And learned to cope on his own.

Chapter Fourteen

The second Monday in July, Nance had designated spring-clean day for Rose's bedroom. Doreen would be arriving two days later. Nance, who prided herself on running her home like clockwork, would not let herself down by having the room less than perfect for her niece.

She sent Agnes up ahead of her to strip the bed and to clear Rose's clutter off the furniture, so that the wood could be cleaned with vinegar on a damp cloth — a process requiring detailed attention: too much vinegar and the wood could be ruined; not enough, and the exercise was pointless. As usual, she would act in a supervisory capacity.

Agnes battled to turn the mattress on its squeaking mesh of springs. Jammed between it and the headboard was a book. *Little Women* by Louisa M. Alcott, read the dust-cover, which had a picture on it of Meg, with a strait-laced expression and lace-collared dress.

As Agnes placed the book on the bedside locker, the dust-cover slipped to reveal another underneath: *Angélique in Love*. In sharp contrast to Meg, Angélique had a voluptuous come-hither look on her face and a joyous bosom bursting out of a too-tight bodice. With a quiver of guilty amazement, Agnes shoved the book far back underneath the mattress.

Under the large oval mat of the dressing-table set she came across the stamped, addressed letter. F.r.a.n.k. F.e.n.n.e.l.l.y. She spelt the letters out slowly. Poor Rose. Such a fuss and sent away so quickly. Either she had not time to post it, or in the rush, had forgotten.

This Agnes could rectify. With a quick over-her-shoulder look to make sure Mrs Horn was not in the vicinity, she slid it into the pocket of her apron.

Agnes had an unspoken empathy with Rose in her recent spate of troubles and would like to have helped her. But Mrs Horn was a demanding taskmistress. As it was, without going looking for trouble, Agnes inadvertently got into more than her share of 'hot water'. Still, in this small way she could make up to Rose. Wednesday was her afternoon off. She would post the letter then.

Once in her room, she took it out of her pocket, put it for safekeeping in a drawer, and promptly forgot it until three weeks later.

From a weather point of view, the first day of carragheen harvesting started inauspiciously with a promise of rain and wads of pewter clouds pressing down on an equally pewter-coloured sea. But Rose and Kate were ecstatic. Much too excited even to notice the weather, much less be affected by it.

'Ye're the only holidaymakers,' Mossie warned.

With a shrug and a sniff, Kate insisted, 'We're not ordinary holidaymakers.'

That Mossie conceded, without even a glimmer of a smile.

Up to now, neither Rose nor Kate had been involved in a community activity like this with young and old striving towards the same goal. They were used to not only the physical, but also the psychological, division between generations. Between themselves and their mothers, particularly, there existed the underlying innuendo, often unspoken, of mistrust. The atmosphere here on the carragheen pick was one of trust and commitment. And the girls responded.

Mossie, very much the man in charge, was the only one of the group of twenty-odd wearing rubber boots, the remainder making do with old shoes or bare feet. In this environment Mossie was a new man, come alive, with a new alertness and air of authority. He and his special brand of organisation were everywhere, co-ordinating, encouraging, cajoling, joking, even glimmering an occasional smile, making serious work an enjoyable occasion. He made sure that professional pickers helped the inexperienced; children were watched over by adults, all working their prescribed patch of ocean.

He caught up with Rose, who had one of Cissie's old shopping bags slung around her shoulders, and her skirt tucked up into the legs of her knickers, making her look, Kate gigglingly told her, as though her bottom had dropped to her knees. Dipping up and down into the water, searching for and bagging that elusive black drifting moss, was hard work but Rose, having found her own rhythm, was an ardent picker. 'Sure, you're a natural,' said Mossie, to her delight.

Working alongside her for a while, he guided her hands in his large ones towards fertile clumps, showing her how to pluck the delicate fronds that moved with the rhythm of the sea. On his huge, brown, wet palm, he spread out a cluster of carragheen, stroking it with the index finger of his other hand. 'Look, isn't it beautiful?' And it was. A filigree of black lace. 'It gets its name from the Gaelic, "carraig", which means rock. Sometimes it's called sea moss, and it even has a Latin name, *Chondrus crispis.*'

Words rolling softly and hanging in the air. For Rose it was like being in heaven. 'It's a seasonal grass and it thrives on a rough tide shore, like this.' From the way Mossie fondled the carragheen, it seemed a living thing; for him it was; for Rose it became so too.

Never before had Rose heard anyone talk about the environment, much less practise conservation. Mossie was ahead of his time, in his appreciation of nature and realisation of the importance of protecting it for posterity. He spoke quietly, but passionately, about the awfulness of ravaging the land and seashore. This, the monosyllabic Mossie!

'Next year's nature project is on the beach. Would it be all right to take shells and bits of seaweed?' Rose wondered.

Mossie scratched his head. 'Yes, but be careful what ya take. Be sure they're not wasted.'

'I'll plan carefully.'

Mossie laughed. 'Ya know the old saying — if ya want to give God a good laugh, make plans.' He moved on to check some detail with another picker.

Up to now Rose had never given much thought to the idea of country versus city. Nor had she reason to. Her father was city born and bred, and her mother had adopted city life with enthusiasm. Rose and her friends considered that life stopped at the suburbs of Dublin.

Well, if it did, she decided, standing thigh-high in the Atlantic, individuality began in the country. There was a freedom. You could afford to be different. Oddness, even real weirdness, could be accommodated. She could not imagine Cissie and Mossie, Mags, Foxy, certainly not Tommo, being absorbed into their neighbourhood. Yet here they were an accepted part of the community.

The exception seemed to be Mikey, the loner.

Despite the discomfort of the job — the water growing colder by the minute and the breeze developing needles of chill — it was a social occasion and fun, and Rose became caught up in the atmosphere of chat and gentle competition around her.

She was not thinking about anything in particular when she sensed she was under observation. Half swivelling her head, she saw, out of the corner of her eye, Mikey watching her, his shirt half on, half off his shoulders, and a grave expression on his face. When their eyes met, he winked. Rose dipped her head in acknowledgement, glad he could not know how much her stomach was contracting and her heart pounding.

The last person Mikey had expected to see picking carragheen was Rose. His wink was a reflex action. A gesture of bravura he did not feel. Mikey's few encounters with the opposite sex at the back of the hall after Sunday night's dance had been the frantic lonely gropings of the sexually driven.

Rose fascinated and frustrated him. He wanted to be close to her. Spend time with her. Get to know her. To peel away, one by one, her layers of reserve and self-protection. He wondered what it would be like to share her world; what a relationship with a girl like Rose involved.

Then there was the dark side of him. The side that wanted to possess her, sample her texture, her smell, her taste, but also to hurt her, to introduce her to the emotional hardship of his world, to make her pay for his unhappiness.

Today, as always when he saw Rose, his head was full of recollections tripping in and out of his mind. Like the Christmas before his mother died. Despite its being a good memory, again the sadness of it tore through him.

Weeks before, he had stirred the plum pudding with his grandmother, following her instructions to do so 'sun-wise', screwing his eyes closed, making a wish, which, she explained, would not come true if he told anyone. He could not remember what he had wished for and whether or not it had ever come true.

What he did remember from that day was Grandma being kind in a way he had not known before, rumpling his hair as he climbed down from the chair.

For Christmas he had a new jersey, a warm one, and he wore it under his tweed coat going to mass in the cold darkness of the morning, holding tightly to his mam's hand.

The schoolhouse, where mass was held, was icy, but he loved the smell of the incense and the brightness of the candles on the altar. To one side baby Jesus was asleep in his manger, shivering, without proper clothes. How cold he must be! Only a bit of cloth across his tummy. And Joseph and Mary all wrapped up in shawls as warm as his grand-mother's.

When he nudged at Mam to tell her, she whished him, putting her lips so close to his ear that he could feel her warm breath. She whispered, 'Stay still. Watch the cows. They're blowing on top of baby Jesus to keep him warm.'

Yes. When he watched closely, he could see the cows' breath, and after a while Jesus stopped shivering.

At dinnertime he ate so much goose and potato stuffing, and the pudding he had stirred, that his own tummy felt like a warm tight drum.

Later, when it was dark, some of his great-aunts and great-uncles called. They sat around the range with Mags, drinking hot port and lemon. He and Mam were outside their circle. But it did not matter. They were often outside circles.

Rose was equally surprised to find Mikey picking carragheen. In no way did it fit his image. Dammit.

And her with her skirt tucked into her knickers. The navy schoolers, no less. Substantial, elastic-legged. Passion-killers.

Compared to Mikey, Frank and the effect he had had on her were in the ha'penny place. She did not even have words to describe it. Profound, intense, passionate, she supposed. And getting worse each time she saw him. Struggling to put him out of her mind, she buried her head in the picking. As tuft after tuft of carragheen weighed down her bag, her strategy worked and she lost track of time until Mossie called a halt to the work.

When she looked around, there was no sign of Mikey. Gratefully she left the water with the other pickers and they climbed the cliff, lugging their laden bags with them.

By now the sullen sky of early morning had disappeared, without the earlier promise of rain having been realised. The wodges of grey clouds had given way to swift-muscled silver ones that chased the sun, intermittently mysteriously cloaking the glare of the sea with their pallor. The sea was no longer just pewter-coloured. It was blue and green, even brown.

Cissie, who would not go near the water even if she had to starve for the winter, was in charge of doling out the food, most of it courtesy of Babs.

As a businesswoman, Babs was a firm believer in there being nothing for nothing and — in this life anyway — getting what you paid for. To ensure that the girls had the best of what Cissie could offer, she paid way above the rate suggested by Father Lehane. At every opportunity, she sent out boxes of food, accompanied by warm messages scribbled on hotel-headed paper about knowing how much young people ate; urging Cissie herself to partake, and to make sure that none of her neighbours went short. The result was that Cissie had earned a reputation for a groaning table of 'town food'.

Everyone was starving, but Mossie insisted the carragheen be spread first.

Cissie, the ends of her skirt hitched up, was help-ing to tip out bundles of carragheen, down on her hands and knees, spreading it out on the sea grass which had been cut back in anticipation the previous week.

Rose and Kate had each been allocated a patch, which they had marked out with the flat grey and white stones of the area. Under Cissie's watchful eye, they disgorged their bags — sorry pickings compared to the locals' — and spread their crop to dry.

Kate, always competitive, gloated, 'I've more than you.'

Certainly her patch covered a larger area than Rose's, but, as Cissie pointed out, only because she had spread her carragheen so thinly.

'Neither of ye'd make a living from carragheen harvestin', so ye'd better pay attention to yer schoolin',' she said.

At last it was time to eat. To the backdrop of quiet chat on the windswept cliff-top, the food was consumed, washed down by tilly cans of cold tea laden with sugar and shy on milk.

'I do love a party,' said Kate, wriggling her buttocks into the grass, tossing back her hair and looking around with the undisguised pleasure of a true sybarite.

'This is no party.' Mags's big face scrunched up in disapproval. Usually she was all over Kate. 'Carragheen pickin's work. Hard work.'

She may have been a killjoy, but she was not the only local who felt that way. The next ten days were vital for the crop. During this time, the carragheen had to be turned at least once. Every night at the end of the Rosary, tacked onto the litany, there were prayers for a mixture of sunshine, gentle showers and heavy dews — the ideal weather conditions to preserve the gel, bleach the carragheen white, wash away the salt and ultimately achieve the best price.

But soon after, an unexpected happening occurred. A happening which, although it appeared almost comical at the time, would set in motion events that would completely overshadow the carragheen harvesting.

CHAPTER FIFTEEN

Kate was full of self-confidence and assurance. She had a very good opinion both of her abilities and of her looks. She had a whole hoard of anecdotes about the compliments she had received over the years and, given any excuse, would launch into them.

She said she could remember sitting in her pram, unknown faces peering in and strange hands stroking her sausagey curls (made each morning by Babs winding the soft damp strands of hair around her fingers). She also swore that on her First Holy Communion day, her teacher had whipped off her veil, the better to display to best advantage her painstakingly ragged ringlets in all their bouncing glory.

This summer Kate particularly loved her hair. She loved its texture, running her fingers through it, tossing it back, shaking it loose, knowing it was full of liquid sunshine. Flirting it at Mikey. Rose was envious of Kate's hair and regularly got fed up of the brouhaha surrounding it. Sometimes she felt like the ugly duckling. She did not get any compliments for her good teeth and bone structure. But then, as she well knew, bones and teeth were not the food of inspiration for poets.

Kate was as changeable as the wind. Still, there

was no side to her and not a trace of malice. As she felt, she was. Funny, sad, selfish, considerate, determined. Her moods varying from one minute to the next.

No matter what had happened during the day, though, the cousins snuggled peacefully together in bed, swapping the latest gossip, Kate invariably raving about Mikey.

Before turning in, it was Cissie's habit to tiptoe in and sprinkle them with the holy water she kept in an old hair-oil bottle on the mantelpiece, beside Susan's head. Piously crossing herself, she would ask God to keep them safe until morning. Shades of Nance when Rose was younger.

Nevertheless, one night, God did not keep Kate's hair safe.

When they awoke, tufts of it were lumped on the bolster. Initially they thought it funny, but when Kate touched her head and a clump came away in her hand, they became frightened.

Kate bawled for Cissie, who burst into the room as though the cottage was on fire. 'What ails ye?'

Wordlessly Kate held out her hand with its tuft of hair in the palm.

Cissie said nothing, but looked grave as she examined Kate's head. 'Stop the cryin'. Ya'll be all right.'

'But I don't want to be bald,' Kate yelled, more bad-tempered than frightened.

'Ya won't. Now hurry up the both of ye and get dressed.'

By the time they sat down to breakfast, Cissie was resplendent in her horrible Sunday coat — long,

brown, with a round collar and big leather buttons —
and black shoes with high heels which tilted her
forward, like a plump plant seeking the light. A
change from her well-worn plimsolls, with cut-outs
to accommodate variously sized bunions, corns and
swollen joints.

Cissie was going out to make a phonecall — her
first, she told them importantly. They watched her
wheel her bike around from the back and up the
path, then pedal off in the direction of the village.

'I bet she's ringing your mother,' Rose told Kate,
thinking that would cheer her up. It had the opposite
effect, driving Kate into a paroxysm of weeping,
though she remembered to hold her head straight in
case her slightest movement would dislodge any
more hair.

Babs, wearing a smart red dress with a matching
edge-to-edge coat, arrived in double-quick time. With
her was their family doctor, Dr Coward, big and bluff
with curly grey hair. While his manner was over-
friendly, he was the kind of adult who ignored
children.

'Get her to stand in the light, Babs, so I can see
properly,' he said grumpily. He had a yellow rosebud
in the lapel of his grey suit, and behaved as though
the state of Kate's hair was Babs's fault.

By now Cissie had put in her teeth and her speech
was all lips and teeth and tip of the tongue. The
doctor ignored her. Kate looked from him to her
mother with a mulish expression on her face and
moved but a fraction of an inch. Rose was glad she
did not give him the satisfaction of crying.

'Over here, *a stór*,' said Cissie kindly, 'into the light,' leading Kate to the small window through which the sun streamed.

The doctor put his hand under Kate's chin and tilted her face upwards. Queasily, as though he could become contaminated, he plucked out with a tweezers a few strands of hair at which he peered. 'Hair loss. A definite loss of hair,' he pronounced.

Po-faced, he crossed the kitchen, lifted the plate on the range, opened the tweezers and allowed Kate's hairs to drop into the flames. They sizzled for a moment.

'Why is this happening?' Babs asked, wondering was she being punished for offloading her children.

'The latest theory is that these things are often psychological,' said the doctor. 'Triggered by stress and, in Kate's case, probably adolescence.'

'Nonsense,' said Cissie sturdily. 'Kate's too young for stress and we all had to grow up.'

The doctor looked scathingly at Cissie, quizzically at Babs, raised his eyebrows and asked where he could wash his hands. Cissie directed him to the back kitchen, brought a fresh wedge of the yellow soap and a thick white towel with a fringe which had come in one of Elizabeth's parcels from America.

He came out, drying his hands, tossed the towel on the table and said to Rose and Kate, 'The two of you run along, outside. Now.'

They did so reluctantly. The final straw was when Dr Coward slammed Cissie's ever-open half-door over on their curiosity. But he had forgotten about the sash window and they stood on tippy-toes listening as the adults held their whispered conference. The only audible words were 'hospital' and 'specialist' because the doctor shouted them.

'Well, I'm not going to any hospital,' said Kate.

Rose put her arm around Kate's shoulders.

'I wish I'd got off with Mikey — even a little, and smoked that cigarette while I had hair,' Kate wailed.

Dr Coward banged out of the door, acknowledged them with a regal nod, and strode to his car, red and sporty, which was parked across the gateway. Tossing his bag into the back, he shoehorned himself into the front and sat drumming his fingers on the steering-wheel.

Babs was not long after him, but she was crying and didn't even seem to notice the girls.

Cissie, linking her arm, was saying, 'It'll be all right. Trust me. The cure'll work. And we'll have Tommo, God help us, to give ya a bit of a break.'

'Oh, not Tommo,' wailed Kate to Rose as her mother was driven off with screeching tyres and crashing gears. 'He's dreadful. It'll be awful with him here.'

Behind them Cissie snorted, 'There's an old Kerry saying that every disease is a doctor. Ya'd think your man would've heard of it. Him with his airs and graces. Psycho … whatever. And stress, at yer age, I ask ya! The way he was going on, ya wouldn't think he was from these parts at all. But I'll show him. If it's the last thing I do.'

Cissie turned on her heel — she was still wearing the high ones — into the kitchen where she put on her plimsolls, removed her teeth and cycled off, a cardigan thrown over her apron, replacing the good coat.

The spunk had gone out of Kate who was white-faced with exhaustion. Rose gave her the copy of *Schoolfriend* and sat quietly opposite her by the range, her head full of romantic thoughts of Mikey and of dread at the idea of Tommo joining Kate and herself. Frank seemed a lifetime away.

Some time later Cissie returned with a parcel wrapped in layers of white paper, which she opened out with a flourish, releasing a pungently sweet smell. Large and medium-sized pieces of bone and glistening knuckles appeared, oozing a yellowish marrow.

Kate, locked into herself, looked on oblivious.

Cissie plunged the bones into a black pot, covered them with water and stood the pot on the range. When it boiled, she skimmed off the scum, replaced the lid and left it, smelling increasingly disgusting, to simmer. After several hours she pulled it to the side of the range and allowed the fire to die out. When the bones cooled she scooped out the marrow, added ashes from the fire and stirred the concoction into a solid paste.

'This will stop your hair falling out,' she said, pushing a lock of her own hair off her forehead.

Kate, jerked into awareness, touched her head, her eyes widening in horror. 'Do I have to eat it?'

'No, *a stór*, it's for putting on your head.'

'No. No. I won't. I won't have that on my hair,' she screeched.

'Ya have to,' Cissie told her, going down to her bedroom and returning with a torn pillowcase which she tore into strips. 'We'll wrap your head in these,' she explained, waving ribbons of pillowcase.

'No you won't. I won't let you,' yelled Kate. 'Rose, tell her. I can't.'

Rose's heart went out to Kate, sitting scrunched up, tears rolling down her cheeks, and she hated herself for wondering could Kate's hair loss be contagious.

Cissie soothed Kate. 'Ya're lucky marrow and ash is my cure. It could be goose dung. Now come on, be a good girl and let's get this done. First, I've to cut your hair, what's left of it.'

Kate looked at her with renewed horror and Rose caught her breath in sympathy. 'How short?' asked Kate.

'Really short.'

'Baldy short?' Kate asked between sobs.

'Yes. I want you to be brave. Don't look.'

Out of the dresser drawer Cissie took a large scissors, which she held discreetly at her side. Kate's hiccuping sobs broke the silence. Rose was near to tears herself and Cissie's eyes were suspiciously bright.

'Just as well the moon isn't waning,' said Cissie. For once, neither girl was interested in her piseogs, but she was not deterred. 'If you cut hair then, it thins and falls out.'

Rose determined for ever more to check on the moon's position before having her hair cut.

Kate held her head high and looked neither to right nor left. While Cissie clipped and snipped, Rose caught the curls in a newspaper. Eventually it was done.

Cissie put the paste on the stubble of Kate's head, winding strips of cotton above her ears. Kate looked like a wounded warrior. Cissie praised her bravery and promised she would have even more beautiful hair when the bandages came off. Kate managed only a very watery smile, though her voice was very strong and determined as, touching her head, she announced, 'I won't go out looking like this.'

'That's all right for now, *a stór*,' said Cissie. 'But ya'll change yer mind. Ya'll be weeks rather than days like this.'

Rose hugged Kate. 'You're a real hero. Sorry, heroine.' Then she ran out into the garden and plucked two scarlet poppies which she tucked into the bandages. Now Kate looked like some exotic native girl, but there was no comforting her and, between sobs, she spluttered that she wished she were dead.

Kate's misfortune precipitated Rose's relationship with Mikey.

Kate stuck to her refusal to venture beyond the garden gate while looking, as she put it, 'like an Egyptian mummy'.

Rose was amazed at how much she had come to rely on her cousin's companionship and the sense of fun she brought to their combined activities. However, after a few days of keeping Kate company in her self-imposed purdah, Rose became restless and decided to put together the beach collection for next year's nature course. Hoping, yet dreading, that she would run into Mikey. Wondering how she would handle him without Kate's backing.

The morning was clear and windy, the horizon etched razor sharp against baby-blue skies as Rose crossed the stile onto the hot, coarse sand of the deserted beach.

Picking her way along the edge of the water towards the outcrop of smooth, tumbled rocks, she collected prickly sea urchins, pearlised conches, navy-blue mussel shells, pointy whelks, and even the odd crab for delicacy and variation of colour.

She loved these rocks. No matter how often she clambered over them, she always made a new discovery: an enchanting bolt-hole, a different vantage point, a secret crevice. When the tide was high, the large rock, around which the waves churned and broke, was a black glossy hump, perhaps the bowed back of the sea god Triton. At low tide, sitting on one of the natural thrones, she imagined the young Triton with his father Poseidon, frolicking around in the shallow waves.

Lost in her own world of sea gods, Rose literally stumbled on Mikey and Maryann. He, sprawled on a rock that cradled him like a throne, at his feet a chipped enamel basin half full of crabs; Maryann, perched to his side, fingering a streel of seaweed. She was wearing a voluminous kaftan of a grubby turquoise. Her hair was long and smooth and her feet bare. She looked at Rose with an expressionless face and flat pebble eyes.

'Hello, Jackeen,' Mikey said. His eyes seemed an even brighter blue than usual.

Rose blushed, answered, 'Hi, Culchie!' and was delighted with her quick repartee. Mikey leaned down, lifted from the basin a small green crab and squeezed it. Then he opened his fist and his palm was smeared with fragments of shell and pink flesh.

A gesture of toughness he immediately regretted. It had been done to impress Rose. It would have the opposite effect, he knew.

Do crabs feel? Rose wondered.

'Come on, so,' Mikey said to Rose, standing up, brushing the debris of the crab onto the sand, ignoring Maryann.

Rose followed him. It never occurred to her to do otherwise. They walked back along the beach, side by side on the flat sand. The waves made silvery lapping sounds, the breeze warm and skittery. Rose kept a distance between them. When she looked back, Maryann was still sitting on the rock, like a disconsolate mermaid.

Picking at the fabric of her dress, Maryann watched them through the curtain of her hair, her eyes following so intently that they seemed to burrow a channel though the air. Wondering what they would talk about, what they would do.

The girl from Dublin was an unknown factor — Maryann had not come across her like before. Unlike Kate, she did not say much. Kate prattled on about everything and anything, words with and without meaning flying out of her mouth with equal intensity. The whole village knew about Kate's hair, knew she would not come out. Without too much expectation, Maryann had hoped Rose would stay in with her.

Maryann was of tough stock. All the O'Briens were. To survive she had to be. But she did not feel tough now. She was full of fear that Mikey would desert her.

She lived with her father and six brothers, three miles out from the village on a mountainy parcel of four acres. Jammy, still regarded as a blow-in from Limerick, was a rough, uncouth man whose wife had died giving birth to Maryann. Blaming his daughter for his wife's death, he shut himself and his sons off from all but minimal contact with the village. The family expected and received nothing from anybody.

For as long as Maryann could remember, her role had been that of general skivvy. Washing, cleaning, cooking, before and after school. That she managed. What she could not cope with was her father's and brothers' abuse. Not that she had the words for what happened most nights. But she knew no other life and thought that was the way things were. The only person who had treated her like a human being, showing her kindness and paying her attention, was Mikey, and her devotion to him was absolute. She loved him with all-consuming intensity. She hated this girl they called Rose, hated the softness in Mikey's eyes when he watched her.

'D'ya always wear socks?' Mikey asked Rose.

Instead of answering, she bent down, removed them, rolled them into a ball, arced her arm and threw them far out to sea, but they landed in the shallows just a few inches from the edge.

Mikey picked up a flattened silver-grey stone, pranced and stanced until positioned to his satisfaction, weighed it in his palm, raised his arm, arced it and skimmed it across the surface of the ocean. It seemed to go on for ever, scuttering diamonds of water in its path.

He looked at Rose sideways, expectantly. She knew enough to acknowledge his expertise but not to labour it. The casualness was taken out of her so-what shrug by her smile. 'I'll swap you?' she said laughingly, holding out her sandals and pointing to his brothel-creepers.

'You're too smart, but you'll do.' He moved closer. Winked, a lazy impudent wink. She had an urge to reach out and touch the slab of his cheek, she loved the angular perfection it gave his face. She read admiration in his voice as he punched her side and called, 'Race you to the pier, so.'

There must have been wings on her feet that day because she won. She dropped her sandals and bag of shells and waited for him. He gave her a thumbs-up sign, then clambered upwards, sure-footed as a mountain goat. Barefoot, she followed him, scrabbling and crabbing for footholds among the forbidden rocks.

When they reached the top, she sat close to him, arms around her legs, chin resting on her knees. She felt like a real teenager, a full-of-notions teenager. Inhaling great gulps of air, breathing in the smell of Mikey. Together they watched a wagtail dance along the edge of the water, the tiny bird continuously poised on the brink of flight, its black and white body constantly alert to danger, head darting from side to side, legs flashing a minuscule jig.

Mikey stood up suddenly and stretched, his arms pointing heavenwards as though embracing the universe. 'See ya around, so.' He skidded down the rocks, heading back in the direction they had come.

Rose remained sitting, perched like Maryann, staring out at the extraordinarily seductive power of the rolling waves. How could their collapse, time after time on the golden sand, seem so full of softness and ease? How could there be such feeling in nature? She pondered what it would be like to walk down into the waves and just keep going.

Then she looked horizonwards at the misty mountains which engulfed the bay, wondering could this encounter with Mikey be classified as a date. Deciding that no, it had not been a proper asking date. How would Kate react? What should she say to her? Did she need to tell Kate at all? It might upset her. Dammit.

Some time later, Rose stood up and carefully made her way down the rocks, stuck her feet into her sandals, gathered up the bag and walked slowly back through the village, back to Kate and Cissie.

If Cissie wondered at the cut of Rose, at her untidiness and exaggerated behaviour — gushing about who she had seen, displaying her shells as though they were precious stones — she said nothing. Merely registered that Rose was behaving most unlike Rose and dismissed her gnawing suspicion.

That night Rose dreamt strange dreams of Frank and spinning bottles, bleating sheep, scudding clouds, puffing cigarettes, and Mikey kissing her. She awoke, wondering was she doing a Monica on Kate. But the light of day put that thought firmly out of her mind. Kate may have fancied Mikey, but it was she, Rose, he had chosen. He had, hadn't he? It made her feel so good. The sexiest fellow ever, fancying her!

Chapter Sixteen

Since the fright of Kate's hair, Babs had developed the habit of taking Wednesday afternoons off and driving out to Fenit to check that all was well. Like Nance, Babs was not an instinctive driver, though she had more self-confidence than her sister. Blissfully unaware of her shortcomings, she chugged along the centre of the road, having managed to crash into third gear, her foot hovering over the clutch.

One afternoon she arrived with Tommo. He shot in the door, head fast-jerking backwards and forwards, lips drooling, eyes unfocused.

Since the Middle Ages the Tommos of the world had been regarded by healers as God's blessed and were seen as good-luck omens. From the minute Cissie set eyes on him she was enchanted and he, seeming to recognise her goodwill, became more placid than he had been for weeks.

He terrified Rose. She thought he was an apparition. She yelped, a mixture of surprise and fright. Having no experience in interpreting his actions, certain he must be having a fit, she backed off.

'He's just pleased to see ya,' Cissie said, giving him a little hug. She was so small and he so tall that her grip was around his waist. Tommo stood loose and gangling, arms doing their usual windmill flap, making little squeaks. Rose supposed that, by stretching the imagination, you could say they were happy little squeaks.

Cissie was concerned about Mrs Mac. She was unlike her usual lively self. Physical tiredness, compounded by worry, had sent her grooming haywire. A smear of lipstick was on her teeth, a ladder ran up the back of her left leg and her nails were chipped. But it was her lack of spirit that was most worrying.

She sent Rose and Kate out the back and handed over Tommo to the care of Mossie, who was thinning carrots. 'What ails ya?' Cissie asked, wetting the tea, bringing out the good willow-pattern cups, reverently placing Mrs Mac's offering of éclairs on a plate.

'Mr MacCarthy's gone again. For the past few days. Not a sight nor light of him. And there's such a lot to be done. The busiest time of the year. And extra business with the Festival and all.'

Cissie, biting into an éclair, nodded understandingly.

'Tommo's acting up. Getting obstreperous.' She shook her head. 'The last thing I want is to have to send him away. I'd to bring him today, even though he's a nightmare in the car. I'm at the end of my tether.'

'Let him here. For as long as ya like,' Cissie urged generously, drawing in a glob of cream with her tongue. 'If ya don't mind him sleepin' on the trestle bed.'

'Oh, I couldn't,' protested Babs. 'He can be so difficult.'

'Mossie'll be around to give me a hand if he gets one of his turns. Sure, it'd be a privilege to have him under my roof.'

'He's only got the clothes he's standing up in.'

'So what. What he needs, we'll borrow off Mossie.'

'Bless you,' said Babs, slumping into the chair, now that a solution had been reached. 'Are you sure, with the girls, and your sister coming and all?'

Cissie was sure.

'It's an awful imposition on you. But Kate and Rose have settled in great. They're so well looked after, it gives me real peace of mind. And Doreen, too, in Dublin. But there's nothing but grumbles from Timmy and the tennis. Not having the worry of the children is the only way I can cope — it allows me get on with the running of the hotel….'

These days Rose was like a hen on a hot griddle. Hugging the memory of Mikey to herself, she said nothing to Kate. Since her hair loss, Kate had been so absorbed in herself that she would hardly notice if the sky fell in on top of her.

Each afternoon Rose climbed up and waited on the rocks where Mikey had left her. Dammit, he had to come. On the fourth day he did, as she knew he eventually would. She sat again, arms hugging her legs, head resting on her knees.

The waves below puttered white-capped and the breeze flurried cold. Shivering in her cardigan, she looked up at him. At his black drainpiped legs tapering into his squelchy, crêpe-soled shoes, the broadness of his white open-necked shirt, the pulse of his throat, the lick of hair falling over his forehead. Waiting for him, willing him to say something.

'Fancy a smoke, so?' he asked, sitting down without preamble, pulling cigarettes and matches from his pocket.

'Good idea,' Rose answered brightly, doing her best to slip into his mood, hoping by actual speech to quieten the mad click-clacking of her mind, trusting that his memories of her last abortive efforts at smoking had blurred. This time, knowing what to expect, she clenched the cigarette firmly between her lips.

Mikey lit his own with a professional flourish and pulled on it, his eyes half closed, his expression soporific. Opening his mouth into an O, three perfectly circumferenced smoke-circles emerged, hovered momentarily, then dissipated on the flirty breeze. Rose watched without commenting.

'Drag at the flame,' he urged her, striking a match and moving closer. So close that their thighs touched. Because of his nearness, the dark bristles on his face and the way he was looking at her, she was incapable of breathing. Much less inhaling.

He took the cigarette from between her unresisting lips, lit it off his own and put it back in her mouth. Their eyes met. And held. Then his hand was in the small of her back. He was leaning towards her and straining her towards him. She didn't know what happened the cigarettes, but suddenly he was kissing her.

Harder and harder. She wanted it to be for ever and ever.

When he withdrew, she felt lost, her lips bruised. She ran her tongue around them and tasted the saltiness of her blood. Reaching up, she touched the plane of his cheek. He winked a slow wink and turned away from her towards the sea.

'Let's see your shells,' Kate demanded when Rose returned late for tea.

'I forgot them,' Rose mumbled, looking at the ground. 'I'll get them tomorrow.'

Cissie took in her distant look and swollen mouth. And knew that her gnawing suspicions had been correct. Rose and Mikey were a lethal combination. Hot-blooded youngsters were devious to the point of insanity, but there was little she could do, except try to keep the pair of them as far apart as possible. She had first-hand experience of love going well and the devastation when it misfired.

Locked evergreen into her mind was the memory of her own feelings at Rose's age.

It was 1937. Cissie had been sent to work as a maid in the home of the Hyland-Sykeses in Montenotte, Cork. The hugeness of the house terrified her. Enormous high-ceilinged rooms, vast double doors, long, wide, lonely corridors.

But the stairs were the most terrifying of all. Cissie had never even seen a stairs before, much less walked up or down one. She knew she could not. And Cook was expecting her to ferry trays of food and buckets of fuel from the basement to the top storey.

Mrs Hyland-Sykes, a delicate woman with a long

face, a snapdragon-shaped lower lip and a penchant for chiffon scarves, spent a considerable amount of time lying on a yellow brocade *chaise longue* in front of the window, looking out to the garden.

Their mistress's wishes were the servants' commands, Cook told Cecily, as she insisted on calling the latest household maid. 'Cissie, a daft bog name,' she had sneered with a fat shrug, giving her two days to overcome her nonsense about going up and down the stairs.

Which is where Robert Hyland-Sykes, the son of the house, found Cissie battling her fear when he returned home from school for the Christmas holidays. Totally absorbed, grasping the banister, she pulled herself up the first two steps, crawled another three, then sat down, surveying the hall. When he stepped out from the shadows, she thought he was a ghost. The tallest, darkest, most handsome ghost imaginable.

For his part he found her buxom figure and auburn colouring, coupled with her naïveté, utterly charming. Within half an hour he had her, if not quite running, certainly walking up and down the stairs.

Two nights later he came to her bedroom down the corridor at the back of the kitchen. Cissie, initially wary, listened to his promises and believed them. She treasured the times they spent together; he brought her to such peaks of ecstasy she wanted to die of happiness.

Innocent and all as she was, before she even told him about the baby during his Easter holidays, she suspected the way it would be. But, of course, she hoped differently. She watched his face shutter over, tongue licking moist lips, eyes sliding sideways. She was the maid; he the son of the house.

She never saw him again. Within an hour his mother had risen from her *chaise longue* and, chiffon scarves awry, had thrown her out on the street.

A stranger in Cork, Cissie knew nobody and had nowhere to go. She walked for hours. In circles, she was sure. And ended up sitting at the back of the Catholic church near the railway station.

Father Michael Lehane, the local curate, found her when he came to lock up. Out of her he drew the age-old story. A story he had heard too many times. He arranged to have her admitted to the hospital, purpose-built in the early 1930s for single, pregnant women.

The next five months were the worst of Cissie's life. Her fear of the future was compounded by degradation, shame, misery and hunger: an endless round of down on her knees, scrubbing wooden floors; washboarding clothes in the freezing laundry; ironing in the moidering steam.

Worst of all was the silent desperation of the other girls. Their lack of hope. Their belief in their unworthiness. Their pathetic attempts at trying to end it all.

Some of them succeeded. Mary with the leaf-green eyes died in agony after drinking bleach; fragile Alice, her life-blood oozing from her wrists, slipped silently away in the small hours of the night; Mamie was cut down from the laundry where she had tried to hang herself, and everyone knew that her baby was stillborn as a result of her actions — she was a murderer.

Cissie gave birth while the home was gripped by a flu epidemic, and Sister Ignatius, the sister in charge, wimple-framed face sheening sweat, eyes dull and glazed, was pleased to leave Cissie to her own devices.

After all these years, Cissie's memory of her baby with its soft down of hair, dewy skin and little starfish hands was crystal clear. Secreted for ever in her personal time capsule. She had plenty of milk. At night she foraged food for herself, stealing down to the cavernous red-tiled kitchen, picking the lock on the pantry door, creeping back, clutching bread and milk, perhaps an apple, or — on one wonderful occasion — a leg of chicken.

Hour after hour she lay on her narrow bed, Brigid on her stomach, stroking, talking. Telling the baby how much she was loved, how she would never be forgotten, willing her a good life, begging her to understand that giving her up for adoption was the hardest thing she had ever done. A gesture of un-selfishness, so she would have the life her mother could not give her.

Sometimes Cissie undressed Brigid and gazed at her in wonder, marvelling at her pink perfection, running the tip of her index finger across her daughter's forehead, down her nose, around her flared nostrils, tracing her lips and outlining the shell ears. Then she would skim the palm of her hand across the infant's shoulders, down her chest, trickling up her arms, streaming down her legs, cupping her buttocks.

Brigid, watching with the huge-irised eyes of babies, smiled, responding. She knew her mother's touch. Of that Cissie was sure.

As the days passed and they were left undisturbed, Cissie began to hope, to believe that she and her daughter might leave this awful place, might make a life for themselves. Somewhere, anywhere.

The morning she heard the rubber of footsteps, the rustle of the habit and the click of Rosary beads along the wooden corridor, she knew it was too late.

Eyes closed, she cowered down, deeper into the bed, shielding Brigid with her body, wishing to suction her back into the safety of her womb. Sister Ignatius, only somewhat recovered from the flu, was brusque, saying, as she reached across Cissie, 'It's past time.'

The nun smelt of stale sweat, bad breath and unwashed clothes. The baby was sweet, milky and soft. Ignatius wrestled Brigid from Cissie.

Cissie jumped up, flinging herself, yelling, pleading, begging, 'Leave her be. Don't take her.' Then she was down on the ground, crawling, nose brushing the nun's lace-ups, arms wrapped around her fat ankles. 'Please, please.'

Ignatius, flailing backwards with jutting hips, stomping legs and aggressive shoes, wrestled free and, holding the baby close, dived headlong down the corridor.

Cissie's memory of the parting was the sudden feeling of searing loss as though the life had been sucked from her, the funnelling rush of the nun, and the thin wail of her daughter drifting back along the narrow, dark corridor.

Her body went hollow and cold, like it was filled with water. She tried to hold in this water but it seeped out through the slits in her eyes. She wrapped an arm across her eyes, covered that arm with the other. Burrowing into the bed, she sobbed silently, not wanting to disturb anyone. But there was no one to disturb.

She became mad afterwards. Quite mad. With her thumping breasts exploding with milk. For many a long day she lay in that moon-grey limbo between the conscious and unconscious, the coarse grey blanket pulled up to her chin. A flicker of memory would come together, construct, then tantalisingly fade beyond her grasp, to be snatched away in the whirlpool of her mind.

Time passed — minutes, hours, days, weeks. Dusk became dawn. And dawn, dusk. Noon became night. And night, noon. Outside her window, skeletal trees soared tall and gangling, frenzied by gusts of wind, creating sinister designs against the steel sky. At night the moon rose, turning from pale pinky-orange to butter-gold and to mother-of-pearl, while the sky deepened from smoky-blue to sapphire and, finally, navy.

Despite everything, this place where Cissie had bonded with her daughter gave her a tenuous identity of her own and was her refuge against the world. She resented intrusion and, strangely, was left alone. Madness disturbed the other girls.

One day Father Lehane came and brought her back with him to his presbytery near the railway station. Sitting her down in the brown wing-chair by the small coal fire in his study, he told her that she would now fill the position left vacant by his house-keeper.

She did so efficiently and without argument. First functioning mechanically, then operating on partial automatic. Gradually, with a small burst of enthusiasm here, a short dart of optimism there, she reached a stage where she could put a sheaf of purple lilac into an empty milk bottle, tie back her hair with a yellow ribbon, make a loaf of spotted dog.

The priest knew that she was on the mend when, against his wishes, she tidied the stacks of paper on his desk. Soon after, he called her into his study, looking up from his battered desk and Sunday's sermon. He had grown fond of this girl — too fond, he realised. She was easy around the place and even easier on the eye.

Her haunted, gaunt look had disappeared; despite herself, youth and health had taken over. She was a far cry from her predecessor, with her haggard expression, constant whining and arthritic complaints.

'Your father's dying,' he told her gently. 'It's time you went home.'

Cissie looked at him, mutely, dumbly. She was used to obeying. In all her life the only person she had argued with was Sister Ignatius. Like the ink-stains on the priest's blotter, fear spread across her mind. The thought of returning home, even to nurse her father, terrified her. There had been no contact

215

between her and her family since Sister Ignatius had informed them of her pregnancy. She dreaded facing them after the terrible sin she had committed. But she knew about duty.

'Can I come back here afterwards?'

'No,' he told her firmly, looking down at the paperwork on his desk to avoid the hurt in her eyes.

Cissie need not have worried. The matter of her baby was not referred to by her parents and she knew they had told nobody. Her father died six months later. The following year, when her mother had initiated Cissie into the secrets of healing, she too passed on peacefully, smiling. Then Cissie was relieved to realise that her secret shame was hers and hers alone.

It was more than twenty years since Brigid had been torn from Cissie. In all that time, while she had never grown totally reconciled to not seeing her again, the sharpness of her pain had blunted. Sometimes she thanked God for the selective amnesia of time. On other occasions, even still, she woke up, her body aching loss; her nostrils filled with the scent of her baby; her ears full of her gurgles. That it was her secret alone made it all the more priceless. Her six days with Brigid were her most precious memory.

The news of the returning Yank had spread like wildfire throughout the village and caused great excitement. The neighbours called in with offers of help and requests to be sure and send Elizabeth down to see them, usually ending with something along the lines of, 'If she hasn't got too big for herself out there in Amerikay.'

Mags nominated herself and her nephew Jamie to be the welcoming committee to meet Elizabeth in Rineanna Airport. Jamie worked in the Munster & Leinster bank in Tralee and had a car. His dark hair was slicked back and his head was narrow on top of padded shoulders. He wore two-piece navy suits and white shirts with detachable collars. He teased Rose and Kate unmercifully about boys and chucked them under their chins like babies. They christened him 'The Drip'.

With an inclination of her head, Cissie accepted the offer graciously. Well she knew that Mags's so-called and much-vaunted generosity was a cover-up. Meeting Elizabeth was her chance to show off her nephew-with-the-car-who-worked-in-the-bank, and had nothing to do with altruism.

Rose would have liked to go to the airport, but Kate said that, even if Mags and Jamie had asked her, there was no way she would — with her hair.

CHAPTER SEVENTEEN

Hair or no hair, no way would Cissie stand for Kate not attending mass. Backing her into the wall and stabbing her with her index finger, she insisted, 'Ye'll go and say your prayers. People have better things to do than be lookin' at yer head.'

Sunday mass, which took place in the schoolhouse at eight in the morning, was the social highlight of the week. The dingy schoolroom with its chalky atmosphere and bleakly postered, scarred walls contrasted starkly with the opulence of the Catholic ceremony — the silver of the chalice and ciborium, studded with precious stones, the luxurious gold-threaded vestments, the richness of the Latin liturgy.

The shawled and head-scarfed women, breast-thumpingly devotional, tried to shush and clatter their children to prayerful order; their men, supporting the walls at the back of the schoolroom, caps in hands, shuffled unease. Mikey was always propped against the wall, too, though he stood alone, apart, with plenty of space for another person on either side of him.

During the week Cissie was not too fussy about the girls' personal appearance. Washing necks, ears or even teeth did not rate high on her agenda, nor did she regard clean socks or polished sandals as being of much importance. But the girls' turnout for mass she saw as a reflection on herself. So Kate's refusal to leave the premises, cutting out their daily swim, was directly responsible for the Saturday bath.

That particular evening it was raining, that insidiously pervasive Kerry rain, sliding off the thatch, slinking over downpipes, gushing into the barrel, stirring the bushes.

Kate, snug beside the range, was flicking through *The Kerryman*. The opening — after twenty years — of the Tralee–Fenit railway line, for the weekends, had been a resounding success, despite the tracks having to be sanded on the first return journey. Kate wondered why none of her Tralee friends had visited her. Then panicked. What would she do if they did? They didn't know she was bald. How could she face them?

After tea, Cissie lifted in the big oval-shaped tin basin usually propped against the wall of the back kitchen. She set it on the floor and started filling it from the ever-simmering kettle on the range.

'What's that for?' Kate eyed her over the news-paper.

'For yer baths.'

'Wha…at?' yelped Rose and Kate in horror.

'Yer baths,' said Cissie in her firm voice. 'Now that ye're not swimmin', ye've to bath.'

'I'm fine,' Kate assured her, looking fragile and patting at the bandages. She had the role of patient dramatised to a fine art. And her head was smelling worse with each passing day.

Cissie ignored her. 'Who's first, so?'

'Rose,' said Kate.

Rose eyed the bath in consternation. She had never bathed in front of anyone except her mother, and that not for years.

'Wait down in the room. I'll call ya,' Cissie told Kate. 'Do ya want me to leave?' she asked Rose in a more kindly voice.

'Yes, please.'

When Rose bathed at home she imagined she was Cleopatra, up to her neck in ass's milk — she liked that story. On one occasion, hoping that her mother would not miss it from the larder, she had poured in three-quarters of a jug of milk. She didn't notice any difference, but knew that her skin must be softer and smoother.

Now she undressed as fast as possible, lowering herself with a shudder into the too-shallow, too-hot water, rubbing the disgusting-smelling slab of yellow soap onto a scratchy face-cloth and running it over her body, lick-and-a-promise fashion, certainly not Cleopatra style.

Despite her rush to be finished with this, the most uncomfortable bath she had ever taken, she could not help noticing that over the past few weeks, her breasts had grown bigger and her nipples rosier.

When she ran the cloth across her nipples, they hardened and stood erect as though to attention. Nice. Then she remembered where she was, blushed beetroot and jumped out of the bath in a flash, terrified someone would come in the front or even back door.

Kate followed, using the same water, and, pronouncing the operation 'positively barbaric', threatened, 'I'll go back to Tralee if I've to have a bath again.'

'That's fine,' Cissie said, taking little notice of her dramatics, getting the girls to lay out their Sunday clothes on their bed. Each week Rose thanked her lucky stars she had left the suit in Tralee and dumped the gloves in the postbox.

Cissie washed in the back kitchen. Not a bath, not even a proper wash, no more than a quick once-over from what they could see, explaining, 'I'm not a great one for too much water.'

While Cissie was kind and friendly towards the girls, like Mossie she was not a great talker about herself. Rose and Kate knew little about her and had grown accustomed to her going busily about her daily tasks without uttering a comment or passing a remark.

However, this night, with Kate giving one of her 'I'm bored' performances, Cissie asked, 'Would ye like to see me shoes?'

They knew she must have a stash. Hadn't they seen the yellow suedes when they arrived, the variety of her mass shoes, and the black ones with the very high heels she wore the day of Kate's hair?

'Yes!' said Rose enthusiastically. Anything was better than Kate's goings-on.

Inside the cupboard in Cissie's bedroom, under a sheet of yellowing newspaper, were two rows of the most beautiful shoes in the world. Tall spindly heels, pointy and peep-toes; there were delicate confections of straps, tiny buckles, delicious bows. The colours ranged from vivid green, glowing red to shiny black, sunshine yellow, from marvellous purple to hot pink and pure white. They stood, toes stuffed with newspaper, in a neat row.

Cissie explained, 'I've different shoes for different occasions.' For mass, she liked to follow the liturgical colours, though she did allow herself a certain amount of leeway so that the shoes would not be at total variance with events in her life. The purple ones were reserved for Advent, funerals or sad events; the yellow and the white were for Easter and joy; red for Christmas and celebrations; green for the majority of Sundays and for St Patrick's Day; and black for funerals and for grieving occasions, though her black ones were not even remotely sad.

Rose and Kate sighed and oohed and aahed, and Cissie looked suitably modest.

When she went to close over the door, Kate clasped her hands and rolled her eyes, like the picture of Maria Goretti who had died at the age of twelve rather than sacrifice her virginity. All Kate was missing was the lily. 'Please, please may I try them on?'

Kate, thought Rose, would make a great martyr, though, having listened to Sister Concepta on the subject, she considered martyrdom mad. Imagine, Saint Brigid wanted to be a nun but her father who was 'a greedy landowner', according to Concepta, with ideas of consolidating the family lands, wanted her to get married. When she called on God for help, what did He do? Had her eye dribble out of its socket and down her cheek, leaving such an ugly welt that,

222

not surprisingly, all her would-be suitors promptly lost interest.

The King of Sicily's plans to marry his daughter, who became Saint Wilgefortis, were foiled when God grew her a beard and moustache. The king was so mad that he had her crucified! Then there was Saint Agatha who was tortured by Sicilian peasants to give up her faith in Jesus. She stuck out the burning, the rack and the cutting off of her breasts, and died giving praise when they rolled hot coals over her.

Looking at Kate's pleading eyes and Rose's solemn ones, Cissie nodded. The girls carried the shoes out to the kitchen table.

'Take them down off that table,' said Cissie sharply. 'Quickly. They'll bring us bad luck.' The girls, well used to Cissie's various superstitions and piseogs, obeyed, hugging them in quick armfuls to the floor.

'I like these best,' said Kate, holding up the most beautiful red suedes with high spindle heels.

'They're my favourites too.' Cissie smiled her gummy baby's smile.

'Where did you get them?' Kate asked.

'From me sister Elizabeth. She sent me them all,' said Cissie proudly.

Kate slipped off her sandals, put on the red shoes and sashayed around the kitchen, quite at home in the high heels, although they were somewhat incongruous with her bandaged head.

Rose tried the green and then the yellow and felt graceful and fluid of movement. They swapped until they had danced around the kitchen in all of them.

Cissie, chin in hand, looked on with sad amusement. Finished, the girls sat back, out of breath.

'The shoes fit Rose and me really well. How do they fit you?' Kate asked, looking dubiously at Cissie's splayed and knobbly feet straining against the canvas of her plimsolls. Kate was very outspoken.

'The red ones were always too small. But that didn't stop me wearing them. I manage with the others.'

'I couldn't,' said Kate. 'Not if they hurt so much. If they're too small for you, can I have them?'

'Ye can, but not till I die.'

'Did you ever buy any shoes yourself?' she asked.

'No. I never would.'

Shaking her head as though to dislodge the foolishness, Cissie returned to the present. 'Look at the hour—' she pointed to the yellow-faced clock over the range, 'and ye've to be up early for mass.'

After the girls had gone to their room, Cissie pulled over the chair to the range, opened the door, raked the ashes and, even though it wasn't cold, huddled in on top of the heat. Events were crowding her. She had always known that nobody could escape their past, but as the years went by, she had been pleased that she had managed to keep hers at bay. Now she had a strange premonition that history, as it were, was repeating itself.

Cissie remembered every detail of the day Sadie Daw died. The way the whole village shuddered to a shocked standstill. And was never the same since.

Mikey, Sadie and Father Florence were in the car. The Rover had been a present to the bishop from his brother, reputed to be a multi-millionaire in Chicago. The bishop, who had never learned to drive, was more than generous in lending the car to his curate in return for chauffeuring, a service of which he never once availed.

That day, for reasons that were never fathomed though it did not stop conjecture, Sadie was driving. She had always been too friendly with Father Florence, they said over and over again, like a refrain. In and out of the presbytery from the time she was a young one. Then off to England when she was eighteen. A year later back with the baby. And that story of a dead husband.

The crash occurred at the Spa corner, a black spot, which over the years had claimed numerous lives. Death for the adults was instantaneous, the steering-wheel embedded in Sadie's chest, and the priest half-way through the windscreen. Mikey was slumped in the back seat, dazed, with blood streaming from his nose. The picnic basket in the boot remained undamaged.

Snots Healy's half-filled bus on the afternoon run from Tralee was the first to arrive on the scene. An elderly woman passenger, with an asthmatic wheeze and swollen ankles, who had been a nurse in England, took charge, ordering Snots away to get help. Snots, being Snots and of limited vision, finished his shift, dropping off his passengers as usual. In the process, the story of the crash spread like wildfire.

On the return journey to the scene of the accident, the bus was packed with the curious and the sensation-seekers, as well as local guard John Joe Sheehy.

On his first posting since finishing training college at Templemore, John Joe was plump, shy and still bemused at his status of *garda síochána* — keeper of the peace. Sitting quietly, podgy pink hands resting on his knees, the young guard had just made up his mind to ask Lizzie Foley to the dance on Sunday night. He really fancied her. Though quiet, like himself, she had a good-humoured way about her and a merry smile.

Snots was in his element, the expert on the story of the year. Facing his passengers, his skinny buttocks propped against the dashboard, he became so animated in the telling and re-telling, elaborating and embroidering, that not a trace of his customary snuffle lingered.

By the time they reached the Spa, straggles of locals from God-knows-where in the underpopulated hinterland had arrived on foot, by push-bike and by donkey and cart.

The nurse comforted Mikey, whose nosebleed had stopped; he leaned against her, a dazed look on his face. The villagers clustered together, blessing themselves, saying their Rosaries, superstitiously eyeing the mangled car, glowering at little Mikey. Their animosity towards what they saw as Sadie's corruption of their Father Florence transferring itself to her son.

Suddenly Mikey, in his blood-splashed jersey and

trousers, his smudged face, hands and legs, was galvanised into action. Jumping up, grabbing at a stone, he climbed onto the bonnet of the mangled car and, lying on his stomach, he hit the priest's head over and over again with the stone, piteously howling, 'My mam. Make my mam wake up. Make her. Make her.'

Having removed the stone from Mikey's grasp, John Joe hesitated, unsure of his next step. Unidentified hands relieved him of the stone and ceremoniously set it aside on the ditch. Someone knew about forensics. It might be required as evidence.

The guard prised Mikey from the bonnet of the car. Like an eel, the boy twisted loose, wriggled into the front seat and tried to snuggle against the body of his mother. It took all of John Joe's strength to pull him away. Cissie joined the group just in time to hear the child's piteous pleas to be allowed to kiss his mother.

'Let him be,' she said. 'Let him kiss her goodbye.'

But they didn't listen to her. Mags yanked Mikey from the guard, shook him and frog-marched him to the periphery of the group.

Out of respect for the Church, up to this the friendship between Sadie and the curate had been a tightly guarded secret, a subject only whispered about. Now it would have its full salacious airing, with a small sobbing boy becoming the village scapegoat.

Cissie wondered how a five-year-old would live with the consequences of what had happened, how much he would remember of his own actions and how he would judge and be judged when he grew older.

Over the years, she had watched him grow up, lonely and isolated. She had grieved with him and for him and offered him small kindnesses, where appropriate. These days, it was no longer fitting. She was answerable to Father Lehane and Mrs Mac; her present duty was to Kate and Rose.

No matter how sympathetic her feelings towards Mikey and her identification with Rose, she could not encourage their relationship.

The only solution that presented itself to her was to try to keep Rose away from Mikey. Easier said than done. She seemed to be fighting a losing battle. It was bad luck about Kate's hair. Even worse that she was so stubborn about going out.

Then she had an idea. Now that she had made one phone call, why not another? To Mrs Mac, to make arrangements for Rose to visit her grandmother in Castlemaine. Not that Cissie would mention the real reason for the call. She could not be seen to fall down in caring for her charges. Hadn't Mrs Mac enough troubles of her own?

Despite Cissie's vigilance, Rose and Mikey sneaked time together nearly every day. No arrangements were made, but invariably he found her wherever she was. Whether fetching messages, collecting shells, or just rambling across the beach. Since the day on the rocks and their one kiss, the tension between them tingled and crackled, but by unspoken agreement, they kept a physical distance between them.

Whenever Rose groped for the words to talk about them and how they were together — the way she and Frank used to — Mikey locked into himself. So, after several abortive attempts, she gave up and lived with him in her head.

For as long as she could remember she had felt different, alone. Not lonely. But alone with her own slumbering thoughts. Different from her family, from her classmates, different even from Frank. But with Mikey, she felt she had found a soulmate. Albeit a monosyllabic one.

Hands jammed into the pockets of her skirt, Rose rambled back across the beach towards Western Cove, looking for samples of sea grass for her project. Strange to think that once there had been a church and a thriving community here. Now only the grave-yard remained as a lonely reminder of the desolate power of the sea. She could see the destruction in the way it reared up before her in a long white wall of foam, before collapsing at her feet and disgorging back into the ocean.

As she wondered about the lonely sailors from the Spanish Armada buried without markers and the even lonelier limbo babies, lumped together in a windswept corner of the old graveyard, she saw a figure cutting across the headland.

For a moment she thought it was Mikey.

But it was a bigger man, head thrown back, striding out, stick in his hand.

With horror she realised it was Jammy O'Brien. Perhaps if she sat down among the few headstones and remained very still, he would not see her, but from the veer he took in her direction, it was obvious that her fleeting moment of optimism had been in vain.

For a few seconds she was like the frightened rabbit of their only other encounter. Terrified by the evil of the man. But she had changed since then. Come a long way. Become more sure of herself.

While she might not have been able to pinpoint and label the precise danger which Jammy afforded her, she knew she had to escape him. She ran, stumbling over the rough terrain of the graveyard, out onto the cliff, in a curve away from him, back the way he had come. In the opposite direction to the village, she realised too late.

He chased after her, moving surprisingly fast for such a big man. Gaining on her. Then she heard her name, sounding as though it were floating on the breeze. She thought it was her imagination but when it came again, she looked back.

Jammy, face red, legs pumping, stick waving, was almost on her.

Behind him and coming from the hinterland ran Mikey. 'Run, Rose, run,' he called.

With a bellow of thwarted rage, Jammy stopped. 'I'll get you yet, girl,' he bellowed, turning on his heel, sloping back the way he had come.

Mikey didn't follow him. Rose was his priority and he went to her. She was sitting, gasping, hugging her knees on the cliff grass.

'Are you all right?'

Rose nodded. Bravery gone, she started to shiver.

Mikey put his arms around her, and, with the palm of his hand, stroked her hair, warning, 'Watch out for him. He's a bad one.' She nestled into his shoulder. 'Be sure and tell Cissie what happened.'

Rose started to sob. The enormity of what could have happened, if Jammy had caught up with her and Mikey had not appeared, was beyond her imagination. Way beyond Monica's sexual drilling. But she knew it would have been bad. Very bad.

'The guards should know,' Mikey insisted. 'Get Cissie to tell John Joe. Get him to keep an eye out.' He kissed her on her forehead, cheeks and chin, and Rose knew she wouldn't mention the incident to Cissie.

'I'd do it,' Mikey said, 'but John Joe wouldn't pay as much attention to me.'

Finally Mikey came to her lips. Not hard and hurting, like the last time. Long, lingering kisses. Tongue-hunting French kissing. Demanding, seeking, caressing. She matched his passion. How could she ever have been disappointed with French kissing? Monica was right. It was the ultimate.

Rose snuggled deeper into Mikey. Encircling her in his arms, he eased her back onto the grass, grasping her so tightly that his thumbs, pressing into her back, were medallions of hurt.

His hands, outlining her body, were experienced. Skimming her breasts, cupping her buttocks. She did nothing to stop him. Did not want the crowdingly delicious sensations ever to cease. Wanted more, wanted it all.

Mikey was so different from Frank. Frank and she had learned together, and with him she had felt protected and safe. Thinking back to Monica and her discussion on the wild passion of experienced men, Mikey, she decided, probably had buckets of practice. Both titillated and apprehensive at the thought of him with other girls, she wondered would he find her dead naïve, concluding that she couldn't go far wrong if where he led, she followed.

And then, he was tugging her blue aertex top free from the waistband of her skirt, slipping his hands inside. Silver fingers running up her spine, down her ribs. The longed-for sensation of his skin on hers. She should do something, not just lie there like a lump of lard. Tentatively she moved her palms up the cotton of his shirt. She could feel his pulses throbbing, hear his blood pounding through his veins.

Then Mikey pulled away. Rolled onto his back.

Dammit. How could she have forgotten? The bloody liberty bodice. The ultimate passion-killer. Who in his right mind would want to make love to a bodice-wearer?

Rose sat up, hugged her arms around her knees, looked out to sea. Mikey reached over for her hand. After a while they walked quietly back over the cliff-top. Still holding hands, but only until they came within sight of the village.

CHAPTER EIGHTEEN

On Monday, Cissie waved Rose off on the morning bus to Tralee and, much to Rose's embarrassment, warned Snots to watch out for her. This, with a gleeful snuffle, he promised.

Halfway through the journey, he shuffled his way down the bus, looked to the right and left and even behind him, leaned over Rose in a conspiratorial manner and whispered, 'When's Elizabeth comin' on th' aeroplane?'

Josie, Nance's youngest sister, was waiting at the railway station, which also doubled as the bus depot. She looked lovely, as always. Slender, blonde, in a short-skirted blue dress, straw clutch bag and white sandals — slingbacks with cork wedge heels, the latest this summer.

Josie hugged Rose. A grown-up hug. As she and Bart had no family, she knew nothing about children, not that Rose considered herself a child.

Rose well remembered, before Josie's marriage, overhearing her mother tell Dolores — who Rose hated having to call Auntie — that it would be over Granny's dead body she would have that black sheep under her roof. It took Rose a while to work out that that black sheep was Bart. Something about Josie having made her bed and having to lie on it. But since marrying, Josie and Bart had lived with Granny. Officially, Josie ran the house, though, according to Nance, she made a right mess of it; unofficially, Josie spent most of her time on the golf course, very successfully.

Josie and Bart had a big old American car, a turquoise-coloured Hudson with the steering-wheel on the left-hand side. Its size was not a problem for Josie, who manoeuvred it with the consummate skill born of endless practice.

'I've a surprise for you, poppet,' she said gaily, turning the car down Castle Street instead of up to Moyderwell and out the Castleisland road. 'We're going to get your ears pierced.'

She drove up on the pavement underneath the clock outside Grunts', the jewellers. One of Rose's dreams realised without even mentioning it! Whenever she mooted the idea at home, Nance, rolling her eyes heavenwards, would ask if she really wanted to be taken for a gypsy?

Inside, the jewellery shop was gloomy, with the hallowed air of a church. Glass case after glass case was filled with earrings — hoops, studs, clusters, drops, fiery diamonds, creamy pearls, gleaming rubies, flashing emeralds, glowing sapphires, smouldering opals — all reclining on black velvet.

'Sleepers to start with. Better for healing,' decided Josie. Rose had a flash of disappointment. Beside the opulence of the others, the small, plain gold hoops looked so ordinary. 'We'll get the carved ones. They're prettier, don't you think? The way they glint in the light?'

With extravagant compliments about his ear-piercing ability, Josie introduced a pot-bellied, bald-headed man called Reuben. Lifting out the earrings with great ceremony, he placed them on a miniature black velvet cushion, no larger than a matchbox, then led the way to the back of the shop.

'Don't want you out front frightening all my other customers away with your screams,' he said cheerfully, pushing Rose firmly into a chair.

Omigod. What had she let herself in for? The chair was just like the dentist's — since her first traumatic visit at the age of six, the dentist had been one of Rose's greatest fears. He still was.

Rose decided that hook-nosed Reuben, with his slender hands and manicured nails, was positively sinister. But there was no escape. Josie, still in the front of the shop, rooting to her heart's content among the display cases, kept up a running commentary on the jewellery in stock.

Reuben approached Rose, holding a small canister in his left hand. Like a frightened horse, her eyes rolling in terror, she reared backwards in the chair. With his right hand he took hold of her chin, steadying her head, and with a quick squirt, the lobes of her ears were numb. As though by magic, an implement rather like the punch Nance used for making holes in leather belts appeared in his hand. Before Rose knew it, with a sharp stab, followed by a meaty clunk, her first, then second, ear was pierced and the earrings were in place.

'You were really brave.' Reuben offered her a glass of water and helped her out the chair. 'Now try and persuade your aunt not to be such a coward.'

Josie came laughing into the back of the shop, saying that never would she submit to such a barbaric practice. Clip-ons would do her fine. Pushing Rose's hair behind her ears, she said, 'You're gorgeous.'

Rose was glad her hair was short — all the better to show off the earrings. She left the jewellers', walking tall and full of courage, with instructions from Reuben about applying peroxide to prevent infection and Vaseline to facilitate turning the earrings.

'So tell me,' Josie said, rummaging in her handbag on the bench seat between them and rifling out a packet of Churchman's with one hand. 'Are Ma and Da having difficulty beating the boys from the door? First love is hard. I'm here if you want to natter. You haven't anybody. Poor poppet. Forget I'm an auntie. Look on me as the big sister you don't have.' She leaned over and squeezed Rose's leg and Rose knew — no matter how gorgeous Josie looked and how generously she behaved, she could never talk to her about those things.

Josie rummaged further in the bag. 'Root out the lighter. I can never find anything in this mess.'

Rose found it, long, lean and gold. 'Go on, light me a cigarette. Don't tell me you don't know, or haven't tried. I'd be ashamed to call you my niece if I didn't think you were properly educated. And not the kind of education your granny means.'

With Rose's newly acquired expertise, she drew out a cigarette from its nestle of white tissue paper, held it between her first and second fingers, clicked the lighter, positioned the flame against the cigarette, inhaled and, to her delight, it glowed satisfactorily.

'Good girl,' praised Josie, settling it, with a sigh of gratification, between her lips.

Annie Clifford's home was a square manor house, set amid trees in a manageable acreage. There was a timelessness about the place and the woman.

These days the high-ceilinged formal dining- and drawing-rooms, with their long windows reaching out to the gardens, mahogany furniture and velvet drapes, were seldom used. The kitchen was the hub of the house, its windows small and deep-set and the furniture no-nonsense oak. The old dresser was crowded with coppery lustre jugs and pewter tankards. The range glowed, winter and summer.

Annie's dark dress skimmed the top of soft ankle boots. Her hair, like Kate's, was her crowning glory, hooshed into a loose topknot with floating wisps of silver. Her lips, dry and feathery, deposited a thistledown kiss on Rose's forehead.

No sooner was Rose sitting down than she had to stand up again to show how much she had grown. 'And you're nice and fat too,' complimented the old woman, to Rose's mortification, prodding at her thigh. What was it with Kerry people? They considered 'fat' a compliment.

Next was Rose's schoolwork. 'Education is very important. It gives a woman freedom, allows her to lead her own life. It's the coming thing for young girls nowadays. Go to university and have a career. Then you can make choices. What will you be?'

'History, I want to do history…' and thinking about her ideas of becoming a romantic novelist, Rose added, 'and maybe English.'

'Good. But make sure you have a career, child, not a job. You can be anything you want.'

Josie made coffee for them in a saucepan, with milk and water and a strip of lemon rind. It was Rose's coffee, which Babs had brought out to Annie on one of her weekly visits. Josie finished off the coffee with a dash of cream from the top of the milk and they drank it, dunking Marietta biscuits, sandwiched with so much butter that the holes oozed golden worms.

Rose's grandfather looked down from the wall. The oval photograph was sepia toned, in a rectangular frame. Dressed in plus-fours, a Norfolk tweed jacket, with a retriever at his feet and a gun under his arm, he presented a jaunty picture of landed gentry.

Rose reminded Annie of herself more than sixty years ago. She had known what it was to rage for freedom, to be a woman in a child's body. From the time of Adam and Eve, being a woman had been hard. But in the old days expectations and roles were clearly defined and life was easier. Those times were gone for ever. Annie sighed. There was no putting back the clock. No halting progress.

'Did you love Grandad?' Rose asked suddenly when Josie had gone out the back.

The old woman looked at Rose out of crinkly, silvery-grey eyes. 'God help us, it's a long time since anyone has asked me that.' She smiled, hands folded in her lap, a dreamy expression on her face. 'I did. In the end as much as life itself.' Her story was the most romantic Rose had ever heard, or even read.

When Moses Foley died in 1895 he left behind his wife Nola and twelve-year-old daughter, Annie. Nola did her best to keep the family shoemaking business going, but she fought a losing battle. She was a homemaker, not a businesswoman. Despite the willingness of the few staff and the kindness of the townsfolk, she did not have the necessary commercial skills and ability. The family home on the outskirts of Tralee was sold, and she and Annie moved into rooms over the workshop.

Uncle R, as Annie called him, was fifty-five. He was a family friend, and she and Nola grieved with him and for him when, three years later, his wife died — choking to death, it was said, on a goitre which just grew and grew. Their five children had emigrated to America. In those days, emigration was for ever.

Uncle R was wealthy. Extremely wealthy. From the time he was a boy in school at Clongowes Wood, his dabbling in the stock market had paid many a dividend. The family business was supplying coaching colts to Wimbush, the London jobmasters. Each year several hundred hunters changed hands. There was also a thriving working farm plus a good acreage of extra grazing and tillage outside the town of Castlemaine. In his leisure time, he bred prize-winning horses and greyhounds on which he regularly placed successful bets.

Uncle R visited the Foleys with increasing frequency and was always received in the parlour. Though tiny, it was a formal room, with crowding furniture, flocked velvet wallpaper and green brocade curtains with silky fringes. When he was expected, Nola lit the fire, squared the antimacassars on the backs of the chairs, polished the brasses and served whiskey and home-made shortbread biscuits from a silver tray.

Annie liked listening to Uncle R, perching on a footstool at his feet as he told stories about Grá, his beloved mare, and Cailín, his favourite greyhound. Annie's fondness for Uncle R related to her mother's happiness. For days before and after he visited, Nola went around smiling to herself and humming soft little tunes.

One April evening, when Annie was fifteen, his hand resting lightly on Annie's head, Uncle R asked permission to escort 'his two ladies', as he called them, to the races the following week at Ballybeggan. They must say yes. That year, 1898, there was only a one-day meeting. They could not disappoint him.

Nola murmured something about it not being seemly for them to be seen together in public. Uncle R nonsensed the idea, assuring her he was not interested in the 'seemly' and didn't she trust him enough to know he would give no cause for talk?

On race day he brought two buttonholes. A red rosebud nestling in maidenhair fern for Annie, and for Nola a scented orchid. They rode the short distance in Uncle R's chaise, drawn by a dancing black horse, up the town, out by Clash. Annie smiling and nodding like real quality, until a mortified Nola stopped her. It was the best day of Annie's life. Uncle R insisted on placing bets for them and his tip, Eddie's Pet, romped comfortably home.

One evening in early September, he was hardly settled in his chair when he said to Annie, 'A whiskey would go down a treat, and don't be in too much of a hurry back.'

Glancing at her mother, Annie knew the meaning of the word 'radiant'. Now the snatches of rumour she had heard around the town made sense. Perhaps Nola would become Uncle R's second wife. Annie would like that. It would provide the stability missing from her life since her father's death. It would be companionship for her mother and would remove the financial strain. Even more importantly, it would allow her to pursue her dream of becoming a nurse.

When she returned, carrying the silver tray, the parlour was silent, Nola's expression unfathomable — a far cry from the radiance of a few minutes ago. Uncle R studied the tip of his brogues, the last pair Moses had made.

His thanks to Annie were perfunctory and Nola said it was time for her to go to her room. Annie opened her mouth to protest but one look at her mother's face dissuaded her from argument.

Next morning Nola was quiet, her eyes red and puffy. Breakfast was eaten in silence, Annie racking her brains for the reason behind her mother's behaviour. While Nola washed the dishes and Annie dried, Nola asked, 'Do you like Uncle R?'

'Mama, you know I do,' said Annie. 'I love him.'

'Enough to marry him?'

Annie started to laugh. 'It's you he's going to….'
A look at her mother's face stopped her in her tracks.
'What is it, Mama?'

'No. It's you he wants. God help us.'

Granny had had her first proposal when she was little
older than Rose! And Rose thought the Dark Ages of
the olden days restrictive, and modern times roaringly
progressive! Forgetting that Uncle R was old enough
to have been Annie's grandfather, Rose's mind
boggled when she tried to imagine either Frank or
Mikey proposing marriage. Wait until she told them
in school! She could hardly breathe with the thrill
of it.

'You must have been very excited?'

Annie looked at her curiously. 'I wasn't. I wanted
to be a nurse, not get married. I didn't even know his
name was Rory. After the last high king of Ireland.'
She gave a little laugh.

'Then why did you marry him?'

'We were penniless. It was Mama's one chance for
security. I couldn't deny her.'

'Why didn't she marry him?'

'That's what a lot of the townsfolk wondered. But
it wasn't as simple as that. It was me he wanted.
When I look back, I know how disappointed and
rejected she must have felt. But we put a good face on
it. I was married the day I turned sixteen. And we
moved in here. It was the finest house in the area.'
Annie wagged a finger at Rose. 'And I'm sure you

know, Castlemaine is the birthplace of Jack Duggan, our very own Wild Colonial Boy.'

Rose was more interested in her own family saga than in this unknown bushranger who had ended up in Australia robbing the rich to feed the poor, and ended up being killed by the mounted police. 'What happened your mother?' she asked.

'She came with us and cared for the babies. We'd ten years together and eight babies. Your mother was my fifth. And when your grandfather died I grieved in a way I didn't think possible. It was only then I knew how much I cared for him.'

Rose, lost in the enchantment of it all, wondered at the power that fired such passion. Granny's story was better than Antony and Cleopatra, Romeo and Juliet, Diarmuid and Gráinne. Even the *Angélique* books, which she considered the epitome of romance, paled to insignificance compared to this drama. 'And what happened afterwards?'

'The flu took Mama the following January. Then I really knew what it was like to be on my own. And the importance of financial security.'

Rose did not know what to say, so she said nothing. They sat opposite each other in companionable silence, each lost in private thoughts, until Josie broke the mood by rattling in the back door, saying Bart would be back soon.

'Come down to the bedroom with me while Josie's getting the tea,' said Annie. Around the time of Josie and Bart's wedding she had moved her bedroom downstairs and had built on an en-suite bathroom, an unheard-of luxury in Kerry, though tales of such extravagance had filtered across the Atlantic from America.

She walked down the corridor ahead of Rose, bent over and slightly swaying. Taking a key from one of several on a chain around her neck, she unlocked the door, pushed it in and re-locked it behind her.

This was a dark room of paraphernalia and memorabilia, crowded by an enormous wardrobe — so old that it had hooks in its back, originally to hang crinolines — a pink marble-topped washstand, a very tall tallboy and a velvet-curtained half-poster bed. There were photographs, mirrors, crochet doilies and framed samplers in abundance.

With an air of mischief, Annie motioned Rose to help her move the tallboy. Despite its height and bulk, being on castors, it shifted easily.

Behind was a concealed cupboard, which Annie hunkered down to open with another key from around her neck. Reaching into the cavity, she grasped a handle, and a trolley rolled forward. On it sat a small trunk. She rolled the trolley over to the bed, and opened the lid of the trunk with another key.

The trunk was three-quarters full of sovereigns. There must have been thousands. Annie scooped handful after handful onto the bed, tinkling gold against the white of the coverlet. With the sun shafting filigreed light through the lace-curtained window, there was an air of surrealism about the scene.

Rose joined her grandmother, scooping and ladling, and when the coins were spilling all over the bed, she raked her fingers through them, raising cupped handfuls, delighting in their musicality as they rained back down. Enjoying the power of holding unlimited wealth.

She received her second lesson of the day in fiscal rectitude. 'These sovereigns represent my freedom and security,' her grandmother told her. 'When you've your own money, you're beholden to nobody. Remember that. And remember this. Mind your money, your body, and be careful who you let know how smart you are, and you'll be all right.'

They counted the coins together, bagging them in hundreds in chamois pouches. As the pouches mounted, Rose lost track of their number. Then they piled them back into the trunk and Annie repeated the procedure with her keys.

'Not a word about this,' she said as they went back down to the kitchen.

By now Bart had come in. He sprawled, reading the *Irish Independent* and smoking a cigarette. When he saw Rose, he jumped up, said how pretty she was — how like Josie; next time she must come and stay with them, not hide out in Fenit. Rose could smell the whiskey off his breath, see the flush of it in his cheeks and glazed eyes. His suit was rumpled and his shoes dirty.

Annie looked through him as he continued to make a fuss of Rose. He wanted to take her to the dogs that evening, but Annie said no. She was too young. But he should go himself. He would not dream of it, he said. He would take Josie and Rose out for a drink. They would go back into Tralee. To the golf club.

What with having her ears pierced and drinking in the golf club, Rose felt very sophisticated and wished she had a grown-up dress.

Josie was having brandy and Bart whiskey. Lemonade or Pepsi seemed childish. While she was still dithering, Bart said, 'Leave it to me. You like coffee, don't you?'

He returned with a stemmed glass full of dark liquid topped with a fine depth of cream. The glass was sitting on a doily on a saucer. It looked gorgeous. 'What is it?' Rose asked.

'A Gaelic coffee,' he said with a flourish. 'Invented by a man not a million miles from here.'

'Who was he?'

'Joe Sherlock, a chef in Shannon Catering in Foynes in the early 1940s, before you were even a twinkle in your parents' eyes,' rattled off Bart.

Rose did not know what a Gaelic coffee was and was not about to find out because Josie stood up, took it back to the bar and returned with an identical-looking concoction but, as Rose subsequently discovered, minus the whiskey.

Next evening, when Josie was driving her back to the bus, Rose was squashed in the bench seat between Bart and herself, he crowding her uncomfortably. There was an edge to Josie's voice when she said, 'Watch it, Bart.'

His leg hot against Rose's, he laughed, 'Now that you're leavin' us, you can tell us what herself does down in the bedroom — counting her millions, no doubt?'

'Leave it, Bart,' warned Josie.

Her warning was Rose's permission not to answer and she was glad when they reached the station.

Rose's body ached all over and her earlobes were swollen and throbbing. Josie came in with her, saw her onto the bus and waited until it drove off. She looked tired and without her usual sparkle. 'Remember, I'm here for you, poppet. Bart and me think of you as our own. I'll come out to Fenit and we'll finish off our chat.' Rose hoped she would not. She hated being called 'poppet'. Hated the way Josie tried so hard. And their chat had not even begun.

Rose's welcome back from Kate was rapturous, the enthusiasm of it well worth the going away.

When Kate spotted her pierced ears she whooped, shouted and screamed around the place. Totally forgetting her hair, she thumped on the table, berating herself for not having accompanied Rose. Going on and on that she could have had her ears pierced too. The way Rose's lobes were feeling, clip-ons seemed a far more sensible option.

Cissie gave Rose an appraising look. Rose was a deep one. Deeper even than she had suspected. Cissie had run into Mikey yesterday afternoon while down at the post office collecting the milk. On the spur of the moment, she had drawn him aside, urging, 'Please, Mikey, stay away from Rose. No good can come of it. Only trouble for the both of ye.'

Up to then she had hoped she had been imagining things, that he would deny contact with Rose. Optimistic foolishness on her part, she realised, when his face darkened and he straightened up high: 'What does Rose say?'

'Nothin'. She's not here.'

'Where's she?'

'At her grandmother's.'

'When'll she be back?'

In view of the circumstances, Cissie had had no compunction about stretching the truth. 'I'm not sure.' Without much expectation, she had wondered if he might take the hint without her having to spell it out further.

Rose did not notice Cissie's look. But she did notice how quiet and locked into herself Cissie was.

'She's been that way,' Kate explained, 'since coming back from seeing her cousin Broody yesterday.' His boil had turned out to be more than a boil. It was cancer.

'He won't live for much longer,' Cissie said. Then, as though reiteration would aid acceptance, 'No man can live for ever and we must be satisfied with the life Broody's had.'

Rose tried to imagine how she would feel if Kate were dying.

'He's satisfied to go,' explained Cissie. 'We who're left behind shouldn't begrudge him.' Blessing herself piously, she said, 'It's the ones who go to meet their Maker still fighting for life that're hard to watch. Thank God we won't have that. Broody'll die with dignity and, one thing for sure, he'll have a wake to remember.'

CHAPTER NINETEEN

This Wednesday, not only had Foxy insisted on accompanying Babs to Fenit, he had also insisted on a morning start. It was not yet eleven when they pulled up outside Cissie's.

Tommo stood gangling in the doorway of the cottage, his head hunched into his shoulders, a vulnerably wide smile set into his face. Babs thought how sweet her eldest son was in his innocence. When he recognised his parents, Tommo jumped back into the kitchen and ran out the back howling like a banshee, it was difficult to tell whether with rage or delight.

Despite Cissie's endless patience and herbal ministrations, Tommo's moments of unpredictability had increased. These days he slipped without warning into a paroxysm of jerks, burst into uncontrollable crying or laughter and jumped around yelping. Slowly Babs was accepting that he was growing worse.

Tommo loved Cissie and she would not hear a word said against him. 'You're the man of the house,' she told him, sitting him at the top of the table. Painstakingly she tried to teach him to dress, and to wash. She helped him to eat, and constantly fussed over him.

Foxy Mac, waving his red tartan cap, was in high form, refusing to allow Tommo to dispel his good humour.

When he saw Rose, he burst into 'The Rose of Tralee', like a signature tune. Kate sulkily told him he was always going on with that nonsense. Didn't he know the real Rose was called Mary O'Connor?

Rose didn't mind Foxy's goings-on. Since he had eaten her beans, she felt an affinity with him. She thought he was great fun, rather like that comedian Jimmy O'Dea who played in the Gaiety Theatre. Nance was a great fan of his and from an early age had introduced Rose and George to his extravagant wardrobe and urban wit.

What Rose did mind was Foxy's appearance, today of all days. She hadn't had a chance to see Mikey since returning the previous evening from her grandmother's and was anxious to have the opportunity of meeting him.

Foxy was a man on a mission. The boot of his car stuffed with food, he was in Fenit to fulfil his promise of a picnic to the Macgillicuddy Reeks. As he stood centre-kitchen, extolling the virtues of picnics in general, and the Kerry mountains in particular, Tommo lurched in from the back kitchen, arms windmilling, wordlessly opening and closing his mouth.

'He doesn't want to go on the picnic,' Cissie translated.

'It's as well — cars disturb him,' said Babs, resplendent in green slacks and a white shirt. She was carrying a mauve jacket and a cartwheel hat with a chiffon bandeau. A pair of white-framed sunglasses nestled in the perfection of her hair.

'He gets sick. Pukes everywhere,' added Kate.

'Don't I know? I'll stay with him,' said Babs magnanimously. 'I wouldn't say no to the chance to put my feet up quietly.'

Tommo was one thing. But a picnic without Babs was a different matter. Foxy would not have her left behind. By God, he determined to make up for his past misdemeanours. But she would have to do her bit as well. He scratched his head, put on his cap and looked petulant, as though going to burst into tears.

Cissie, elbows dimpling, cutting soda bread, said, 'Tommo and I'll stay here, so.'

'You could do with the break.' Babs had made herself comfortable on Tommo's trestle bed.

'I've no need for a break.' The pursuit of leisure had not reached Fenit, certainly not Cissie. When she sat, she prepared vegetables, worked on herbal remedies, or mended clothes. 'If I've the time, it would be better served gettin' Mossie to bring us over to Broody. And Tommo'll come with us.'

Triumphantly turning to Babs, Foxy said, 'There now. There's no reason for you to stay. The picnic'll do you good.'

Kate interrupted: 'I'll be staying here too.'

'And may I ask why?' thundered Foxy, turkey-cock red.

'My hair. I don't go out.'

Over Foxy's dead body would his daughter miss the picnic. Hair or no hair, she was coming.

Kate, recognising when she was beaten, appeared

a few minutes later wearing a yellow head-scarf, fashioned into a turban.

Babs passed no comment.

Unlike Foxy. 'All you'd need is a grass skirt and you could join those savages in Africa,' he bellowed, striding ahead to his beloved Vauxhall, Babs running to keep up with him, followed by Rose, and with Kate trailing behind.

Suddenly Kate gave a strangled yelp, shot past Rose and, head down, dived into the car. She had seen Mikey, swinging up the road. Her first sighting of him since her hair.

When Mikey saw the group emerging from Cissie's, he hesitated, unsure. Glad Rose was back.

Out of the corner of his eye, Foxy, halfway into the driver's seat, saw him, stopped and stared. At the top of his voice, over the roof of the car, he called to Babs, 'A teddy boy. Here. You wouldn't expect that in a place like this. Bad enough in town.'

Then he got into the car, shut the door gently and took off smoothly. Foxy behind the wheel was a model of decorum and bore little relation to his usual self.

Rose wondered about Mikey and what he would do for the remainder of the day. 'Mikey was too far away to hear,' she comforted Kate.

At Babs's insistence, they headed towards Killarney. 'I refuse to go into the wilds of the mountains for a picnic. The lakes are a nice place to relax — a good crowd of people around and the car right beside us. I'm sure Rose would prefer it.'

Rose's ears were so sore that she could not care

less. With the car's each bump and pothole, a hot judder ran from her lobes into her head.

'Over-commercialised place, Killarney,' muttered Foxy. 'Far better to enjoy scenery than people.'

His wife shushed him firmly and, above the roar of the engine, Rose and Kate could distinctly hear the words 'Dublin', 'whiskey' and 'cars'. At his insistence, they were taking the scenic route.

'You know,' said Foxy, many miles later and after a surfeit of the luscious scenery of the area, 'there's the best mushrooming field ever just down this boreen.'

Babs was not keen. 'What do we want with mushrooms? You've enough food to feed an army.'

'Oh, just let's go to Killarney and get it over with,' Kate said sulkily.

Foxy would not be deterred and, to the chorus of Babs's grumpy complaints, butted the car down a rutted lane coiling between a patchwork of small fields. With gentle revs, he stopped abruptly and turned off the engine. He got out, rubbed a bit of dust off the bonnet, stretched, inhaled deeply and exhaled noisily.

It was a glowing day of crackling air. After the night's heavy rain, a newly washed blue sky arched over distant fields. Following Foxy, Rose and Kate wriggled through a hawthorn hedge. There it was. A field full of mushrooms the size of plates.

'It's a magic field,' Foxy told the girls, stuffing the pockets of his sports jacket with mushrooms, taking off his cap, filling it to overflowing. Kate looked at him sceptically. 'Mushrooms come out in the morning, but this field produces for me no matter when I come. Pick them carefully so you don't damage the spoors.'

Rose filled her skirt with the pink-underbellied delicacies. It was beautiful in this cool, grassy lap of earth, this song-filled field.

Foxy, like an enthusiastic child, waddling from clump to clump, extolled how mushrooms actually grew before their very eyes. Well, almost. Kate, distanced from her father, plucked the nodding ox-eye daisies that rimmed the hedgerow.

Clucking impatience, Babs peered over the hedge, cartwheel hat and glasses firmly in place, giving her a comically mushroom-like appearance. She announced her intention of driving back to Fenit on her own if they did not come immediately.

Foxy responded with alacrity; the thought of Babs crashing the gears of his beloved Wyvern was beyond contemplation. He loaded the mushrooms into the boot and reversed carefully back up the laneway.

By now everyone was hungry and Foxy's suggestion of stopping to eat was greeted with enthusiasm. He knew just the spot, he said, making an elaborate turning to the left, down another rutted laneway, peaking the brow of a hillock, where he parked, looking down over a small lake.

Bustling around, he issued orders with military precision. 'I'll get the primus going. Babs, you're to oversee laying out the food. Kate's in charge of spreading the rug and tablecloth and putting out the cutlery and dishes. Rose is in for the lesson of a lifetime in the art of cooking mushrooms.'

On a biscuit-tin lid he put a generous lump of

butter, and held this makeshift frying pan over the flame of the primus, deaf to Babs's protestations that she was dying for a cup of tea. Rose prepared the mushrooms.

'Wiped. Never peeled.' Foxy shuddered at the idea. 'Ruins the flavour.'

The mushrooms he stood upwards on the lid, with a mini knob of butter and a dribble of salt in each cup, then fried, 'until soft, never limp'. Served on buttered brown soda bread, they were a feast fit for a king.

The picnic took so long and everyone was so relaxed that when Babs finally looked at her watch and drew Foxy's attention to the time, he said, in mock dismay, 'Oh, dear, Killarney will have to wait for another day.'

Easing back on his elbows in anticipation of further relaxation, he asked, 'Does anyone know where the first picnic took place?' Nobody did and nobody looked as though they cared until he said, 'Right here.' Rose's interest was pricked. She was continually fascinated with the richness and variety of the local history.

'Kerry is the kingdom of the picnic,' he assured them and, showman that he was and believer in the tension of silence, waited for someone to ask for an explanation. Predictably it was Rose. With a great chortle, Foxy Mac jumped to his feet and spread his arms wide. 'In times gone by, the great Macgillicuddy used to sit here in the drivin' rain lookin' down to the water's edge, eatin' smoked salmon and Irish soda bread.'

Foxy had won. Despite themselves, they had picnicked in the foothills of the Macgillicuddy mountains. And enjoyed it. Babs, mellowed by the day out, shot her husband a fond look and remarked, 'I might have known you'd get your own way.'

Foxy smirked, 'It's seldom enough I manage to outwit you.'

Kate, pulling at his sleeve, asked in a small voice, 'Please, will you come when my bandages are being taken off?'

'I wouldn't miss it for anything,' he assured her in the loud voice of the reformed man wallowing in the joys of family life.

Rose did not see Mikey that evening, but next day was carragheen sale day. A real opportunity. Between them Cissie and Rose had looked after and turned Kate's crop.

Kate was mercenary and acquisitive where money was concerned, but even the enticement of payment would not tempt her out. Striking a dramatic pose, she announced, 'I'd sooner do without my money than have Mikey see me like this. Remember, Mossie says the going rate is seven and six a stone. I should have that.'

'I wouldn't think so,' interrupted Cissie, busy chopping cabbage. 'It takes a lot of carragheen to make up the stone.'

The agent who weighed and paid was talked about in whispers. The fact that he was not a subject for local gossip only added to his mystery. He seemed to come out of nowhere and return to nowhere. Stories abounded about how clever he was. What an astute businessman. It was said he was as sharp as a cut-throat razor and there was not a trick in the book which would take him in.

One young fellow had meticulously scattered small stones throughout his carragheen to add to the weight. Without as much as a contrary word, but with everyone looking on, the agent had him tip his crop out on the grass. With his fraud common knowledge, the perpetrator and his family were shamed, though if he had got away with it, he would have been a local hero.

Cissie and Rose stood with the other women at the edge of the strand, waiting for the agent, Rose jigging from one foot to the other, with a mixture of ill-concealed excitement and impatience; traditionally the men congregated with the mounded carragheen at the back of the strand.

Eventually a donkey and cart could be seen zig-zagging through the tufty field which lay on the hinterland. As it drew closer, Rose could see the cart laden with weighing scales and black weights and a stack of hessian sacks.

Not the slightest indication of awareness did the agent give as he dismounted to lead the donkey over the rough terrain. He was a bottle-shouldered, dark-coated man of indeterminate years, with a felt hat crushed down on his head. Skinny, bow-legged and narrow-faced. His black overcoat was tinged green with age, and his belt was a fraying rope. No way an awesome figure.

Rose wished Kate were with her to share the ludicrousness of the moment and trade outrageous remarks. In straggling bunches at a suitably reverent distance, the group, Rose trotting demurely beside Cissie, followed the agent across the top of the strand.

Mossie was much in evidence at the sale site, dealing with the agent, corralling the sellers into order, and negotiating money. The quality of the carragheen played an important part in finalising the price. Though the crop was small, this had been a good year.

Most families kept back a certain amount of carragheen to take home to make into blancmange-like puddings and drinks for colds and flu — well spiked with poteen for the men. If all the stories were to be believed, a feed of carragheen worked miracles for sickly calves, cattle and even donkeys. The women who laundered the priest's vestments blessed the stiffening properties of the water carragheen was steeped in.

Neither girl made the stone weight. Rose's carragheen yielded six shillings and eleven pence and, much to Kate's disgust, she received five pence less.

There was no sign of Mikey. Rose fretted and Cissie hoped he had taken her hint.

CHAPTER TWENTY

'I feel awful.' Kate, just rumpled out of bed, was grinning widely as she came out to the back kitchen, rubbing her eyes. Cissie, her morning face crumpling concern, asked, 'What's wrong, *a stór*?'

'I'd love some turnover for breakfast and I feel awful asking Rose to get it,' said Kate, mischievously, her eyes laughing, her hand across her mouth.

Cissie, despite her good intentions about not spoiling Kate, fulfilled most of her whims. 'Not to worry, I'll get it. When I'm finished here.'

Kate, hand on heart, answered, 'Now I do feel awful, putting you to all that trouble.' It was not her way to back off and settle for the freshly made spotted dog, propped up on the windowsill, cooling, wrapped in a towel to keep the crust soft.

These days Rose knew Cissie watched her every move and used all kinds of lame excuses to keep her around. 'I'll go,' she said and, before Cissie could protest, was out the door and up the path into the blue-sky morning, with warm air and a vagrant breeze playing hide-and-seek with the flirty white clouds.

As she meandered back clutching the flimsily wrapped loaf, Mikey appeared out from Tansey's gate. It was five days since they had seen each other. He gave her such a fright that she dropped the bread on the road. He must have been waiting. As though they had spoken only a few minutes ago, he asked, 'D'ya like dolphins?'

Rose, remembering their last time on the cliff-top, was flustered. Dusting off the bread with her skirt, she replied, 'I don't know. I've to get back. Kate wants this for breakfast. And Cissie's like a jailer.'

The shadows on the road between them shifted capriciously, blown by the wind. As though he had not heard, Mikey asked, 'So, d'ya want to come and see one?'

'Are you sure it isn't a mermaid?' she joked.

Only the other day Kate had read out a snippet from the paper about a mermaid being seen in Darby's Bed in Ballybunion.

Instead of joking with him, Rose wanted to tell Mikey she had missed him, to put her arms around him. Wouldn't she go visit the devil himself in his company? This would be her first real date with him. A proper asking date. Wondering how she would escape Cissie, she stalled for time. 'Isn't the dolphin supposed to be a bit of a lucky mascot?'

She had heard that, rather like the Swans of Lir, the Fenit dolphin was destined to remain in the area. The story was that when his mate was taken ill, he had escorted her to Cahirciveen where she had beached and died. Afterwards he had swum around to Fenit and there he remained.

She did know a bit about dolphins. On her attic-tidying sojourn when she had been reunited with Susan's head, she had come across an old book of her father's. A slim volume on the archaeological digs in

Crete, showing dolphins as an integral part of the culture as far back as 2000 BC.

Squatting on the dusty floor of the attic, with motes of dust circling the waggling light-bulb which swung from a fraying three-strand flex, Rose had been transported back in time to when dolphins had had the status of friendly gods. She had never known there were dolphins in Ireland.

Rubbing her right foot against the back of her left leg, Rose decided to keep quiet about her bit of knowledge.

'I could introduce you to him,' Mikey enticed, watching the expressions flit across Rose's face. He felt overawed in an awkward way by her very presence. Since the incident on the cliff-top, she invoked in him, even more than lust, a protective tenderness. It was a sensation he had not known existed, one with which he was unfamiliar, but which made him feel manly and in control. He would get that bastard Jammy O'Brien yet, but not with Rose around.

An introduction to a dolphin? That, Rose thought, seemed a bit far-fetched. 'Where is this dolphin?' she asked.

'Off the shore a bit. He likes to swim with humans.'

'I'll go. Before tea.' She hoped she would be able to get out.

'Make it later. He's more playful around sunset,' said Mikey. 'See ya, so, by the pier, then.'

He went through the gate, into the field, as quickly and as silently as he had come. When Rose looked back, she thought she saw another figure. It looked like Maryann, but she could not be certain. Perhaps she was imagining things.

The gods smiled on Rose that afternoon. Cissie and Mossie were visiting Broody, and Tommo, who would never miss a chance of riding with the donkey and cart, had gone with them.

Cissie, a strong believer in the devil tempting idle hands, left Rose and Kate with a scissors apiece and a plentiful supply of *The Kerryman*.

On the front page was a picture of a bride-to-be, at her kitchen shower, grinning like a Cheshire cat.

'Daft, isn't she, getting excited about that?' Kate wrinkled her nose. 'When I get married, it won't be pots and pans I'll be thinking of. I bet Mikey won't either.' And she turned the page.

Rose did not comment. She felt awkward when the subject of Mikey came up. Sooner or later, Kate would have to know. The longer the deception continued, the worse Rose felt. But Mikey was her biggest slumbering thought ever. One she could never, no matter what, imagine releasing into the public domain.

'Don't you wish we could go to Puck Fair?' Kate was still on about that.

Rose would never get used to Kate's habit of butterflying from one subject to another. 'Yes,' she said with more enthusiasm than she felt, relieved at the change of subject.

'Imagine, it's going to be on television. And so's the Festival. We'll be able to see that in Hurley's shop on the Mall. Poor you, you'll be gone.'

Rose would be back in Dublin by the end of

August. Only a few weeks before school opened, when she would know the results of her Inter Cert. As the time drew near and she thought more about it, she felt increasingly confident that she would achieve good honours.

She had to get a new gymslip, cardigan and blouses. Thankfully, the last she would ever need, as it was an outfit which must have been chosen by the nuns to inflict the most hideous shape on its wearer. And new books for the Leaving Certificate which she would sit in two years' time. Then freedom. She couldn't wait for it.

But for now there was Mikey. And the dolphin. She had no option, on this occasion, but to take Kate into her confidence.

Keep it off-hand, she told herself. Embroidering Mikey's invitation with casual humour. Going as far as to say that, of course, Kate was welcome too. For a horrible moment, Kate's face lit up with mischief and it looked as though she could be tempted. So much so that her question took Rose by surprise.

'You're going with him, aren't you?' she asked in a sad little voice, her eyes full of hurt.

'What do you mean?' Rose stalled.

'You know … going out with him? You are. You could have told me. It wasn't fair not to.'

'I'm not sure we're going out. He's never said.'

'What's stopping you asking him? Isn't it about time you knew where you stood?' snapped Kate, turning back to the paper.

Kate was right. Dammit. Life was so complicated. But she wouldn't think about it now. She had better get going. She would deal with the matter later. She really would.

In for a penny, in for a pound, Rose thought, slipping into their bedroom, opening the chest of drawers and sliding out Doreen's bra.

'What are you doing?' Kate called. She was always so on the ball.

'Just getting my togs,' assured Rose, stripping silently, hoping Kate would stay where she was. She wedged her bodice under the mattress on her side of the bed and slipped her arms into the bra. It felt gorgeous. Soft and satiny. Firm and sophisticated. She had to turn it around to the front to fasten the clasp. It would take practice to be able to do it up at the back.

She wished her breasts were bigger as she eased them into the cups. However, when she slipped her aertex shirt back on, she was pleased with her womanly shape. So pleased that she thought she had better take a cardigan to cover it up from Kate.

By the time Rose arrived at the pier, she had convinced herself that Mikey would not turn up. But he was there before her, leaning over the wall, staring down into the sea, chopping grey, cold and forbidding with little white-capped ripply waves lip-lapping the pier wall.

At the bottom of the steps a small, pointed-prow currach rattled in its mooring, rather like a Viking ship. Rose had thought they would swim out to the dolphin.

Mikey went first, steadying the rocking of the boat while she climbed down the steps, clutching her towel-wrapped togs. Omigod, he had no togs! Gesturing her towards the back, he took the middle section and fitted the oars into the locks. Dipping and pulling. Oars and ocean in harmony, and they were soon out of the harbour.

'What about you and Maryann?' she blurted out after a while, unnerved by the way he was watching her. No sooner were the words out of her mouth than she wanted to suck them back. She had never meant to mention Maryann. She had intended to follow Kate's advice. To ask about them, their relationship.

He paused in his rowing. 'What about Maryann and me?'

'Is she your girlfriend, or what?' Rose's voice sounded very small in the expanse of water.

'If ya think that, what're ya doing here?'

'I wondered.'

'Can't ya let it be?' he said. 'And don't listen to everything ya hear.'

Rose couldn't. 'You're always with her. I saw you this morning.'

'Maryann's not your business.' His voice was cold and the shore seemed far away.

'Am I your girlfriend?' As soon as it was out, Rose tried to swallow back the question; her voice had emerged as a pathetic little squeak.

Again Mikey rested on his oars and looked at her. 'What do ya think?'

After the other day, surely Rose did not need to ask. She should know she was the only girl he wanted. Hadn't he proved it by not messing with her? Stopping kissing her had taken every vestige of his willpower. She must know that. He should be the one wondering. The way she had disappeared for days. And Cissie telling him to back off.

When she did not answer, he started rowing again. As he rowed, the pink-streaked sunset turned to gold, dimpling in its final burning haze. When he stopped, the currach rested in a pool of cold flame.

Rose put down her hand and stroked the sea's calm surface. Perhaps for luck. Maybe to call up the dolphin. They sat, she and Mikey, in silence, each locked in their private thoughts. At least he no longer winked. That was some consolation.

After a while, a dorsal fin, curved like a gondola, broke the smooth water. In the last light the dolphin's body burnished jonquil-coloured. Then it arched upwards. Rose and Mikey watched in wonder as it romped near the boat, arching, bending, curving, diving, emitting shrill sounds of pleasure.

Mikey stood up, the currach rocking wildly from side to side. He yanked off his shirt, undid the great silver buckle of his belt, kicked off the thick crêpe-soled shoes, pulled off his socks by their toes. Horrified, Rose averted her eyes as he undid the buttons of his fly and wriggled out of his tight black drainpipes. His togs were blue, like her father's.

'Come on, so. Get in.' With an even fiercer rocking action, Mikey disappeared over the side of the currach to be immediately joined by the dolphin.

Rose hesitated, torn between leaping in, clothes and all, and wriggling into a bathing suit in a wobbling boat. Decisions. Decisions. She kicked off her sandals and jumped in, her blue cotton skirt umbrella-ing wildly around her. Omigod. She had forgotten. Doreen's bra. It would get soaked in the sea.

With a great whoosh, the dolphin was in front of her, seeming to tread water. He was so close she could reach out and touch his snout. And his eyes were soft and gentle, his mouth curved in a smile. Silence stretched between them. For one exquisite moment, Rose was — just was. Complete in being. That one moment was enough. She would remember it for the rest of her life.

Then the tempo changed. The dolphin became full of playful cavorting, leaping balletically, trumpeting joy. Mikey joined them and his face was full of wonder. 'This one sure likes the wimen,' he said with an admiring look at Rose.

The dolphin was kneading the water in front of her, assessing her, watching her through his button eyes, his mouth wide open in a laugh. He had little pearly teeth, just like a baby's. And she laughed back at him. Then, in another mood change, he emitted a series of squeaks and high-pitched sounds.

'He's talkin' to ya,' said Mikey, swimming alongside her, his limbs long and pale. 'Answer him.'

And Rose talked back with incomprehensible soundings which came from she knew not where. But they made sense to both girl and dolphin.

'After watchin' the pair o'ye, I can believe that, after us humans, dolphins are the most intelligent beings on earth,' admitted Mikey. 'Probably more intelligent than some of us.'

That evening off the coast of Kerry Rose felt that a primitive tableau as old as time was being enacted.

She could feel a universal harmony, and nature seemed to be holding its breath, as she, female human, and the dolphin, male animal, communicated. The sea gods were in attendance. Of that she was sure. And Mikey's face was bathed golden in the sunset.

Then the magic was over. The dolphin hooted, leapt once more into the air, dived into the sea and was gone. With his passing, he left her bereft. Her life-force sapped, she felt cold, laden down with her lumbering clothes.

After such an experience and in this dizzy place of magic, to return to reality Rose needed the mundane, the ordinary, needed to hear her voice, to listen to Mikey talk. Above all, she craved his touch.

He too, even as he dragged her into the currach, was lost in his own world, locked into himself. Profoundly moved. He wanted to reach out to Rose. Hold her, stroke her gently. Not with the passion that had flared between them. Not yet. The intensity of that had frightened him. He wondered did she think him soft, the way he had pulled back.

Pulling up his trousers, he jammed on his shoes, stabbed his arms into his shirt and stuck the oars into their locks. With a set look on his face and his eyes cast down, he started the silent row back.

In the fast-diminishing light, Rose saw in the water a spectrum of colours, even more wondrous than on the day she had picked carragheen: the deep, almost black blue that glittered then paled through every shade of blue until it became green, a thousand greens and greys and browns until it met the silvery line of the horizon.

Mikey watched the range of expressions flit across Rose's face. Wistful, sad, thoughtful, embarrassed. When she looked at him and smiled, it was as though the sun had come out. He wished he had the words to tell her what was in his heart. Instead he said, 'You're cold. D'ya want my shirt?'

'No. I'm fine.' And then, 'Thanks.'

It was not dark yet. Maybe he would bring her around the back of the boathouse. It would be quiet there now. Nobody about. He would insist she take his shirt. They could talk. He would explain to her about Maryann. About a lot of things. It began to rain as they reached the jetty. Luckily the boathouse was sheltered.

While Mikey was tying up the boat, Rose touched him lightly on the shoulder. 'I'll be off.' He let her go without comment, watching as she ran up the pier.

Head high, confused and bewildered, she walked in her sodden clothes in the wet darkness, through the village, without meeting anyone. It seemed as though the gods continued to smile on her when she found that Kate had fallen asleep on the trestle, and Cissie and Tommo had not yet returned.

Rose put Doreen's bra into the oven of the range to dry off. After all her trouble, Mikey had not even known she was wearing it. Such a waste.

The gods had not been smiling on Rose. They had been mocking her, playing a joke, lulling her into a false sense of security.

The fact that she had not seen anyone on her

damp journey back from the pier to Cissie's did not mean that she had not been seen. The village had eyes and ears in every wall, a thriving network of innuendo and communication.

Cissie, Mossie and Tommo were late returning from Broody's. Just when they were about to leave, Broody took a turn for the worse. Cissie, promising she would help him 'pass over', took off her coat again and sat down, then placidly gave out the Rosary.

When he drifted off to sleep, she had two of his cousins move the head of his bed to the south, the healing position. Broody had insisted it stay north, the way he remembered it from childhood. An hour later, Cissie was not in the least surprised when he sat up and demanded a shot of poteen.

Next morning, Mags hotfooted it up to Cissie's, puffed with self-importance, her eyes sparkling gossip. First she enquired after Broody, nodding her head at the sadness of it, *ochón*ing as she dry-washed her hands. 'And there's nothing you can do for him?' she asked, the tone of her voice casting aspersions on Cissie's integrity as a healer.

That end of business dispensed with, she got down to the real reason for her visit. Tattle about her grandson's and Rose's nocturnal doings. She prattled with malicious delight, sitting at the range, her knees wide apart, slurping from a mug of tea. Rose had been seen walking through the village, then on the pier getting into a currach with Mikey. Rose's wet and dripping return had also been noted.

After the trouble she had gone to in the interests of Rose's welfare, Mags was bitterly disappointed at evoking no more than a deadpan reaction from Cissie, and not a sign of Rose being called to account.

Cissie was too wise for that. Neither would she go behind Rose's back to Kate. She would not put either of them in the position of having to lie. And didn't she need Mags and Jamie to bring Elizabeth from the airport in three days' time?

CHAPTER TWENTY-ONE

Rose was beginning to get used to Kate's fluctuating moods, which these days involved more silent sulking than good humour. Following Cissie's example, she tried to ignore them, though every now and again she had an attack of guilt, sure that her relationship with Mikey was contributing to Kate's misery. Rose was glad Kate had not referred to him since the evening of the dolphin. She still did not know where she stood with him.

The bra she had returned to the back of its drawer. As far as she knew, Kate had never worn it. Other than feeling a bit scratchy and smelling a bit salty, it didn't appear to be any the worse for its watery outing.

Elizabeth arrived in a swirl of clothes, bags, cases and parcels, teetering down the little path in white stilettos, the bouffant skirt of her blue dress puffed out with loads of starched petticoats, her waist nipped in to hourglass proportions by a wide white belt.

Jamie, sweating and red-faced, was laden to the chin with her luggage. Mags, the dead heat of the afternoon getting to her, trailed tiredly behind, though she still managed a triumphant smirk.

It was difficult to believe that Elizabeth was Cissie's sister. Even though she was ancient, the girls thought she was gorgeous, like a Hollywood film star. Talking non-stop in a real Yankee accent. Laughing in a wide-mouthed way that showed off her big teeth, waving her hands around with their red-painted nails. She was without inhibition, shouting and laughing as humour and emotions took her.

'What a reception committee,' she drawled after kissing everyone on both cheeks, 'Mother Macree and the Playboy of the Western World. If I'd known what I was in for I'd have turned around and taken the next flight back.' And she roared with laughter.

Rose and Kate grinned widely; Jamie smiled nervously; and Mags twitched uneasily. Cissie fussed with the kettle. Mossie, puffing away on his pipe, paid no attention to the atmosphere of hyperbole.

Drawing her shawl firmly around her, Mags, with an overload of dignity, said, 'If Jamie and myself aren't required for anything else, we'll be going.' The distinct implication was that they had been worked to the bone and for little thanks. When nobody replied one way or the other, she added importantly, 'As Jamie's to drive to Tralee tonight. For the bank. Tomorrow, ya know, I'll take him below and do a fry-up for him.'

'We've a cold chicken and salad,' Cissie could not resist saying. The chicken, courtesy of Babs, was one-up on a fry. Everyone knew that. 'And ye're welcome to stay.'

'Jamie's a man who enjoys his fry,' decreed Mags.

Elizabeth lavished praise and cooed thanks on aunt and nephew for their kindness in taking pity on a poor returning emigrant! How would she have managed without them? Mags lapped up the approbation, shooting triumphant glances at Cissie.

When they were gone, Elizabeth heaved a gusty sigh of relief, raised her arms above her head and, to the amazement of all, touched the floor without bending her knees, her puffy petticoats fluffing out like a dancer's tutu. She repeated the exercise three times.

'Yoga,' she explained. 'Great for relaxation and for keeping your figure. The latest thing in America.' In a quick movement, she knelt down, clicked open a tan leather suitcase and began to scrabble through its contents. 'Time for presents.' With a rueful little laugh, she apologised, 'Didn't know my sister'd be entertaining two gorgeous girls and a handsome hunk of a guy.'

Rose and Kate were mesmerised by Elizabeth; they had never come across such vivacity, much less been on the receiving end of it. Tommo, thumping his bottom against the wall, could not take his eyes off her.

For Cissie there was an oblong box in red foil paper. For Mossie a cob pipe, which he quickly put in his pocket, nodding his thanks to Elizabeth. Cissie's box contained a pair of shoes. Silver with red velvet bows, nestling in white tissue paper. Cissie lifted them out, held them up, shook her head, and looked at them from all sides. Despite having her teeth in, her smile was warm.

Tommo clapped his hands, rocking backwards and forwards on his heels. Cissie set the shoes on the floor, where they wobbled for a moment, then straightened and seemed to stand to attention. Tommo lay down beside them on his stomach. Stroking and crooning. Faster and faster. Until he knocked them over. Cissie, putting a restraining hand on his arm, motioned him upwards, sat him at the table, and handed him the closed box.

Tongue protruding from the side of his mouth, he eased off the lid. Inside was the crumpled tissue paper, which he lifted out and, with awkward sweeps of his hands, set about smoothing. It flittered in long tears.

Tommo looked in disbelief, then, with a bellow of rage, leapt to his feet. Arms flailing, paper scattering, he threw the box on the floor and jumped up and down on it until it was flattened. Face crumpling into great racking sobs, he fell back onto the trestle bed. Cissie, arms around him, drew his head to her breast, crooning and stroking his hair until he calmed down.

While this was going on, Elizabeth, helped by Rose and Kate, transferred her luggage to the bedroom she would share with Cissie. She tipped over her suitcases and out spilled a froth of the most beautiful clothes in the most wondrous colours and materials. Crisp yellow cotton trimmed with rosy strawberries; a slender-skirted lime-green Moygashel; pale-pink gingham; blue voile with navy braid; white piqué with green roses. Too many to absorb. Some of the dresses had the latest cap-sleeves, others were sleeveless, more had short sleeves. A few had matching puffy under-skirts. Some even had toning shoes and cardigans.

'What do you think?' Elizabeth drawled, hands on hips, scarlet lips pursed in concentration. 'What's your favourite?' Rose's turquoise-blue party dress paled into insignificance beside the magnificence of these American clothes. 'Go on. Choose one,' she urged. 'As a present.'

Elizabeth talked in short, sharp, staccato bursts, with a nasal twang that made her seem like a real film star. Her hair was very short and very black, sitting like a cap on her head, with jaggy bits firmly plastered to her forehead.

Rose held the lime against her, while Kate tried the blue. Rose had to hand it to Elizabeth. Not only did she appear not to notice Kate's bandaged head, but she did not bat an eyelid at the smell. Decidedly ripe, like rotting marrow, Rose supposed. Kate seemed oblivious. Cissie never commented. Rose said nothing either. It didn't seem right to complain about something as minor as a smell when Kate could be facing a life of baldness.

Elizabeth, sitting on the bed, legs tucked under her, shook her head, huge white hoop earrings jangling madly. 'The colours do nothing for either of you.' They swapped but still did not meet with Elizabeth's approval. She pulled out the yellow for Rose and the pink gingham for Kate.

'That's more like it. Try them on,' she urged.

But they would not undress in front of a virtual stranger. Clutching the dresses, they crossed the kitchen to their bedroom. There, without ceremony, shapeless cardigans, grey divided skirts and aertex shirts were yanked off. They stood in their flesh-coloured bodices and substantial cotton knickers with elasticated legs.

'This calls for the bra,' said Kate, gleefully turning her back on Rose, stripping off her bodice and, to Rose's horror, reaching into the drawer. So absorbed was Kate with sticking out her chest, sucking in her stomach and admiring her shape in the minuscule mirror, that she noticed nothing amiss with her sister's bra. With a sigh, she said, 'I wish I'd taken the set.'

'What do you mean?'

'Doreen has cami-knickers to match.'

Rose envied Doreen. 'Can I try the bra with my dress?' she asked.

'Certainly not.' Kate busily buttoned the dress all the way down the front and tied the belt with its little white tassels.

'You said I could. Sometime.'

'Well, you can't. I've changed my mind.'

At times like this, when Kate was sharp and spiteful, Rose almost hated her.

Rose might not have a bra, but the dress had its own nylon slip. The top was quite like a bra. A flattish kind of bra with lacy straps and a little bow which nestled between her breasts.

Turning her back on Kate, she slipped out of her bodice and into the dress. It was gorgeous enough to die for; full-skirted with a dropped waist, stopping just below her knees. The little strawberries around the neck looked good enough to eat.

Kate was fulsome in her compliments and Rose reciprocated, casting envious glances at her cousin's jutting bustline.

After they had had their fill of pirouetting, they

sashayed out to the kitchen to show off. As expected, Cissie confirmed how beautiful they were. Ignoring the bulging flesh of her feet, they told her that she, too, was beautiful in her new shoes.

Elizabeth, delighted with the success of the dresses, handed Tommo a silver coin. 'An American dollar. Specially for you,' she twanged. 'Keep it in your pocket always and it'll bring you luck.' Tommo gave a few leaps of delight and a couple of blood-curdling yelps.

The sunshine-yellow dress gave Rose a boost of unexpected confidence. She felt all womanly, and wanted to seek Mikey out actively. 'I think I'll go for a walk,' she said, hoping Cissie's attention would be occupied with Elizabeth.

'Good idea,' answered Elizabeth. 'Won't the pair of you cause a stir, in your finery?' Then, with a gutsy laugh: 'Ye'd better take Tommo with you for protection.'

'Not me. I don't go out,' cried Kate.

'Why ever not?'

'My hair. Look at it.'

'Looks to me as though it's under control,' drawled Elizabeth. 'But suit yourself. So it's up to Rose and Tommo to take the village by storm.'

'I don't think Tommo…' Cissie began. Tommo gave a little twirl, clapped his hands, and grasped at Rose's dress. Sharply, Cissie told him to stop. Usually he obeyed her instantly. This time he kept his grip on the skirt.

Rose, terrified by his strength, smacked his hand away and moved back from him. As he made a grab for her, Cissie stepped between them. Tommo raised his right arm. For an instant it looked as though he would hit her, but instead he dropped his arm, fell back on the trestle and put his head in his hands. 'You're going nowhere today, *a stór*,' said Cissie sadly.

CHAPTER TWENTY-TWO

Rose went out as far as the gate and looked up and down the roadway, but her own innate shyness, and Sister Concepta's homilies about the sin of vanity, made her reluctant to parade through the village to the pier, showing off her finery.

She ran the palms of her hands over her stomach, swaying her hips to the ruffle of the fabric, enjoying the smoothness of the nylon against her breasts. And wished she had a decent pair of flatties or, even better, wedge sandals, like her aunt Josie. At least she had stopped wearing socks. There was a great freedom in the uninhibited wriggling of toes.

Thinking of Mikey, she strolled a little way down the road. Her throbbing body and slumbering thoughts made her feel so deliciously sexy, she knew this had to be real love. She cringed at her immaturity of a few months before. How far she had come since Frank.

Monica said real love was when you would go all the way with someone without even thinking of the consequences. Rose thought she would with Mikey. Well, maybe not quite all the way, not as far as the having-a-baby bit — but would she be able to stop in time? She hoped so. Unless she got carried away on this roller-coaster of passion about which Monica knew so much.

In a way she had been unable to with Frank, she could imagine uncontrollable passion flaring between Mikey and herself, starting with the same lingering, tongue-hunting kisses they had experienced on the cliff. But this time there would be no pulling away, no breaking off. They would progress to undressing each other, in a tearing passion. From the *Angélique* books, Rose knew this was what real lovers did. He yanking her skirt to the floor. She kicking away his drainpipes. He dragging her shirt over her head, her mane of hair tumbling in disarray (pity it was so short). He entranced by her satin bra (never again would she be caught wearing a liberty bodice). He nuzzling her breasts. Imagine, once she had been so green she had wondered did boys even touch breasts. The nuzzling bit she fancied.

She still was not too sure what came next. The all-enveloping vibration of delight which she had dreamed about before ever even meeting Frank, she supposed. Silver paths of touching that would have their bodies humming. Then surrender. Sex blooming between them like a wild flower. And the rush of joyous relief. She knew about that too, but only from reading. Monica had never got that far.

Rose stopped. The outcome of such passion could be terrifying. Pregnancy, the wrath of the Church, not to mention social ostracism.

She shivered in the sunshine as she thought about the consequences. Forever washing and ironing clothes in the moidering heat of the Magdalene Laundry. Sometimes she saw them, the inmates, these fallen women scurrying in pairs through

Donnybrook. Clipped hair, chapped cheeks, red hands, unfocused expressions. Omigod, she would prefer to be dead than to end up like that.

Then she heard a familiar, 'Psst. There ya are.'

Rose expected his eyes to fill with admiration. Hadn't he even noticed her sunshine-yellow dress? 'So I am,' she answered, parodying Kate, fluffing out the skirt. Feeling really confident. 'Look, Cissie's sister gave me a present.' She moved coyly, modelling the dress, proudly showing off her body.

'It's nice.' He took her in with a quick embarrassed glance. She looked so beautiful. Like a lady. Almost untouchable. Quite unlike the rumpled Rose he knew. He thought of Cissie's warning, 'No good can come of it. Only trouble for the both of ye.'

Mikey was no stranger to trouble, he had lived with it all his life. 'Will ya come into the woods?' he asked Rose. Today he would tell her about Maryann.

Carefully, she climbed the five-bar gate and walked tall beside him, through the fields, towards the woods. Black-and-white cows grazed like scattered dominoes, and from the field beyond came the tetchy bleating of sheep. After last night's rain the wood still steamed and pestled, a rank, sexy, undergrowth smell.

Mikey caught her hand, interlocked their fingers and squeezed tightly as they approached his hiding-place. Rose wanted him never to let go.

Her left ear was still hot and throbbing and Cissie was threatening treatment. Pierced ears were definitely not a good idea. Gingerly she rubbed at it.

'What's up with yer ears?' He touched her lobe.

Slowly, hesitantly, as though remembering from a distance: 'My mam had her ears pierced too. She'd the same earrings.' Mikey enfolded Rose in his arms. 'She died on my birthday, the year I was five.'

Rose said nothing. Mikey drew her down to the mossy undergrowth, burying his head in her shoulder, drawing her in close to him.

Rose was certain this was going to be the day. Thanks be to God, she'd removed the bodice and had on the yellow dress. She hoped it wouldn't be ruined. She would have to stop him before the pregnancy bit — better still, keep him above the waist. From Monica she knew that would be dead safe.

She need not have worried. Today there was no passion in Mikey. Just tenderness and sadness. Rose, who craved skin on skin, instead found herself asking, 'What about your father?'

Mikey's face emerged from her shoulder. 'I dunno,' he replied, but without conviction, and his soul was in his eyes. Then he was talking. Telling her. Slowly at first. Then warming to his subject.

Since his mother's death, he had dreamt of finding his father. Despite Mags's scepticism, he had gone to London, Kilburn to be precise, on a kind of pilgrimage, to trace his roots. To look for his father's family. His mother had told him the story, so often that he knew it by heart. The laughing man. High up on the scaffolding. Why did he have to fall?

Mikey had no luck in Kilburn. He met nobody who had known Mick Daw. But it was the place where he tried to shed his Irish identity, to become more like his father, where he got his gear and had his hair cut. His change of image did not bring him any nearer to the father he never knew, and in no way alleviated the ache in his heart.

Since he had come back, his grandmother had worn her what-did-you-expect face, though she had remained silent on the subject.

'And your mother. What happened?' Rose asked, disentangling from him, rising up on her elbow.

'I don't know. I don't remember that birthday, except it's the day my mam died.' Shaking himself, like a sparrow after a bath, fluffing himself up, folding himself down, Mikey ended up shuttered in on himself. Trembling.

His vulnerability brought a new dimension to their relationship. Rose forgot about passion. She felt powerful, in control. In a protective, tender way. Now she was able to reach out, take Mikey in her arms, stroke his hair, murmur endearments. When she looked into his eyes, they held the certainty of love. She knew they were going together, she had no need of verbal confirmation. And she did not even consider Maryann.

Gradually his quivering stopped, and for a time they remained quiet, wrapped together in the silence of twilight. With a shrug, he disentangled himself, lit a cigarette and the silence between them was no longer as easy.

'Come on, so.' Mikey jumped up, eyes blazing, fighting for restoration of his macho image. Raging with himself. Why had he gone on with all that stuff about his parents? And he had still not told Rose about Maryann. He was not about to now. She must think him really soft. He yanked her to her feet and, swinging hands, they walked out from the woods to the meadow where swallows dived after insects and a blushing sun retreated behind the woods.

Rose, a mass of conflicting emotions, but with a new security in her step, thought she would die of happiness.

Now she knew what real love was about. Knew it was much more than uncontrollable passion. Knew that when you have found the real somebody, that somebody special, all that matters is now. Time narrows to an intake of breath, a pulse of sweat. A laugh of eagerness. Sprawling and aching in secret. Dry whispers blurring each other's lips.

To her own amazement, Nance was deriving great pleasure from being with her niece. Doreen's initial sulky shyness had been replaced by a sunny nature and a willing helpfulness. Her neatness and precision appealed and she was very domesticated. Happy to follow her aunt around like a disciple. Nance was in her element.

Doreen too enjoyed being with her aunt. Whether pottering around the house and garden, cooking or just wandering around town, window-shopping. Nance was the mother she wished she had had. Babs was not maternal, always busy, with the hotel on her mind. She never seemed to have time just to sit down and be. Doreen loved the evening meal when they lingered over the last cup of tea, discussing current affairs, the theatre and books. Real conversation.

The outings when Uncle Trevor joined them were brilliant — he was so different from her father. Reliable. Knowledgeable. A mine of information on local history. Be it walking Dún Laoghaire pier, strolling around Howth Head, or visiting St Kevin's settlement in Glendalough. And, of course, his enthusiasm for James Joyce was infectious.

The three of them laughed themselves sick at Maureen Potter and Jimmy O'Dea's summer show in the Gaiety Theatre. After the success of that, Trevor booked for *Juno and the Paycock* at the Abbey Theatre. A powerful play and a great production, they all agreed. Strangely, it was their discussion when they got home, over cocoa and Nance's shortbread biscuits, that paved the way for the confidences next morning between Nance and Doreen: 'The characterisation and language is realistically Dublin,' Trevor insisted.

'That may be so,' Nance conceded, 'but, in my opinion, Sean O'Casey overdid it, to beyond the point of entertainment. What do you think, Doreen?'

Doreen savoured being asked for her opinion, as though it really mattered. She agreed with Nance. She had not known people lived or communicated like that.

Throwing up his hands in a gesture of defeat, with a broad smile, Trevor said, 'Joyce was right. A man born in this country has nets flung at him to hold him back. I'm off to bed. The pair of you are so protected and spoiled, you've no idea of the real world.'

'Wait a minute. I'll be with you,' said Nance, giving him her special little smile.

'Rose is so lucky having a mother like you,' was the way Doreen started next morning. 'The way you can discuss things. Even bad language.'

Doreen could never remember agreeing with her mother, much less having an intellectual discussion. Pushing the wheelbarrow, she trailed around the garden after Nance who was deadheading flowers, a daily chore during the summer months. She hated looking out the windows at dead blooms.

Nance straightened up, tossed a fistful of rumpled pansies into the barrow. 'I wouldn't be sure she thinks that way. But it's nice of you to say so.'

'It's kind of hard at our age…' began Doreen, biting at her lip, 'boys and things….'

'I know,' said Nance. 'But it's important not to grow up too soon.' She snipped off a dead rose-head, scattering red petals on the green lawn. 'Childhood is so precious.' She bent down, scooping up the petals.

'But I'm not a child. And neither is Rose. And because Mammy didn't trust me and wouldn't listen to my side of things, I ended up lying to her. She was so mad. And then I was sent up here. Not that I mind,' she assured. 'I'm having a lovely time.'

Nance laid aside the secateurs, patted a place for Doreen to join her on the garden seat. She had never done this with Rosemary. Never once had they sat together in the garden just chatting. Always she had lectured.

She and Rosemary had been close on the day they had shopped for her party dress. Nance had enjoyed the occasion, remembered feeling lucky and grateful to have the companionship of a daughter. And full of plans for the future. How had it gone so wrong? Though, now that she thought about it, the conversation had been decidedly one-sided. Her side. She had not taken the opportunity to draw Rosemary out.

From Doreen she heard all about Jack, his life of difficulty at home, his ambitions to own his own bar. And, most importantly, how much they loved each other.

'We only ever kiss, you know,' Doreen confided. 'Jack respects me.'

In a way that her friend Dolores, with her seedy memories, never did, Doreen brought Nance back to the early days with Trevor. Their hopes, their dreams, their love for each other. What had gone wrong? Though, strangely, since Doreen's arrival, things between them had been much better. Condoms and all, she had lost herself in their lovemaking last night without even the smallest twinge of guilt. 'Do you miss him?' Nance asked.

'Yes, of course. But he'll be there when I get back.'

'Do you write to each other?' Nance had only noticed the occasional scribble to Doreen from Babs.

'We thought it better not to.' Doreen grinned.

How honourable the pair of them were. 'He's a lucky boy,' Nance told her.

'I'm lucky too,' Doreen assured. Then, 'I bet you trust Rose.'

Nance took a deep breath. 'I'm afraid not. And I never had the full story. There was a boy. They were seeing each other. After school, I believe. We put a stop to it.'

'Who's we?'

'Your uncle, the nuns and myself.'

'Who was he?' Doreen was curious, certain this boyfriend had to have some major defect. Her mind ran riot. A thief? A cheat? Dishonourable in some awful way?

'I'm not really sure.'

'You mean you stopped Rose's friendship just because it was with a boy?' Doreen was incredulous. 'That's unlike Uncle Trevor.'

'And the nuns,' Nance justified. Hurt Doreen had not queried her role in the affair.

'Don't mind the nuns. They're away with the birds. What would they know about life, locked up in a convent?'

Nance sat up a little straighter on the bench. 'In our defence, Rosemary wasn't straight with us.'

'When Mammy disapproves of something, it's very hard to talk to her. She just won't listen. And often I don't even try. Maybe that's what happened with Rose?'

Nance nodded. 'Perhaps. Sometimes it's easier to play the parentally heavy hand than to listen.'

Kindly, Doreen justified, 'Mammy's a lot to put up with. Daddy — the way he drinks. He's most unreliable. Having to run the business on her own. And Tommo. And, I suppose, now me. I'm probably the last straw.'

'It's hard for all of you. Though it could be worse. You've a lovely home, don't want for anything,' said Nance briskly, standing up, touching Doreen affectionately on the shoulder. 'You've been a great help. I do see things more from Rosemary's perspective now. Perhaps I was hard on her.'

'Tell her. Talk to her and let her talk to you.'

'I will. And I won't wait until she comes back,' Nance promised. 'I'll write to her while she's still in Fenit.'

CHAPTER TWENTY-THREE

Rose and Kate were fascinated by Elizabeth. She lived in her own glamorous world and took little part in either the domestics of the household or the general activity of the village.

A great one for staying on in bed, resting, she did not emerge before noon, always looking stunning, in a bouffant skirt, high-heeled white shoes, jangly earrings and immaculate make-up. The most she took before leaving on the early afternoon bus to Tralee was a few sips of tea.

For Kate, America was Hollywood. She paid no attention to the fact that Elizabeth lived in New York, on the opposite coast, thousands of miles away. Considering herself an expert on film stars and their goings-on, she justified Elizabeth's lifestyle with, 'That's the way film stars live. Out drinking champagne until the small hours of the morning. So, of course, they've to get their beauty sleep. And they always wear make-up.'

Often Rose did not bother contradicting Kate's flamboyant statements. But on this subject she could not resist: 'She's not a film star. She's always home on the last bus. I wouldn't think she's drinking champagne, not even in Tralee.' This last remark was in deference to Kate, and the trendiness of her home town, particularly this year, with the Festival, its complement of horse racing, civic receptions, street entertainment and competitions.

'She's very mysterious. Probably has a past,' Rose conceded one noon, watching Elizabeth teeter up the garden path, leaving behind a legacy of crimson lipstick on her cup.

'Probably an unhappy love affair — maybe several,' mused Kate, helping herself to a bite of the bread and jam Cissie had optimistically prepared for her sister. 'Bet she's had at least one Hollywood film star as a lover, probably several, she knows such a lot about them and their love affairs.'

'Maybe she's more into millionaires. There's a lot of them in America. And she doesn't live anywhere near Hollywood,' finished Rose defiantly.

'Film stars are always travelling.' Kate was determined to have the last word.

A few days later, when the girls came in from the back meadow, parked across the gateway was Foxy's Vauxhall. He was already inside, drinking tea, and Cissie was acting somewhat too polite. The bright yellow legs and feet of a chicken stuck out of a brown paper bag on the table, alongside a half tin of Afternoon Tea biscuits.

When Foxy saw the girls, he lurched to his feet, knocking over the chair, grasping the edge of the table to prevent himself from falling over. Sitting back down with a bump. His eyes were red-rimmed and underlined with dark scoops of tiredness.

'Oh, God,' whispered Kate to her cousin. 'He's on the booze again. This is so embarrassing.' Like a punctured balloon, she shrivelled into herself.

Cissie hushed at her, saying it would be all right and not to worry, but Kate broke away from her, stood in front of Foxy, and screamed, 'Get out. Go away. I don't ever want to see you again.' Dashing into the bedroom, she slammed the door. Cissie went after her.

Rose, looking at Foxy, recognising the hardship and heartbreak of his drinking, understood for the first time that there was nothing amusing about him or his behaviour.

He swayed upright, muttering about rudeness, and his daughter not having the manners to greet her father with the respect that was his due. Shaking his head, he blinked rapidly, trying to focus on Rose, stuck his face into hers and started humming the first few bars of 'The Rose of Tralee'. He was pathetic. She backed away towards the range and, when he kept coming, she picked up and speared the poker at him.

'Bloody hell,' he slurred, peering myopically at her. 'Put that down, girl. 'Cos of you, I'm here.'

He patted over his person, again and again, with increasingly frantic gestures, eyeing Rose and the poker warily. 'Woman,' he bellowed at the closed door of the bedroom, 'where's the letter?'

'Where ya put it,' said Cissie, emerging from the bedroom, pointing. There it was, propped behind the vigil light. Taking in Rose's white face and determined expression, she removed the poker from her grasp.

'It ... is ... for ... you,' Foxy enunciated slowly

and with great clarity as though Rose were a stranger to the English language. He made a swaying effort to cross the room. Forestalling him, Cissie reached up and handed the letter to Rose, who recognised Frank's tilting-backwards writing and shoved the envelope into the side pocket of her skirt.

With the astuteness that comes from being half sozzled, Foxy reckoned he was not particularly welcome. Kate, with her prissy attitude, was a real killjoy. Cissie had been polite, but hardly waving the flag of welcome which he considered his due. But Rose's attitude was new. Aggressive and ungrateful. And him driving out all that distance with a letter.

'I … came … out … specially … to … give … it … to you … the letter,' he reminded Rose.

When he got no good out of her, or the others, he said goodbye and huffily staggered out the door and up the little garden.

Rose held Frank's letter, running her fingers over the square creaminess of the envelope. He must have asked Barbara for her address. Certainly her mother would not have given it to him.

Why did life have to be so complicated? Communication had broken down between them and she had not known how to handle it. Well, she had, but had lacked the courage to face up to her parents and the nuns. She had messed up. She was tired of playing and replaying in her mind the Frank scenario until it was like a swarm of flies, going round and round, the continual buzzing making it impossible for her to make sense of it. Still, it was an unresolved issue. And Rose liked her ends neatly tied up.

Using her little finger as a paper-knife, she eased it under the flap of the envelope. Inside were two flute-edged pages. Written on both sides. As Rose read, she became increasingly confused.

Frank apologised for what he referred to as his 'pigheadedness'. He shouldn't have invited Monica to the party. Dublin was miserable. When was she coming back? He hadn't known she was in Kerry. He hoped she was having a good time. Not too good, though.

Then came the really confusing part. He wouldn't have had the nerve to write if he hadn't received her letter. Was it a joke? If so, not a very good one. Surely she knew that sarcasm was the lowest form of wit. And the nerve of her, always going on about his jokes. But it had given him the courage to sound Barbara out. He finished with a row of exclamation marks. After his comment about always knowing that they had a lot in common, but not realising before that it even extended to choice of notepaper. Rose had no idea what he meant.

Omigod. Could Barbara, off her own bat, have decided to act as go-between? Writing Frank a letter purporting to come from her? Perhaps it was out of kindness, trying to mend their rift. No, she decided. That was not Barbara's style.

That night, Rose and Kate sat around the range with Cissie who was working on a bundle of Mossie's heavy woollen socks. Tommo was down with Mossie. He was minus his whittling knife — these days

Cissie only let him have that when he was actually whittling, and where she could keep an eye on him. He was safe with Mossie — out of harm's way — and Mossie had the strength to control his antics if necessary.

'Ugh. They're horrible,' said Kate, looking at the socks. 'Why doesn't he throw them out rather than have you sew them?'

Rose, who, after the hard slog of her tapestry, considered herself a bit of an expert on needlecraft, interrupted her cousin loftily with: 'That's darning, not sewing.'

Cissie corrected the two of them. She was 'turning', not sewing or darning. Turning was a real skill, she told her uninterested audience.

Rose was thinking about Mikey, remembering the way he looked at her; how his shirt rumpled around his neck; the dark hairs on his arms; the warmth of his breath. Above all, his smell — a mixture of sweat and smoke and sea; sometimes it would waft over her so realistically she would believe he was right there beside her. Smells were peculiar. For example, overnight, the pong from Kate's head had disappeared. It was time for the bandages to come off, Cissie had decreed.

Rose knew she had only a skeletal part of Mikey's story. On many occasions she had tried to pluck up the courage to ask Cissie about him and his family. Cissie's kindness and non-judgmental attitude made her intolerance of Mikey all the more unusual.

While acknowledging the heartache Mikey had brought to the village, Cissie had a soft spot for him.

Well she knew that she was the last one who could afford to cast the first stone. Or indeed any stone. None of the circumstances had been Mikey's fault. If fault were to be apportioned, the largest part of it had to lie with Father Florence. That was a frequently occurring heretical thought which she quickly squashed, though every time Mikey's name was mentioned, she was eternally grateful her own Brigid was adopted and safe. She had done the right thing. She could not bear to have Brigid ostracised like Mikey had been and still was.

CHAPTER TWENTY-FOUR

The day the bandages were to be removed from Kate's hair, Mossie appeared shortly after dawn at the back door, with a bucket of water, which Cissie took from him with hardly an acknowledgement and not even the offer of a cup of tea.

Kate, up unusually early, was particularly fractious: snapping at Rose, niggling at Tommo, clinging to Cissie, trailing backwards and forwards to the bedroom.

'When will Mammy be out? Wouldn't you think she'd be here by now?' Biting a chunk from a wedge of bread. 'Maybe it would be better if she didn't come.' Her eyes enormous in her face, wondering whether her father would show up. Seeming to have forgotten her screaming at him that she never wanted to see him again.

Cissie, very much in command, issued instructions in a positive way, determining the placement of Mossie's bucket of water in relation to the slant of the sun with such precision that Rose likened her to Einstein.

Finally satisfied, Cissie sat Kate on a chair at the kitchen table and began unwinding the bandages. The kitchen was silent except for the tick-tock of the clock and the spluttering of the fire from the range.

Tommo, sitting at the table, tongue sticking out the corner of his mouth, grunted concentration. Quiet now, and calm enough to be allowed the whittling knife which he was using on a slab of wood, he paid scant attention to what was going on around him.

His introduction to wood-carving, by Mossie, had been successful beyond anyone's imagination; as well as showing an instinctive feeling for the wood, he had taken to the actual whittling like the proverbial duck to water.

Already he had accumulated several pieces — large hens and tiny cows, his favourite subjects. He had no idea of the size relationship between his subjects, and became red-faced, rattled and aggressive when Mossie pointed out, and even went as far as showing him, that in real life cattle were bigger than fowl.

Neither Cissie nor Rose spoke; they hardly dared breathe. Tommo's breathing continued heavy and laboured, seeming to keep time with each stroke of his knife.

Full of trepidation, Rose watched. Suppose Kate's head had rotted away! As the last of the bandages began to slide off, she offered a quick silent prayer to St Jude — yeah, she knew, always seeming to return to the patron saint of hopeless cases, and her an avowed non-believer. Over the past weeks, she had been so wrapped up in Mikey that the enormity of Kate's predicament had not properly registered.

Cissie, an inscrutable expression on her face, and the pair of round-shaped, wire-framed glasses she and Mossie shared perched on the end of her nose, stood over Kate, running fat, sensitive fingers over her scalp, which was encrusted in a black flaking scab. Kate sat motionless, face scrunched, eyes closed, lips trembling; Rose's fingers were double-crossed, and she hardly dared breathe.

Straightening up, Cissie smiled, her gummy smile of spontaneous delight. 'It's all right, *a stór*, look.'

Kate could not see herself, but she smiled, a watery smile. When Rose scrutinised Kate's head, she could see a faint chicken-like fluff growing on the scabby bald patches.

Tommo jumped up from the table and began dancing around, flailing his arms, stabbing the air with the knife, singing noisily and tunelessly.

Cissie looked sharply at him. 'Take it easy, Tommo. Easy. Quieten down now.'

He obeyed instantly, going back to his whittling. It looked like being one of his more biddable days. Cissie sighed with relief. 'Tommo's a real Kerryman. Always on for a bit of a celebration.'

And to prove he was, he let out a few blood-curdling yelps and whoops.

Cissie told Kate not to look into the mirror until her hair had been washed. In the circumstances, Rose reckoned, good advice.

'No, Kate, ya'll not wash it yerself. There's a special way to do it. Into the back with ya.'

From behind the curtained cupboard under the wash-stand, Cissie fetched out a jamjar containing a foul-looking, muddy green paste.

'What's that?' asked Kate nervously.

'Special herbs for yer hair.' Cissie never talked much about her various cures and concoctions.

Kate looked shocked. 'Do I have to eat it?'

'No. Don't be daft. It's for washin'.'

Dotting a dollop of the glunk over Kate's head, she massaged it in, left it for a few minutes and rinsed it off with the water Mossie had brought.

Kate yowled at its coldness.

'Be grateful. I could have brought ya to the spring rather than have Mossie bring the spring to ya.' After patting the hair dry, Cissie lifted off the mirror from the wall and brought it over to Kate whose eyes, after a quick look, again pooled tears.

'Kate, you're beautiful,' Rose told her. 'Most unusual. Exotically different.' The lack of hair showed off Kate's long neck, sculpted head and delicate features. The coolness that had grown between them was temporarily suspended. Rose's heart went out to Kate in her vulnerable state and she wished they could revert to their old spontaneous footing.

Lips pursed in concentration, Kate turned her head from side to side, swivelling to get full value from the small mirror. 'Would you think I'm anything like Audrey Hepburn?' she asked hesitantly.

'Now you mention it, you are. A blonde Audrey Hepburn,' Rose conceded generously. Generosity going a little way to assuage her guilt. She had given up on her own dream of looking even a little like the film star, realising she was just too chubby-cheeked.

'What do you think, Cissie?' Kate struck a pose, hand on hip, head thrown back, her former vivacity and self-preoccupation returned.

Cissie knew nothing about film stars, had never heard of Audrey Hepburn and was not even remotely interested in Kate's looks. To her, only the cure was important. 'Enough of that going on,' she chided, attacking the floor with the broom, slapping in her teeth and wedging her feet into the celebratory red shoes.

When the doctor's red MG screeched to a halt up outside the gate, Babs's headscarfed head visible in the passenger seat, Kate shrieked like a banshee.

'What's wrong with ya now?' asked Cissie sharply.

'It's Daddy. He hasn't come,' she wailed.

'Of course, he has,' soothed Cissie.

'No. no. He hasn't.' Kate's good humour had been short-lived. She thumped the table with a bunched-up fist. 'He'd come in his own car.'

Tommo, thinking this was a new game, joined in, slapping at the scrubbed wood with the blade of his knife. Cissie quietened him, removed the knife and tucked it for safekeeping behind the votive lamp. The last thing she wanted was Mrs Mac upset.

'Maybe Mr Mac is following,' she comforted Kate.

'Mammy'd come with him, not old Coward,' sobbed Kate.

Babs, dressed in a Kelly-green two-piece, lots of gilt jewellery, and high heels, was handed out of the car by the doctor. He wore a striped navy suit with an orange tie, a yellow spotty handkerchief spilling out of his pocket. Untying the headscarf, patting her hair into place, Babs picked her way down the path.

Rose ran into the garden, pulled her aunt aside, and whispered. When Babs entered the kitchen, she hugged Kate, kissed the top of her head and held her at arm's length. 'My, aren't you lovely? Now which film star do you remind me of — the pretty one who won the Oscar in *Roman Holiday*?'

'Audrey Hepburn!' said Kate delightedly, with more than a flash of her old exuberance. Babs shot Rose a look of thanks.

'Where's Daddy?' asked Kate.

'He's not coming. He's not himself.'

Kate started to cry.

Babs intervened. 'It's better he didn't come. There's no point in hiding it. We've all known for a long time, we just can't depend on him.'

Today she was glad to be without her husband. Throughout their married life, Foxy's rumbustious attendance at various family functions and commitments had regularly created hassle and chaos. His presence had the ability to reduce high points to low points rapidly.

Unless he was in the initial guilt-ridden stages of drying out, Kate's hair could never compete with the excitement of the dogs. The inaugural meeting in Abbeydorney would keep Foxy well occupied. Probably for days. No more covering up for him, she had decided — the children were old enough to accept their father and his behaviour.

Swinging his medical bag, Leslie Coward strode into Cissie's kitchen as though he owned it, brushed off the table — nothing to brush off — and, putting his bag on the edge, clicked it open and made a big production of rooting around in it. He took out a stethoscope and a thermometer.

'There's no need for those,' said Babs, an edge to her voice. 'Can't you see how well Kate is? And look at the way her hair's growing back.'

He left the instruments on the table and examined Kate's head without touching it, saying 'Mmm', and murmuring something about her being 'a lucky girl'.

'Could it happen again?' asked Babs tentatively. 'Kate's hair fall out?'

Head cocked to one side, palm cupping his chin, Leslie Coward prevaricated, 'Well … I suppose … stress … as I said earlier.'

'Nonsense,' said Cissie stoutly, cutting across him. 'Kate'll be all right from now.'

The girls were too young to appreciate Cissie's powers but they did know that Babs was firmly convinced. She did not say much, just sat there nodding and smiling, enjoying a cup of tea and a wedge of Cissie's spotted dog.

The doctor hid his curiosity under a transparent mantle of enforced friendliness. They all knew he was mightily impressed because his nonchalance was so desperately artificial. He drank a lot of tea, and asked a lot of questions, to which Cissie gave him very short answers.

That evening, Elizabeth returned early. As she teetered down the little path, carrying a big square cake box from Latchford's Bakery in Tralee, her skirt seemed fuller, her heels higher, and her smile wider than usual. Cissie rose to meet her.

'It's happened. Really and truly happened.'

Cissie hugged her, and Elizabeth danced a few steps of joy. Then placed the box on the table. 'Eclairs to celebrate. It's not every day a girl gets engaged.'

Kate's eyes widened. Rose held her breath. The girls were sure Elizabeth's fiancé had to be either a Hollywood star or a millionaire.

They were gobsmacked — totally gobsmacked — on learning that she was engaged to Snots Healy. Snots Healy, of all people!

'Won't you miss the excitement in America and the film stars? And the clothes?' asked Kate.

'No, I won't. Not for one minute,' Elizabeth assured her.

Kate could not let it rest. Her voice incredulous, she asked, 'Do you really love him?'

'Yes.'

Kate's look of incredulity was almost laughable.

To break the deadlock, Rose asked, 'Will you be married before you go back?'

Between laughing and crying and a mouthful of éclair, Elizabeth said, 'No more going back. We'll be living in Tralee.'

'I'm going to live in Hollywood,' said Kate importantly. Elizabeth just smiled and asked had they heard that Jammy O'Brien had been so badly beaten up that he was on crutches.

Every now and again, Rose had a pang about returning to Dublin. She was no longer the girl who had come to Kerry. How would she cope with the physical and psychological restrictions of home and school?

Wait until her parents, especially her mother, saw how she had grown up and the notions she had acquired on the way. Mammy thinking by sending her to the country she was removing her from city temptations!

Never had Rose known that so many experiences could be packed into so few weeks. Carragheen-picking, counting sovereigns, swimming with a dolphin, ear-piercing. The variety of people she had met: Cissie, Mossie, Elizabeth, Mags, even drippy Jamie.

How much more she knew about sex. What with Jammy's and her uncle Bart's overtures. Dangerous, but no denying the thrill of it. And Mikey and she nearly making the most passionate of love.

Still, the letter from her mother gave her some hope, actually recognising she was no longer a child. If only she were allowed to grow up naturally, Rose was sure she would not be so preoccupied with being a teenager and a woman. Stuck in the time warp of being treated as an opinionless child was a hard place to be.

She wished she and her mother could talk. Really talk. About life and growing up. Shared confidences. Like the day they had shopped for the party dress. That had been good. Hearing how her mother and father had met.

Her mother. Omigod. Her letter. The same cream notepaper with the fluted edges as Frank's letter. The same paper as the love letter she had hidden away! That was what he had meant. Now it made sense. How could he have got hold of that letter? She had stuck it somewhere. Somewhere safe. But where? She couldn't remember.

306

It was so much easier being a child. Life as an adult, even a beginner adult, was so complicated, so full of conscience, so packed with do's and don't's.

The hardest thing Rose had ever had to do in her life was to come clean to Kate, to tell her the whole truth about herself and Mikey. But Kate deserved an explanation. She found it much harder than the session with her parents and the nuns about Frank, probably because she chose to do this, whereas that had been thrust upon her.

Her internal debates in justification of her silence had raged long and hard, but she could no longer live with the consequences. After several ineffective stabs, eventually, one night when she could not sleep and even the moon boat offered no comfort, she reached across to Kate. 'I want to try to explain about Mikey.'

'I don't want to hear,' said Kate, turning her back. A definite cold shoulder.

'Please. The least you can do is listen to my side,' urged Rose, more firmly than she felt.

'Oh, go on, so,' Kate grudged.

Rose was as honest as she could be, telling Kate how she had first seen him on the train to Tralee, labelled him gorgeous but was not interested as she was still heartbroken over Frank; two days later on the bus he had winked. Kate remembered that, didn't she? Then there had been the sheep-shearing incident. Rose had not known what to think of that — it was the O'Briens, not Mikey, who had frightened her. Though he did make her feel uncomfortable. And all those other times — the way he watched her.

'But I thought he fancied you, Kate, the way the two of you were always talking and laughing and joking.'

Kate turned onto her back, arms above her head, and, hope in her voice, said, 'Did you really?'

'Cross my heart and hope to die. Yes.'

'Go on, so.'

'Remember when you wouldn't leave the house with your hair and I went to get shells for my project? That's when it started. Mikey and me. We had a race along the beach. And I won.'

'Bet he let you. So when did you, you know…?'

'A few days later.'

'I bet he's a great kisser.'

'He is.'

'I hope you're not serious about him.'

Rose didn't answer.

Primly Kate said, 'He's unsuitable. Even more unsuitable than Doreen's Jack.'

'I'm really sorry about not telling you. If it wasn't for your hair, I bet it's you who'd be with him.'

'No it wouldn't. He didn't mind kidding around with me, but it was always you he fancied,' Kate conceded. 'What'll happen when you go back to Dublin?'

'I don't know.'

'But you are going with him?'

'Oh, yes.'

'You might have told me. When did he ask you?'

'He didn't. I just know.'

'Huh. Just wait until my hair grows a bit, I'll give you a run for him.'

Rose had no reply to that. But she was not worried. Instead she asked, 'Are we okay again?'

'I suppose so.' At the least, Kate's acceptance was reluctant.

'Now do you think I could have a loan of Doreen's bra?'

Kate reared up on one elbow, indignant. 'Certainly not. Never.'

Rose resigned herself to being bra-less. But she slept easier that night, knowing that she had done the right thing, accepting that you can't necessarily expect instant forgiveness. And she was not about to ruin the peace which had been achieved with Kate by admitting to having already borrowed the bra.

CHAPTER TWENTY-FIVE

While Kate was all talk about Mikey, promising Rose a run for him, she was still reluctant to venture out. Rose could see her point. She really was very baldy, though Cissie assured, 'In a month's time, ya won't know yerself.'

'Well, I'll certainly be pleased to meet myself then,' Kate assured her pertly.

Despite Broody's deteriorating condition, Tommo's increased aggressiveness and Elizabeth's forthcoming wedding, Cissie still kept a watchful eye on Rose's comings and goings. And despite her acknowledgement that love was more than passion, Rose still dreamed of even a bit of passion with Mikey.

It was one of those still, silent, stifling afternoons. Rare in Kerry. Since the previous night the air had been as hot outside as inside. As though nature held her breath in anticipation of a momentous occurrence.

When Rose came out of Cissie's gateway, bodice-less and wearing the yellow dress, as though on cue, Mikey appeared. 'There y'are. I was looking for ya. Come on. Quick. With me. Into the woods.'

So absorbed was Rose thinking about him and their bodies together that she attributed his wild-eyed panting to anticipation of what was about to flare between them.

He went ahead, gasping, half running, half walking, his white shirt drenched tight against his back. Caught up in the momentum of what she interpreted as his uncontrollable desire, she ran across the field too, circumventing cowpats, wading through tufts of damp grass, towards the trees. Yes, their place. But she could not keep up with him and flagged behind.

Then she heard it. Never had she heard the like of it before. And never did she want to again. A cry of terror. Like a wounded animal. In ferocious pain.

Rose skidded to a halt. 'What's that?' She had to shout to be heard, as Mikey was now some distance away, and she knew her voice pooled on the still air, but Mikey, registering the gist of her tone, turned around.

'It's Maryann. Come. Come on. Quick.'

'What's wrong with her?'

He kept running.

'You've got to tell me.' Rose stood stock-still. 'I'm not going to move until you do.'

The worst she could think of was that Maryann had broken her leg. Mikey came back, grasped her by the elbow. Not even the tiniest bit of ardour. His expression was panicky, his eyes sliding sideways, and she could smell the fear of his sweat.

Mikey was afraid, unsure of what to do. He had never felt so alone. Though he knew he had to see this out. Finish this business with Maryann. Rose's appearance was like a miracle. Her very presence gentling.

'Just come on,' he said. 'Please.' Then the cry came again. 'Hurry.'

Despite herself, Rose obeyed. Both of them sprinting like March hares over the last few hundred yards.

Maryann was sitting on the ground, her back against the trunk of the broad-leafed chestnut, a few haphazard branches from Mikey's hideout affording some privacy. Her skirt was high around her thighs, blood oozed from between her legs. She was sobbing, whimpering like a wounded animal.

'Ya'll be all right,' Mikey told her in a gentle voice. The voice he had used on the afternoon he had spoken to Rose about his parents, right here in these woods. 'Rose and me'll take care of ya.'

'I don't want her. Get her away,' yelled Maryann.

'What's wrong?' asked Rose, not wanting to stay. There was something unnerving about Maryann. 'She's bleeding.'

'She's having a baby,' Mikey said, as nonchalantly as though Maryann had a bit of a cold.

Rose felt as though a bucket of cold water had been thrown over her. Then butterflies were gnawing at her stomach. This she could not absorb. It was worse — much worse — than Monica's betrayal. So awful that she could not take in the enormity of what she was hearing. 'I'll get Cissie.' It was all she could think of.

'Ya can't,' Maryann screamed. 'Don't let her, Mikey. Ya can't tell anyone. Me da'll kill me. Ya know he will. And if he doesn't, me brothers will. Let her go. You, don't leave me again.'

'Ya're to stay here,' Mikey ordered Rose, as though she were a stranger to him. For Mikey, the only thing that mattered for now was getting Maryann through the birth. Afterwards, there would be all the time in the world for Rose. And for explanations. How he wished he hadn't neglected to tell her. Why had he let her go after their swim with the dolphin? Why, instead of whinging on about his mother and father, hadn't he told her here in the woods?

Rose felt as though she were in another world, an unreal world where time was suspended. You had to do IT to have a baby. With somebody. A boyfriend. She refused to think about the boyfriend bit. Who might Maryann's boyfriend be? Babies were born in hospitals, not in woods, weren't they?

Scrunching closed her eyes, she pinched herself, hard, on the fleshy part of her hand near her thumb. It had to be a dream. When she looked again, nothing had changed. It was not a dream, it was a nightmare. Mikey and Maryann doing IT? No. No way. It was not possible.

In the all-enveloping heat, Rose watched and listened. Maryann whimpering and howling in turn, grasping at Mikey's hand, Mikey bent over her murmuring, stroking her forehead.

Rose shut her mind inwards, away from the thought of them, focusing instead on the pain of having a baby. It must be bad. Very bad, the way Maryann was going on. And Rose bet she was tougher and braver than her. Bad enough to die, as Aunt Babs had said, or to be cut in two, like Mammy.

Rose's own worst pain had been the toothache she had had once, and that was only a baby tooth. She tried to imagine what Maryann was going through.

Increasing the intensity a hundredfold and magnifying to the size of her stomach the way it was with that little tooth in that one little corner of her mouth. Rose had been only six and she could still remember after all these years.

Despite Nance's experience of childbirth, she had scant sympathy for anyone else's pain. So, when Rose complained about her tooth, she peered in, chucked her on the chin and said, 'It'll be better before you're twice married.' Instead, it got worse.

Trevor bought oil of cloves from the chemist, which Nance dribbled onto a pad of gauze and then wedged into Rose's mouth. 'You'll be better before you know it,' she assured, sniffing luxuriously at her fingers. Rose was not. The pain was so bad that sometime during the night she got a mouthful of brandy.

Next day, after lunch, Nance put on her cherry-red coat and hat, and she and Rose got the bus into town and walked over to Fitzwilliam Square, where the dentist had his practice. Not that Rose knew what a dentist was. Then.

Mr Cronin was his name. And Rose hated him on sight. After setting Nance in the waiting-room, he brought her into his surgery. It smelled scary, like the hospital where she had visited Grandma Laetitia the time she had broken her hip.

The dentist's chair was huge and black, and he wrapped a big bib around Rose and told her to open her mouth. Wide. Some sort of jabbing instrument touched her sore spot and she yelled. Good and loud.

'Behave yourself,' he said, picking up a long needle and doing a few test squirts. Rose's tummy was full of butterflies and she closed her eyes and opened her mouth. Very slowly, he stuck the needle in, his hand blocking off her breath for ages.

Next came an implement, rather like their silvery nutcracker. This grasped and rocked the tooth. The pain was awful. Rose tongued his hand out of her mouth and told him so.

'Nonsense,' he said, breathing hard, pinning her to the chair with his elbow. 'You're not feeling a thing.'

'I am, I am,' she squealed through pliers and fist which were back in place.

He pushed his face close. 'You're not. You've had an injection.'

The pliers plunged, deep, grabbed the tooth. This time rocked it backwards and forwards. Then yanked. And all the time bursting clouds of pain. Rocking, yanking. Then the creaking sound. Sort of like a splintering. It was that which finally broke Rose.

She bit down on Mr Cronin. Good and hard. Where thumb joins hand. With a yelp, he jumped back, removing the remainder of his hand and the pliers from her mouth. His blood gushed, red globules down his white coat. And his breathing was hard, really hard.

By now Nance had rushed into the surgery. Quick as a flash, she hauled Rose out of the chair, apologised for her behaviour while buttoning her coat, and whisked her into the street. There she gave her a shake and a lecture about making a show of herself. They were halfway home on the bus before she

315

discovered that the tooth was still in position. Rose could not remember whatever happened it. But she did remember that it was her worst pain. Ever.

Her eyes full of unshed tears, Rose watched Mikey's gentleness with Maryann.

'Lie down, Maryann.' Mikey tried to ease her backwards, but she fought at him in a weary way, batting ineffectual hands, forwarding tired shoulders, agitating limp knees. 'It's better,' he told her, his hand pressing her down, 'easier for birth.'

'What d'ya know about it?' Whereas previously Maryann had been monosyllabically sullen, now she was verbosely truculent.

'Sheep,' he answered succinctly, taking off his shirt, tucking it under her head. He squatted beside her, interlocking his fingers with hers, the way he had done with Rose. Maryann no longer whimpered; it was continuous howls interspersed with gasps.

Rose stood apart from them, as though this had nothing to do with her. In a strange way, it did not. She was isolated from this act of birth. Yet it did affect her, profoundly. Tears spilled out of her eyes, rolled unchecked down her cheeks.

Watching the tableau unfold, she felt her heart break, as though she would die, as though she were being torn in two. She wanted to be in Dublin, in familiar surroundings, away from this relationship which had got out of hand and of which she no longer felt in control. Home with her mother and father and George and Agnes. Even in school with the nuns.

She began saying the Rosary, counting on her fingers, starting with The Annunciation — the first of the Joyful Mysteries. The repetition was familiar and comforting: the strength of the Our Father, followed by the softness of the Hail Mary and the hope of the Glory Be. Prayers flowing out of her like a mantra. A kind of shivery acceptance that she did not belong here washed over her during the saying of the five Sorrowful Mysteries. Around her the earth was redolent with the decay of undergrowth; the heavy sun lurking sullen behind pre-storm clouds; birdsong reduced to a sad whisper as she started into the Glorious Mysteries; and, when she had finished with The Coronation of the Blessed Virgin, she began the cycle of fifteen all over again.

By Rose's count, the baby was born at the end of The Agony in the Garden, the first mystery of the Sorrowfuls. Silent and red and purple, it emerged into the world, with a little fuzz of matted black hair. Mikey placed it, cord and all, on Maryann's stomach and knelt beside her. She lay without moving, blood gushing from between her legs, staring into space, shivering in the wan evening light that dappled shadows on her and her infant.

Some time later, without even a backward glance, Rose left the two of them and the dead baby and walked away, back to Cissie's.

She ignored Mikey calling after her, ignored the sound of him thrashing through the woods. Just kept walking, slowly and definitely, out of his life. A hard decision. But there was nowhere to go to escape from the pain. Except forward.

Even though it was nine o'clock, she had not been missed. Though Tommo was missing. When he had not been around during the afternoon, Cissie had presumed that, despite being forbidden to go off on his own, he had gone down to Mossie. But Mossie had been on the beach since early morning, loading up on seaweed, and had not seen sight nor light of him since the previous evening.

Rose went through the motions of worrying about Tommo, though she found it hard to get caught up in Cissie's fear. The neighbours gathered — the women assuring he would be back any minute; the men saying he was a strong broth of a boy and to give him time.

In the light of the general optimism, Cissie decided not to worry Mrs Mac. Everyone except Cissie politely ignored Tommo's abnormality. Nobody except Cissie knew that the knife he used for whittling was missing from behind the votive lamp.

Rose, disassociated from the lot of them, felt not the slightest need to mention what she had witnessed. As the throbbing grey of the clouds began to darken the August evening, she laid the sunshine-yellow dress with its trim of red strawberries on Elizabeth's side of Cissie's bed. She would never wear it again.

In the purple dusk, she walked with Kate as far as the pier, ostensibly out looking for Tommo, in reality to escape the claustrophobia of the cottage.

That night Broody died. And Cissie kept a private vigil for Tommo by her range. Broody was gone beyond her. It was Tommo she prayed for and worried about. By morning he still had not returned.

At 8.30, as Garda John Joe Sheehy drank his second mug of breakfast tea in the family quarters attached to the station, the bell above his head thunked. He took another slurp, rose from the table, hitched up his trousers and ambled out to the bilious green office with its scarred furniture.

Tommo, dolorous eyes and downcast mouth, leaned across the cracked counter, elbows supporting him. He was distraught and panting, his trousers mud-stained and his shirt wrinkled and dirty.

With the kindly ponderousness that was his hallmark, John Joe asked, 'Have you been home, Tommo? Cissie's worried.'

Tommo shook his head and licked his lips, as if moistening them would make the words come out more easily. But all he managed was a repetitive muttering of two words. Sounded like 'baby' and 'wood'. John Joe, unable to make head nor tail of him, brought him into the kitchen where his wife, Lizzie, gave him a mug of tea. She thought Tommo might be talking about whittling the figure of a baby from his block of wood.

The guard gave Tommo a crossbar back to Cissie's, an experience he determined never to repeat. As they passed Tansey's gate, Tommo became so disturbed that the two of them toppled off the bike. Tommo, sitting on the roadway, pointed agitatedly across the fields, muttering the same 'baby' and 'wood' words.

He calmed down when John Joe, enunciating the words slowly, told him to stop his worrying — that he would take care of the matter, but he was disgruntled at having to walk the remaining few hundred yards.

Tommo's return was marked by Cissie with rapturous scolding. Out of his depth in such displays of emotion, John Joe beat a hasty retreat. As he was right beside the woods, he would take a look. Though from the cut of Tommo, even if you could understand him, you could not be sure of a word out of his mouth.

Removing the clips from his trousers, he braceleted them to the handlebars and rested the bicycle against the grassy mound at the entrance to the property. Undoing the makeshift clasp, he opened the gate, let himself in, closed it and carefully re-knotted the twist of wire.

Oblivious to the dewy hush of the morning, the meadow streaked with buttercups and daisies, the hedgerows garlanded by wild roses and the distant hayfields quivering in the thick heat, he meandered towards the woods, thinking of nothing more than his dream that one day his eldest son would make the county hurling team. That the boy expressed a decided reluctance even to hold a hurley, much less wield it competitively, did not in the least faze his father.

With the exception of that awful incident of the bishop's car crash, John Joe's term of office in Fenit had been uneventful — just the occasional squabble over land boundaries, missing livestock and a disappearing bicycle or two. Married to Lizzie, his life had been placid: fulfilled by fatherhood, he enjoyed dreaming up unrealistic ambitions for his eight children.

The one thorn in his flesh could be the O'Briens, if he let them. But they seldom came down from the mountains and, when they did, it was an easy matter to avoid them. He had heard about Jammy being beaten up, but as there had been no formal complaint, he had happily turned a blind eye to the incident.

Nothing in his life had prepared him for the sight that met his eyes a few minutes later.

Maryann, dress rucked around her thighs, the baby nestling into her stomach, still attached to its umbilical cord, lay like an abandoned rag doll at the base of the tree. Her eyes were closed to the grey light filtering through the leaves and lighting up the chestnut candles, her white face tinged a mauvey-grey, and her hair knotted and matted with bits of twigs and leaves.

The air and ground around her were alive with flies and beetles, and the smell was of pungent sweetness. When John Joe realised that Maryann's life-blood had drained out of her and seeped into the ground, his ruddy face rumpled in distress, his breath left him and an electric tingle of grief coursed through his limbs.

He had no notebook in which to record anything, but then he would not have known what to record. He did kneel beside Maryann and offer a prayer for the repose of her soul and that of her child. Desperately he wanted to take off his jacket and cover up the two bodies, but he remembered enough from his training to leave undisturbed what could turn out to be a crime scene.

He noticed signs of digging around the back of

the tree. Perhaps something to do with the tarry rag lying a few feet away from Maryann? Whatever it was, it was hardly buried treasure. Just as he was thinking how much he wanted out of here, he noticed a glint. A silver glint. It looked like a half-crown. On closer examination, it proved to be a silver dollar. Nothing to do with poor Maryann O'Brien, he was sure. Still, he would have to hand it in. And if it was returned to him, he might — just might — offer it as an incentive to his son to try to make the hurling team.

In breathless spurts, he ran his fastest back through the meadow to summon help.

Cissie was ages getting the messages in the village. The community was alive and buzzing at the turn of events. Not primarily Tommo's absence and subsequent return, though Cissie was as relieved at the discovery of his whittling knife tucked under the trestle as she was at having him safe under her roof again. No, the big subject was Maryann giving birth. Nobody had even known she was pregnant. But now everyone knew who the father was. Weren't she and Mikey always together? Didn't the fact that there was no sign of him around today only confirm his guilt? Cissie hated herself for holding her silence.

Mags had the post office determinedly open. However, she was tucked behind the grille, doling out stamps and postal orders rather than serving groceries or knitting on her porch. And her breathing was particularly wheezy.

As though queuing to buy stamps, they came, her neighbours, in a meek shuffling line, to offer their condolences. 'Sorry for yer troubles,' they said, bobbing their heads, one after another. She was about to remind them there had not been a death in her family when she realised if what they said about Mikey was true — and she would put nothing past him — she had lost a great grandson.

Condoling done, outside on the street the villagers gathered in a huddle, talking about Mikey. Good riddance, they said. Bad blood, they confirmed. Like mother, like son, they supposed. Poor Mags. Maryann rated even less sympathy than Mikey. Her family were outsiders. In life she had never been one of them; in death, particularly after committing the worst of all sins, she certainly would not qualify.

When the O'Briens appeared at the edge of the village, the massive father wielding his crutches like weapons, flanked by his six hulking sons, they made straight for the garda station, pausing for a moment by the open door.

Jammy ordered, 'Say nothin'. I'll do the talkin'. Do ye hear me?' Their collective nods were almost imperceptible. 'Remember, the baby weren't nothin' to do with us. Do ya hear?'

To the astonishment of John Joe, Jammy O'Brien, backed by his sons, after denying knowledge of Maryann's condition, rejected all responsibility and disowned the baby. Father and brothers declined to see the corpses. They did not want anything to do with the funeral and were not interested in how, where or when the burial would take place.

Their attitude went against all the family values John Joe held so dear. Never a particularly courageous man, to his own amazement he found himself insisting they pay for a coffin. Jammy did so without argument, peeling notes off from a bundle he had pulled out of his back pocket.

Cissie returned home, silent and disturbed, wondering about the events that were starting to rock the small community. It was even worse than the day Sadie and Father Florence had been killed. But Mikey was not the father of Maryann's baby. Of that she was sure.

She wondered how the affair would affect Rose.

And knew what she must do.

How much of the past slides its tentacles into the present, curling and tightening in secret around this soul and that heart, strangling, crushing? All of it, Cissie knew, and she also knew that it was too much. No matter how she tried, she would never be free of the daughter she had passed on for adoption. But she could make some form of reparation.

During the afternoon, she called into the station. John Joe, delighted that the birth and deaths were not to be classified as a crime, had no objection to her suggestion. Indeed, he welcomed it as a solution.

Next morning, with gulls scimitaring the pale air, the sea dead grey, with a mean breeze whipping up whitecaps the colour of pewter, Mossie's donkey and cart brought the bodies of Maryann and her son along the beach to the disused graveyard. He was accompanied by Garda John Joe Sheehy, sole representative of the establishment, and Cissie for the village.

The two men dug the grave in the far corner. Next to the limbo babies. With the unyielding, rocky ground, it took them a long time. There, mother and son were buried, together. Without ceremony and without mark. Because the infant was unbaptised, and regarded by the Church as stained with original sin, it was destined to remain forever in limbo. Never to reach Heaven. And his body was unwelcome in hallowed ground.

Cissie had desperately wanted mother and child to lie together in death.

As the tiny group of mourners walked back over the top of the beach, the glowering scarlet vestiges of the storm lit the clouds from behind. The wind, a guerrilla force sneaking up, attacked from one side to the other, whiplashing the paler sky. The pewter whitecaps, gathering momentum, churned the bay to fury.

EPILOGUE

Dublin, 1979

Cissie felt sick. A combination of excitement and apprehension.

She looked up and down the platform. The Tralee–Dublin train was in five minutes early and there was nobody to meet her.

It was difficult to believe she was here standing in Heuston Station, her greatest dream about to be realised. She shifted her small overnight bag from one hand to the other. Her feet were killing her. Swollen from the long journey. For the occasion she had not been able to resist the red shoes. Shabby now, but still celebratory.

Then she saw Rose, running towards her along the platform. They hugged. Cissie, holding her at arm's length, praised, 'You're looking well. Nice and fat.' Rose flinched. She would never get used to Cissie's blunt greeting. But try telling her that fatness was no compliment. 'Though a bit of good Kerry air wouldn't go amiss. Put a bit of colour in yer face.' Commenting on Rose's appearance gave the day a semblance of normality.

Despite Cissie's comments on her weight, Rose loved the easy camaraderie which had grown out of their Fenit days. So long ago. So much compressed into so few weeks. But that was youth: great technicoloured happenings, the heightened passion of it all.

Herself and Mikey. The crackling dynamics between them, the intensity of feeling, not just lust and passion which in the end had never been realised. But pity and love and sadness. And the numbness that got her through the days after Maryann's terrible ending. She had learned to label those emotions. The clarity of time and distance, she supposed. As well as maturity.

The story was that the O'Briens had got Mikey. Payback time, it was said. And they had either buried him somewhere or thrown his body out to sea. The rumour was compounded when John Joe Sheehy had interviewed father and sons, but nothing had come of it.

Rose accepted the story of Mikey's death. Dead was final. Anyway, she had not been capable of speculating one way or the other. Nor had she needed to mourn him; she had done all her grieving for him and their relationship during the birth of the baby.

Despite trying to keep the day ordinary, Cissie knew that there was nothing ordinary about today. The way it had come about was a miracle. Arrived at by a confession. The full circle of life. Wrong being made right. Bad becoming good. Today, no matter what way it went, was due to Rose.

It was believed to be the sight of Maryann and the dead baby that had finally flipped Tommo. A few hours after the burial, he had had his worst and longest fit ever. Eyes wild, lips drooling, gabbling and blubbering, locked into his own incomprehensible place. Cissie unable to get through to him. With an arm rigid across his eyes, he perpetually sought sanctuary from the world.

The night after he was committed to the asylum in Killarney, Cissie, Elizabeth, Rose and Kate sat around the range, with its red hearth fire and black lead dust. Each lost in the threads of her own thoughts.

It was then that Cissie spoke. For the first time telling the story of her daughter, unrehearsed and unplanned. Triggered by the enormity of what had happened to Maryann, the reaction in the village, and the disintegration and incarceration of Tommo.

The urgency to acknowledge Brigid, to give her substance by speaking her name aloud — to tell her story — had been overwhelming. More than the time being appropriate, more than an easing of a burden, more than a need to share. It was further reparation for years of denial. Cissie could no longer remain quiet.

When she had finished, the silence was broken only by the ticking of the clock and the splutter of the fire.

Elizabeth had thought her life in the States lonely, but this sure took the biscuit. 'Why didn't you tell me, let me help? Going through that on your own must have been awful.'

'There was nothing else for it,' Cissie said with a briskness she did not feel, but with a great sense of relief.

Five years on, like a bolt from the blue, came the letter from Australia. Addressed to Cissie. Mikey explaining his relationship with Maryann. It was as she had suspected. He had tried to protect her from her father and brothers. When she became pregnant by one of them, it was his idea to say and do nothing for as long as possible. He planned to help her get away afterwards.

Would Cissie please make Rose understand? He was building a new life for himself in Australia. It was okay, but lonely. He often wondered about Rose.

Cissie replied. But it took her six months. And it was a good year before she mentioned the matter to Rose.

For several weeks Rose thought about Mikey. She even composed a letter to him in her head but something held her back from writing it. By now she, too, had built her own life. Had reconciled Mikey and that summer of '59 to memory. Wonderful, warm, funny memories. In her mind Mikey had become her very own Wild Colonial Boy. Never would she forget him. Never did she have to, now she knew that Mikey was not the father of Maryann's baby.

Eventually she asked Cissie to give him her address. She never heard from him. Dammit. And he stopped corresponding with Cissie.

'Today. The most important day of your life. How can you even notice whether I'm fat or thin?' Rose took the bag from Cissie and ushered her outside to where she had double-parked the car at the entrance to the station. Settling Cissie in the passenger seat, she confided, 'I'm feeling decidedly fat. Kate was up last week. She's pregnant again. Not that that stopped her buying up the place.'

'I know, I met her in Tralee.' Cissie stretched out her legs gratefully, resisting the urge to remove her shoes. Too difficult to get on again. 'She told me ye'd a right good time. And looking very well, she is.'

Cissie liked Kate rounded in pregnancy. She took scrawniness, as she called it, as a personal affront. She was delighted when her girls had grown close again, though the final rift had not been healed until Kate's marriage.

'She's dreadful. Cakes and chocolates. And I'm as bad as her. After the birth, she'll revert back to a size ten. As for me, the coffee creams and Walnut Whirls are permanently lodged here.' Rose thumped her offending thighs. 'No willpower, that's my trouble.'

'How are the pets?' Cissie asked, changing the subject. This new-fangled dieting talk was beyond her. She had known and seen enough hunger in her time to be ever grateful for a full belly. She loved Rose's children and spoiled them at every opportunity.

'Wonderful. Maddening. I love them to distraction. But, God, I could kill them on occasions. Viola has this geek of a boyfriend. Totally obsessed with him, she is. A hop, if you don't mind, she wants to go to on Saturday night. In St Mary's tennis club....'

Cissie laughed, 'No different from her mother? And what about the boys?'

'Francis is no trouble. Born wise. An old head on young shoulders. Insists on being called FR, if you don't mind. Modelling himself on JR out of *Dallas*, on the television. Compulsory viewing for all ages,' she explained, realising Cissie would not even know what she was talking about. 'And Trevor's a delight. Still at the biddable stage. You'll see them for yourself. I'm jabbering. I couldn't be more nervous if it was myself.' She started up the car.

'And himself? How's the boss?'

Rose smiled. Even the thought of him made her smile. Funny, the way that had worked out.

On her return to Dublin after Fenit, a new and closer relationship had developed between herself and her mother, though not totally devoid of the occasional spats and personality clashes. That would have been asking too much. But Nance listened and Rose confided. Well, most of the time, both of them did. And there was no longer a problem with Frank, or any other boy. Her right of choice would be respected, within reason, of course.

Frank and herself got back together for a while. But with the perversity of teenhood, she no longer fancied him. Now that he had the freedom of their home and she had parental permission to have a social life, much of the excitement was gone from their relationship. He tried to instigate a relationship again in UCD, but Rose held him at arm's length while he studied Civil Engineering and she did History and English.

She heard his news one summer evening in Kiely's in Donnybrook, the in-pub for their crowd that year. It was just after Barbara had told her that

Monica was back in hospital again — her weight down to five and a half stone. Frank's news was the talk of the place. The air thick with the smell of pints and smoke, motes of dust floating on the soft summer light. Frank Fennelly had been 'milk-runned'. A five-year contract in Bolivia, building bridges. Rose, standing at the bar with Barbara, was devastated. Poleaxed. Five years. And so far away.

Then Frank was beside them, buying a round of drinks. She had not even known he was in the pub. She chose her congratulatory words carefully, treading a guarded path through the emotional quagmire in her mind. But her flushed face and tear-filled eyes gave her away.

'I'll miss you,' she blurted. It was the last thing she intended saying.

He paid for the drinks, guided her outside to the street and they walked the few yards down to the entrance of Bective Rugby grounds.

'What's a three-legged donkey called?' he asked.

'A wonkey, of course.'

'You remember.'

'How could I forget? I don't know anyone else who tells such excruciating jokes.'

Rose accepted his proposal without hesitation. Afterwards thinking she seemed to have been waiting for it for ever. They married within three months. When Frank's contract expired, they returned to Ireland, after what they described as an extended honeymoon, with their three children.

Rose's own happiness made her realise the importance of family, and she often thought about Cissie and her Brigid. Cissie had not said to keep it a secret, though she locked the subject into herself again and refused to be drawn. Rose and Kate had talked about it among themselves, particularly since the birth of their own children, but they had never broken her confidence.

About three years before this visit, Rose had broached the subject of trying to trace Brigid.

Initially Cissie refused even to listen. Eventually, fluctuating between hope and despair, she gave Rose permission to start enquiries on her behalf. That very night, on her knees in the quiet of her bedroom, Cissie began a private novena to Saint Anthony, the patron saint of the lost and missing.

Rose started her search in Cork, in the hospital where Cissie had given birth. While her enquires did not meet with resistance as such, the sister in charge was quietly and firmly uncooperative. Her long thin face set in a mournful mask, she murmured about incomplete records and accidents with papers, and even cast apologetic aspersions on the hospital's own documentation.

Eventually perseverance paid off. Rose discovered that Brigid had not been placed in the good home Cissie had hoped for, but had been sent to the Catholic Protection Society in Dublin. Cajoles and threats gained Rose further glimmers of information, and hearsay filled in the gaps.

In 1948, four years before the Adoption Act had come into being, Brigid had become a statistic in 'the boarded-out' file, when she joined the ranks of parentless children sent to families throughout the country. Rose understood why they were called the lost children: old enough to act as unpaid skivvies, never to be fully adopted, nor properly fostered. Limbo kids.

Brigid was one of the lucky ones. She went to Gweedore in Donegal to the Bonar family. They had seven children of their own and she slotted in happily after the eldest, becoming a willing pair of hands on the rocky farm and in the sparse kitchen. Eventually, like the other children, she moved away to work in a factory in Birmingham. There she met and married a Donegal man from Gortahork.

They returned to Gweedore in the mid-1970s so that Brigid could take care of her foster-mother. Which is how she came to open the door the day Rose came calling. Brigid was the spit of Cissie, the same warmth, the same stocky build. Even down to wearing a pair of too-high heels.

The traffic was terrible. Dublin was one of the worst European cities for bottlenecks. Out from the complicated snarl of the station, down the quays, up O'Connell Street, past the Rotunda Hospital, around Parnell Square. Rose paid scant attention to other drivers, muttering to herself, with intakes of breath and exhalations of relief. She could never remember the new one-way systems. City driving was a nightmare. She drew up with a flourish outside the Gresham Hotel.

'Will ya come in?' Cissie pleaded. She had a firm grasp on the Rosary beads in the pocket of her Sunday coat, the horrible brown's current replacement being a soft midnight blue.

'You'll be better on your own. I'll be back in an hour. You'll love each other.' Rose gave her a hug. 'Best of luck.'

As she drove off, Cissie stood on the shallow steps of the hotel looking too fragile and vulnerable to have to go through this on her own.

So would I be, thought Rose, if I were meeting my only child for the first time in forty years.

GLOSSARY

Alickadoo	Rugby club official or committee member, especially as referred to by younger members
Amadán	fool
A stór	darling, a term of endearment
Banshee	a female fairy renowned for wailing and shrieking. (In Irish mythology her wailing and shrieking signified death to a member of the family to whom she was attached.)
Boreen	lane, byroad
Bowsie	gurrier, lout
Cailín	girl
Currach	long fishing boat of similar construction to a coracle
Dáil	Irish parliament
Garda síochána	(lit. trans. — keeper of the peace) Irish police force or a member of it
Grá	love
Ochón	lament
Piseog	superstitious practice or belief
Plámás	flattery, cajolery
Poteen	illicitly distilled Irish whiskey
Radio Éireann	Irish national radio station
Súgán (chair)	type of Irish chair with a seat